KEPT SECRETS

Other books and audio books by

Traci Hunter Abramson

Undercurrents Series

Undercurrents

Ripple Effect

The Deep End

Saint Squad Series

Freefall

Lockdown

Crossfire

Backlash

Smoke Screen

Code Word

Lock and Key

Drop Zone

Spotlight

Royal Series

Royal Target

Royal Secrets

Royal Brides

Stand-alones

Obsession

Deep Cover

Failsafe

Chances Are

Twisted Fate

Kept Secrets

KEPT SECRETS

A NOVEL

TRACI HUNTER ABRAMSON

Covenant Communications, Inc.

Cover image *Chinese Lanterns* © caoyu36.

Cover design copyright © 2016 by Covenant Communications, Inc.

Published by Covenant Communications, Inc.
American Fork, Utah

Printed in the United States of America
First Printing: October 2016

22 21 20 19 18 17 16   10 9 8 7 6 5 4 3 2 1

ISBN 978-1-52440-109-2

For Christina
Thank you for sharing your love of all things Asian.

Acknowledgments

EVERY BOOK I WRITE REMINDS me of how valuable a good editor can be as I navigate the journey from idea to finished product. For the past dozen books, I have been fortunate to have an amazing editor who has truly helped me progress as a writer. Thank you, Samantha Millburn, for all you do.

My continued appreciation to everyone at Covenant who puts so much effort into every aspect of my books. Thank you to Stephanie Lacey for your tireless efforts and for being willing to think outside the box. Thanks to my writing partners, Paige Edwards, Jen Leigh, and Ellie Whitney, for your editing advice through those early scenes and for being my sounding board, and to Mandy Abramson for your help in the early editing process.

I also want to thank Paige Edwards and Lara Abramson for helping me create a particularly unique scene in San Francisco. Without you, the journey wouldn't have been nearly as enjoyable.

My gratitude also goes out to the rest of my family who continue to support my career as an author, and I especially want to thank my sisters, Stephany Osborn, for giving me the idea of a planned elopement in Las Vegas, and Tiffany Hunter for creating so many memories that ended up in these pages.

Thank you to the CIA Publication Review Board for your continued support and diligence. Finally, thank you to my readers, who make creating these stories so worthwhile.

Chapter 1

FAI MENG MADE HIS WAY through the hallway of the executive suites of Revival Financial. The brokerage firm had earned worldwide recognition over the past decade as one of the top in its industry. What the world didn't know was that among the successful brokers were a few select individuals who also doubled as spies for the Chinese government.

Fai's position in Hong Kong opened the way for him to operate freely while spying on foreign nationals from the Western world.

He walked over to the corner office where his associate in both careers maintained his appearance as a senior executive at Revival and knocked on the door that hung ajar. As soon as he was summoned inside, he entered and closed the door behind him.

"I have something I think you should see." Fai crossed to where Qing Yao sat behind his desk. He handed a paper to the older man.

"What's this?"

"A job application for our company."

Qing's shrewd eyes narrowed, the whites disappearing beneath eyelids that drooped with age. "Who is Devin Shanahan?"

"I believe he can be a valuable asset, one who can bridge a void we have been hoping to fill."

"I'm listening." Qing motioned for Fai to take a seat.

Fai lowered himself into the padded chair and leaned forward slightly. "A source indicated the CIA was pursuing Mr. Shanahan to work with them. Our background research shows he is an only child, raised primarily by a Chinese nanny. We also know the cook in his household is a native of Hong Kong, and Mr. Shanahan is fluent in both Mandarin and Cantonese."

"And his feelings about the United States? Clearly the Central Intelligence Agency believes him to be a loyal American if they are contemplating bringing him into their employ."

"Yes, but everyone has a weakness."

"What is his?"

"We know he lacks a solid family structure, and our psychological profile indicates this is something he seeks."

"You think we can provide what he seeks here?"

"That, or we find another weakness. He's probably got another one." Fai straightened in his seat. "I believe if you look at his personal information, you will find he has other attributes that will serve us well."

Qing looked down at the application, his heightened awareness apparent when he lifted his gaze. He steepled his fingers, tapping his forefingers together. "We may need to find a position for Mr. Shanahan. I believe we have a problem employee who can be disposed of."

"Kyle Rode?"

"He has been accessing files he shouldn't be looking at." Qing's eyes went hard. "Do we know who Mr. Rode is really working for? The British? The Americans?"

"The British." Fai's voice lowered to nearly a whisper. He had planned to offer the information to Qing and feared what would happen now that it had been demanded before he had the opportunity.

"You were going to tell me this?"

"Yes, sir. That is one of the reasons I am here."

"I see." Silence filled the room and stretched for two long minutes. "I believe this will be an excellent opportunity to teach some lessons."

He was afraid to ask the question and more afraid not to. "What lesson would that be?"

"Kill Mr. Rode."

"I thought you wanted to question him in the hope we could turn him into a double agent."

"Shanahan will give us what we need. This man must die. He will be an example of what happens when we are crossed."

"Yes, sir." Fai swallowed hard. "I will take care of it."

"Make Devin Shanahan the offer, and put him under surveillance. Also, verify the proper security is in place to make sure he has nothing to take back to his CIA while we make our play."

"Yes, sir."

* * *

Las Vegas.

Devin didn't have to read the signs to know they had arrived. The strip was alight with neon billboards and towering casinos. Pedestrians streamed up and down sidewalks, and the pulse of adventure filled the air.

After spending the past five and a half years with his nose in a book and interning for the CIA every summer, Devin was ready for a new adventure. One more semester, he reminded himself, and he'd achieve his goal: an MBA from Stanford, followed by a career in intelligence.

His friends and family didn't know about the intelligence part, of course. The likelihood of his working undercover prevented him from being able to share anything beyond his cover story.

What would they think if they knew the truth?

He glanced at the man in the driver's seat beside him. Caleb's blond hair had recently been cut short, and his blue eyes were usually filled with humor . . . or mischief. Devin could hardly remember any part of high school and college that Caleb hadn't been a part of.

"Are you sure this is where you want to get married?" Devin asked. "Seems to me that most girls want the whole flowers and bridesmaid thing."

"Molly definitely wants the flowers and bridesmaids. What she didn't want was months of stressing out over whether the tablecloths matched the napkins or whatever it is the mother of the bride likes to worry about."

"I gather Molly's mother was getting carried away on the wedding plans."

"Oh yeah. She wanted the country club, a string quartet, and five hundred guests. Not to mention the first available date was almost a year out. We don't want to wait that long to get married."

"On the bright side, that would have meant five hundred presents," Devin offered.

"I'd rather forgo the gifts and start on the marriage." He glanced over at Devin. "What about you? Ever thought about getting married? You and Ashley have been together for five months. That's a long time for you."

"We *were* together for five months," he corrected. At Caleb's raised eyebrows, he added, "We broke up a few weeks ago."

"What happened?"

"Nothing happened. I guess she thought the same thing you did and expected me to put a ring on her finger when we celebrated her birthday last month."

"Sorry about that."

"Don't be. It was fun while it lasted, but I don't think we ever really had a future together."

"I thought it was getting serious," Caleb said. "You haven't lasted that long with anyone since Grace Harrington our senior year in high school."

Devin experienced the same little stab in the heart he always did when he thought of Grace. He hadn't seen her since graduation, but that didn't change the fact that she was the only girl he had ever loved. He wished he had recognized that fact when he was seventeen. Maybe then he wouldn't have made the biggest mistake of his life.

Caleb slowed when the GPS announced their destination was on the right. He pulled into the drive in front of their hotel. "Here we are."

"When is Molly supposed to get here?" Devin asked.

"She should already be here. She was supposed to fly in this afternoon."

"I'm surprised she isn't sitting in the lobby waiting for you."

Caleb turned off the engine and grinned. "What makes you think she isn't?"

They both climbed out of the car and stepped onto the sidewalk. Not thirty seconds passed before the doors slid open and Molly rushed outside into Caleb's arms. Her straight blonde hair framed her face, and her green eyes filled with pleasure.

The sheer delight in her expression made Devin smile. "You two had better be careful, or people are going to think you're in love."

Caleb gave his fiancée a hard smacking kiss before turning to grin at Devin. "You're just jealous that I get to marry the prettiest girl in Arizona."

"That must be it," Devin agreed easily. "It's not too late, Molly. You can still dump him and run away with me."

She shot an amused look at him as the automatic doors opened again. "Tempting, but I think I'll keep him."

"You're breaking my heart." He put his hand up to his chest in mock despair.

A familiar female voice broke in, a hint of the South carrying humor. "I don't think a girl alive has managed to dent that heart of yours, much less break it."

Devin turned, then took a step back, stumbling off the curb and barely managing to keep his balance. It couldn't be. His eyes narrowed and then widened with delight. Speak of the devil . . . "Grace Harrington? Is that you?"

"In the flesh." Her hazel eyes held warmth, and she moved toward him, her arms outstretched for a hug.

He moved forward, careful not to trip over the curb a second time, and pulled her against him in a welcoming gesture. The scent of vanilla clung to her hair, courtesy of her shampoo, no doubt, and a wave of emotions crashed over him as he held her for that brief embrace. He shifted back to look at her, suddenly transported into the past. Before Grace, he had dated dozens of girls in high school, never letting anything get too serious.

But she had lasted longer than most, over six months, until his buddies had convinced him to move on. Prom was approaching, and he needed someone who was more the prom-queen type. With her solid build and wildly curly hair, Grace hadn't fit the mold.

The thought made him cringe inwardly. Had he really been that shallow? Or had he let his friends nudge him into the breakup because his feelings for Grace had started to scare him?

Her hair was straight today, hanging past her shoulders, light catching in the golden streaks against darker brown. The transition from teenager to twenty-three had enhanced her natural beauty. Instead of solid, her body looked long and lean, her subtle curves evident despite her loose-fitting T-shirt. Beyond her appearance, she seemed more confident and secure.

Devin struggled to find his voice. "I didn't know you were going to be here."

"You didn't know Molly is my cousin?" Grace asked.

"Your cousin is marrying my best friend? What are the odds?"

"The odds were pretty good considering she introduced us," Molly said.

Devin turned an accusing eye on Caleb. "You never told me Grace introduced you."

Caleb shrugged good-naturedly. "I thought I had."

"Come on." Molly grabbed Caleb's hand and took a step toward the door. "Let's go inside and get you two checked in. I'm sure you're both ready for some dinner."

Devin fell into step beside Grace and glanced at her again. There was no doubt about it. She looked like the prom-queen type now.

Chapter 2

DEVIN SHANAHAN. GRACE ROLLED HIS name over in her mind as she dressed for dinner. He had changed over the years since she had seen him last. He had grown a couple more inches, now standing about six two, and his shoulders were much broader than they'd been in high school. A faint scar trailed up the side of his left temple before disappearing beneath his dark red hair, which was cut stylishly short. It irritated her that she wanted to know the origin of the scar.

She hadn't seen Devin since he had graduated high school a year ahead of her. They had shared a number of classes over her two years in Sedona, despite their difference in grade. Grace had been a year ahead of most students in math and science when she moved from Virginia to Sedona at the beginning of her sophomore year. Two seasons of running track together beneath the Arizona red rocks had given them the foundation of a friendship. When he had asked her out the first time, she'd thought she'd stepped into glass slippers and a fairy tale. Unfortunately the fairy tale had lasted only twenty-seven weeks.

He had tried hard not to break her heart. She could give him that. Their talk had ultimately been about his concern that they were getting too serious. She couldn't deny that at the time, she had started thinking of herself as half of a couple instead of as an individual. She had also recognized how much stock everyone in school had put in the fact that she had lasted longer than any of his other girlfriends—Devin had been known for breaking things off before he ever reached a one-month anniversary.

That knowledge hadn't stopped her from falling in love with him before the end of their first date. It hadn't simply been her infatuation with the handsome senior or that her friendship with Devin had developed into a crush long before he'd asked her out. No, what had captured her heart had been his innate kindness.

That first date hadn't gone as expected. Their picnic at Grasshopper Point had been interrupted by a terrified three-year-old who had approached, tears in her little eyes and very much alone. They learned later the little girl had managed to wander off while her mother was changing her baby brother's diaper.

Devin had given the child a water bottle to drink before leaving her in Grace's care and going in search of the mother. His presence of mind had been admirable, as had his sensitivity and reassurance when the mother and daughter were finally reunited.

Grace shook away the memories and slipped her hotel key into her purse.

"Are you about ready?" Molly called from the bathroom, where she was reapplying her makeup. The girl had flawless skin, yet she was always powdering something.

Grace ran her fingers through her hair, raking it into place. "Yeah."

Molly emerged from the bathroom, and her gaze swept over Grace's black evening gown, the hem of which grazed the top of her knees. The cap sleeves and scoop neck were more modest than what she knew most women her age tended to wear, but Grace had always loved the classics in everything from movies to fashion.

"You look great." Molly wiggled her perfectly plucked eyebrows. "You're going to have the men eating out of your hand tonight."

"I doubt that." Thirty minutes with her straightener had helped tame her naturally curly hair into smooth waves, and she couldn't deny that moving out on her own had benefited her waistline. The extra pounds she carried during her teenage years had slowly melted away once she was no longer tempted by the cookies and other desserts her mother had often baked for the family. None of those changes convinced her that the guys would suddenly start noticing her tonight.

Her heart squeezed a little at the thought of her parents, and she drew a deep breath to push away the memories. She was here in Vegas to make happy memories, not to dwell on what she had lost.

"I can't believe I'm getting married in five days," Molly said.

"Neither can I." Grace tucked her purse under her arm and offered her cousin a smile. "You're going to make a gorgeous bride."

"Do you think my mom will get over the whole Vegas wedding thing?"

"She just wants you to be happy," Grace assured her. Aunt Marie might be a little over the top with a lot of things, but she had a good heart. When she slowed down long enough to listen, she could usually be persuaded that other people were entitled to their own opinions too. "Come on. Caleb is probably downstairs pacing the lobby, waiting on you."

The two women left their hotel room and started down the hall. "So what's the deal with you and Devin?"

"I don't know what you're talking about," Grace said, reluctantly admitting to herself that she looked forward to seeing him again at dinner.

"He looked pretty excited to see you. How do you know him?"

"Same way I know Caleb. We all went to high school together. You know that."

They stepped into an empty elevator, and Molly turned her green eyes on Grace. "And?"

"And nothing." Grace deliberately turned to face the front of the elevator so she could avoid her cousin's scrutiny and that reporter's intuition she had honed during the past year working for the local television station in Phoenix. Feeling Molly's gaze still on her, she added, "Sorry, Molly, but there's no story here."

"In my profession, I know better," Molly insisted. "There's always a story."

* * *

Devin scanned the interior of the comedy club as he entered. Round tables stood throughout the room, the chairs angled so everyone could see the stage along the far wall. The comedy show had been Cody's choice. Caleb's older brother and best man had flown in from LA the day before and had taken it upon himself to arrange for the entertainment this weekend.

Cody waved at Devin and Caleb from a table in the center of the room, where he sat beside Sean, Caleb's old college roommate. Devin thought it odd that except for the happy couple's parents, all of the attendees at the wedding on Saturday were also in the wedding party. Caleb and Molly had wanted simple, and that was what they were getting.

"Hey, bro." Cody clapped his hand on his brother's back and gave him a hard hug.

"About time you got here," Sean said.

"Yeah, well, not all of us have Daddy's private plane to fly us wherever we want to go," Caleb said.

"What can I say? It's tough being a rich kid." Sean's father owned several car dealerships around Arizona and had done well for himself over the years. Sean extended a hand to Devin. "Good to see you again, Devin."

"Yeah, you too."

They all settled into their seats, and Devin took a spot with an empty chair on either side of him. He didn't realize he was watching for Grace until she appeared in the doorway, her hair falling in waves past her shoulders. A jolt of anticipation shot through him, and he frowned slightly. Where had that come from?

"Is that Gracie Harrington?" Cody asked from across the table.

Devin shot an irritated glance at Cody. He knew Grace hated it when people called her Gracie. "Yes, that's Grace."

"Wow. She looks great."

She's always looked great, Devin thought to himself. Sure, she'd been a little overweight in high school, but she had always been pretty. Her straight nose and expressive hazel eyes were set in a perfectly oval face. Then and now, he found her attractive enough to capture his attention regardless of her waistline. The sequins on her black dress reflected the overhead lights and shimmered as she moved.

All four men stood as the women approached. Devin had been so focused on Grace, he hadn't noticed the other two women following her and Molly until they'd wound their way through the tables and were nearly to them. He now recognized one of them as Caleb's younger sister, Ellie. Her blonde hair was cut short, fringy bangs wisping across her forehead. He didn't recognize the other woman, a willowy redhead wearing a fitted blue dress.

He saw the interest in the redhead's eyes when they approached, but his gaze shifted to Grace and held there.

Molly greeted Caleb with a kiss before offering introductions. "Elyse, this is Cody, Sean, and Devin. I think everyone else knows each other."

They all exchanged greetings, and Devin pulled out the chair to his left intending to offer it to Grace. Elyse beat her to it.

Grace clearly read his intentions but gave only a slight shrug before taking the only other available seat between Sean and Cody.

Sean immediately turned to Grace. Devin couldn't hear him, but Grace's responding laughter carried to him. Distracted from whatever Elyse had said, Devin tried to focus on her now. "I'm sorry. What did you say?"

Elyse smiled and scooted closer. "I asked where you're from."

Swallowing an inward sigh, he focused on his end of the conversation. He learned that Elyse had attended Arizona State University with everyone else there, and even though he was disappointed he hadn't been able to sit beside Grace, he could admit that Elyse was easy to talk to and appeared to be genuinely nice. She was even the sort he would consider dating if his attention hadn't already strayed elsewhere.

When Elyse mentioned studying accounting with Grace, Devin looked across the table.

How was it that he had never run into Grace on campus while he was completing his undergraduate degree before moving on to Stanford? Come to think of it, how had he missed her every time he'd gone home to Sedona to visit?

He wanted to ask her what she had been doing since high school, but with the din in the room, conversation with Grace wasn't feasible unless he wanted to shout. He considered the possibility.

When Elyse started chatting again, he wondered how long the comedy show would last. Even though it hadn't started yet, he was already looking forward to it ending so he could spend some time with Grace.

* * *

Grace could feel Devin's gaze on her. She lifted her eyes to meet his, and she saw the interest reflected there. Was she seeing things, or was it possible there was still a spark between them after all these years?

The lights dimmed, and the host walked on stage. The first comedian engaged the crowd and used the perfect balance of self-deprecating humor and a slanted look at life to have the crowd roaring with laughter.

The second comedian started out with a commentary on his relationship with his parents and the past twelve years living in their basement. Images of the past crashed over Grace, an unexpected reminder of what she had lost when her parents had died in a car crash a few days after high school graduation. She shifted uncomfortably in her seat and fought against the familiar well of emotions.

When the topic shifted, the short, wiry man on stage related his attempts to attract the right woman, describing his view of exactly what she would look like. When the jokes went from raunchy to downright crude, Grace decided it was the perfect time to take a walk.

She collected her purse and whispered to Molly, "I need to get some air."

Molly nodded briefly before turning her attention back to the show.

Grace reached the lobby, not sure what to do next. She wasn't ready to head back to her room, but she didn't care to watch the show any longer. Even before the jokes had turned edgy, she had been more than ready to put some distance between herself and Elyse.

She was pretty sure Devin had been about to offer her the seat next to him when Elyse had claimed it. Watching the way she had poured on the charm had felt just like the first time she had seen Devin with Bethany Whitaker only a week after he had broken up with her.

"Not interested in comedy?"

Grace turned to see Devin standing behind her. "Not that particular brand anyway." She motioned toward the club entrance. "What about you? Why aren't you still in there?"

"I thought maybe I could convince you to go for a walk with me."

"What about Caleb and Molly?"

"I'm sure they'll be fine without us." He held out a hand. "Come on. Let's go see what's outside."

She automatically put her hand in his. "I'd like that."

When his hand closed around hers, her heart experienced the same little lift it had when he had hugged her earlier. She remembered the sensation well from their dating days. Come to think of it, she couldn't remember feeling like that with anyone she had dated since.

Odd, she thought to herself, that she could still feel a connection to him after so many years.

"Molly said you're finishing your MBA," Grace said.

"Yeah. One semester left." He released her hand so he could push open the glass door leading outside. "What about you? I assume you've graduated college."

"I'm finishing my MBA too." She shivered when she stepped outside into the crisp December air. "We'll graduate around the same time."

Devin shrugged out of his jacket and draped it around her shoulders.

"Thank you." She pulled the jacket tighter around her, appreciating the gesture.

"You're welcome." Devin guided her forward. "Where are you studying? ASU?"

"Yes."

"How is it I didn't see you the whole time we were going to school together there?"

"I actually did my undergraduate work at Colorado State."

He turned a curious gaze on her, taking her hand in his once more. "I thought you went to Arizona State like everyone else here."

"Not until I started my master's." She knew she should tell him the circumstances of her quick departure from Arizona and the events that had changed her life so drastically once she had moved to Colorado, but with the neon lights flashing overhead and his hand warm in hers, she decided such heavy topics could wait for another time.

She pointed toward the roller coaster that cut through the New York–New York Hotel, a replica of the Statue of Liberty beside it. "What do you think? Are you up for it?"

He gave her a crooked grin. "I am if you are."

"Then let's go." She tugged on his hand, and they left the wedding party behind in search of their own adventure.

Chapter 3

His FIRST MORNING IN LAS Vegas, Devin awoke thinking about her. He rolled over and picked up his phone, pulling up a picture they had taken after their ride on the roller coaster. Grace's hair was windblown, her cheeks flushed.

A smile lit his face when he thought of the way she had thrown her hands up when they had reached the pinnacle right before the roller coaster had started its wild descent.

He checked the time. 8:00 a.m. How was it that he was already awake? He hadn't arrived back at his room until nearly two.

Though he knew he should probably wait an hour or two before he texted Grace, he sent a message anyway. *Breakfast? Call me when you get up.*

Expecting that she was still sleeping, Devin rolled out of bed and pulled on some sweatpants and a fresh T-shirt. After donning his running shoes, he headed for the workout room.

A few people were already inside, two on the ellipticals and a woman on a treadmill, her ponytail bouncing with each stride. Devin drew closer, intending to leave a treadmill between them. Then he did a double take.

"Grace." He stepped onto the treadmill beside her, but she didn't turn her head. He noticed the earbuds and the cord leading from her cell phone to her ears.

Grinning to himself, he started his treadmill at a walking pace. He lifted his cell phone and texted Grace. *Look to your right.*

As soon as he pressed send, he increased the speed, watching her out of the corner of his eye. He was a little frustrated that she didn't look at her incoming text right away, apparently content to ignore it while she finished her workout. The rest of her run took another twenty minutes.

He was finishing his third mile when she slowed her treadmill for a cooldown. Hearing the motor slow, he glanced at her again, his amusement bubbling up inside him when she finally looked at the screen on her phone.

She looked to her right. Stunned disbelief quickly faded behind an eye roll, then laughter. She pulled her earbuds free and asked, "How long have you been down here?"

"Oh," he glanced at the monitor, "a little over three miles' worth." He slowed his treadmill to walking pace once more so he could chat with her without stopping his workout completely.

"I texted you a while ago to see if you wanted to grab breakfast, but I didn't think you were up yet. I guess I was wrong."

"I'm not very good at sleeping past six."

"Admirable," Devin stated. "Crazy but admirable."

"If you've already put in three miles, you're on the crazy side too."

"Maybe a little," Devin said. "I want to put in a couple more miles. Want to meet for breakfast in an hour or so?"

"Sounds great." She grabbed a towel from a nearby basket and wiped the sweat off her face. "Where do you want to meet?"

"I'll come by your room, and we can walk down together."

"See you then."

Devin punched up the speed once more, but the increased pace didn't keep him from watching Grace toss her towel into the hamper and walk out the door.

* * *

Grace opened the door and fought against a frown. Did her heart have to pick up speed just because Devin was looking at her?

"Ready?" he asked.

"Yes. Let me grab my purse." She crossed to where she had left it on her bed, her thoughts racing. Last night had been so much fun, and she wondered how their friendship could feel so easy after so many years apart.

He took her hand in his when she stepped into the hall beside him, and her heart experienced a slow, slippery meltdown. She straightened her shoulders and reminded herself that she probably wouldn't see him again after this week.

Enjoy the moment, she told herself.

"Do you have any idea what the plan is for today?" Devin asked.

"We have a luncheon at one and a dinner show at seven. Thankfully, they decided to skip the traditional bachelor and bachelorette parties."

Devin chuckled. "That's not surprising. Those two are practically inseparable."

"I know. It took some major effort to get Molly to fly up early with me to take care of the wedding details."

"How did you manage that?" Devin asked.

"I reminded her that she gets carsick." They stepped into the elevator. "That's also the reason they decided to spend their honeymoon in San Diego instead of on a cruise ship."

"Good call." Devin punched the button for the lobby. "That also explains why I get to drive Caleb's car back to Phoenix."

"What?" Grace looked at him with a combination of surprise and concern. "I thought I was going to drive his car back for him."

"Sounds like someone got their wires crossed." Devin leaned against the back of the elevator. "I gather you don't have other transportation back home?"

Slowly she shook her head. "What about you?"

"My plan was to drive to Sedona to see my folks before continuing to Phoenix to catch my flight back to school." He gave her hand a squeeze. "Don't worry. We'll figure something out. Worst case, we can drive down to Sedona together, and you can drop me off."

"That would work." She let out a sigh. "For a simple wedding, Caleb and Molly have sure managed to make it complicated."

"How so?"

"First, they couldn't pick a date. Then they chose a wedding chapel, but when we got here, Molly hated it, so we had to find a new one. And instead of a weekend in Vegas, they wanted almost a whole week. Now the car." Grace shrugged. "I'm starting to think eloping in the traditional sense might hold some appeal."

"I don't think your parents would approve of that idea."

She swallowed hard, then drew a deep breath and prepared to tell him the truth. The elevator doors slid open, and before she could form the words, Devin led her into the lobby and they found themselves face-to-face with Molly and Caleb. Disappointed that they were interrupted, Grace tried to push aside the past and focus on the present.

"Looks like old times," Caleb said. "You know, it's not too late to turn this into a double wedding."

Grace could feel her cheeks heat up. She tried to pull her hand free, but Devin had anticipated the attempt and held firm.

"Not a bad idea." Devin pulled her another step forward and shocked her when he pressed on and asked, "What do you say, Grace? Do you want to get married?"

The romantic in her had imagined dozens of ways her future husband might propose. An off-the-cuff comment in a crowded Las Vegas lobby didn't measure up to any of them. The ill-timed delivery didn't prevent the image of such a future together from forming in her mind.

"I think I'll wait a bit longer to get married, but thanks anyway."

"Are you sure?" Molly asked, half serious. "You two do make a cute couple."

Grace shot her a look that told Molly she was venturing into a sensitive area.

Gratefully, Devin changed the subject. "We're going to grab some breakfast. Did you want to join us?"

"No, we're heading out to pick up our parents at the airport," Caleb said. "You two have fun though. Let us know if you change your mind about the double wedding."

"See you later." Devin tugged on Grace's hand and led her to the hotel restaurant. The hostess took them to a table near the center of the room. As soon as they were seated, menus in hand, Devin said, "You know, we really could get married with Caleb and Molly."

"Getting married isn't like deciding to go skiing together. I think it should take a bit more thought than a random suggestion."

He cocked his head to one side. "Maybe you're my one true love, the person I've been pining for ever since high school."

"You broke up with me, remember?" Her voice was light, even though she experienced a little stab in her heart when she thought of that day once again.

"Definitely the biggest mistake of my life."

"Right."

"Seriously. I saw you yesterday and couldn't believe I'd been that stupid." He brushed his fingers over hers. "Can you ever forgive me?"

Never had she expected to hear such words from him. "I think that forgiveness was granted quite a few years ago."

"That's a relief." He leaned closer and, to her surprise, pressed his lips against hers.

Shock prevented her from pulling away, that and the rush of attraction that flowed through her. She shouldn't let him kiss her like this, but that thought floated away when he cupped a hand behind her neck and changed the angle of the kiss.

Past and present collided, the dreams of her younger self blossoming into something more permanent. She didn't want to still love him, but her heart wasn't listening. Regardless of their time apart, Devin Shanahan was the only man who had ever made her yearn for a happily ever after.

When he pulled back, she glanced around, suddenly aware of the other patrons scattered around the room. As though the years between them had never happened, he edged back and said, "So you'll marry me, right?"

She laughed. She couldn't help it. "You're impossible."

"Part of my charm." He gave her another quick kiss and picked up his menu. "Have you decided what you want?"

Grace didn't have to look at the menu to know her stomach wouldn't handle much more than toast and orange juice. "Yeah. How about you?"

He nodded and lifted a hand to signal the waitress. After the woman took their order, Devin and Grace fell into a comfortable conversation, catching up on the past few years.

Grace skirted the topic of her family situation, partially because she didn't want to broach the depressing topic and partially because it never seemed to be a good time to change the subject.

After paying the bill, Devin glanced at his watch. "We still have a few hours before we'll have to meet everyone for lunch. That's plenty of time to go apply for our marriage license."

"We aren't getting married."

"Ever?" He didn't give her the chance to answer before he shook his head and added, "That's not an answer I can live with."

"I don't remember you being so dramatic in high school."

Devin stood and took her hand. "If you don't want to deal with paperwork right now, we can check out the casinos first."

Grace didn't know whether to be flattered or frustrated that he kept bringing up marriage. "I'm not much of a gambler."

"What do you want to do, then?" They left the restaurant and reached the main lobby. "We could go shopping. I still need to get some Christmas presents for my folks."

"That sounds good." Grace's stomach tightened, and she decided to take the opening before it closed. "How are your parents doing?"

"The same. Dad spends most of his time away on business trips, and Mom spends his money redecorating."

Grace heard the touch of bitterness in his voice. "I always thought your family was close."

"Not really. In fact, I'm only going to see my parents for a few hours before they leave for Paris for the holidays."

She pushed aside her disappointment that he would be going back to school so quickly while she would once again be left behind with the what ifs. So much for him loving her. "Aren't you going with them?"

"Hanging out in Paris by myself while my mom shops and my dad squeezes in meetings while he pretends to be on vacation isn't my idea of Christmas. I'd much rather hit the ski slopes." He headed for one of the hotel boutiques. "What about you? What are your plans for Christmas?"

"I was planning to fly to Colorado to spend the holiday with my grandfather."

"Are your parents meeting you there?"

"No." She took a painful breath but couldn't force the words out.

Devin stopped walking and looked at her. "Grace?"

Dozens of words filtered through her mind, but she couldn't find a way to string them together. How did one announce the loss of lives so precious? Or explain how life would never be the same again because her parents were gone? Would he be able to fathom the depth of hurt and loneliness that had followed the accident?

The unspoken questions in Devin's eyes were replaced with concern. "Is there a reason you aren't going to be with your parents this Christmas?"

Grace blinked hard against the tears that threatened. She took a breath and forced herself to look up at him. "My parents were killed in a car accident right after I graduated from high school."

Shock, sympathy, and concern all crossed his face, and she could feel her own grief threatening to swallow her again.

He put his hands on either side of her face and pressed a kiss to her forehead before looking her in the eye. "I am so sorry. I had no idea."

"Most people don't know." She forced herself to keep her eyes on his. "My dad lost his job at the end of my junior year, and we moved in with my grandfather. It was too hard to tell everyone in Sedona what had happened, so I just let everyone assume everything was fine."

He pulled her into a hug and held on, his chin resting on the top of her head. She blinked against the tears welling up in her eyes. She knew she should be used to the way emotions could rise up and swamp over her like this, but she still wished she could somehow find a way to keep them in check.

Devin led her into an alcove near the boutique entrance, where they were afforded some privacy. He ran his hands down her arms. "We don't have to go shopping. This time of year must be really hard on you."

"It's okay. Really. I still have my grandpa to shop for." She wasn't going to mention that she purchased his gift three weeks ago and had already shipped it to him.

He wrapped her in another embrace and held on as a minute stretched into two. When he finally pulled back, he said, "I don't know how you do it."

"Do what?"

"How you always roll with whatever life throws at you."

"What do you mean?"

"Remember when you moved to Sedona, and they kept changing your schedule? And then you lost your spot on the sprint relay when you sprained your wrist." He kept his hands loosely around her waist. "You never complained."

"How do you remember that stuff? I hardly knew you back then."

"Maybe not at first, but I certainly knew you when we toilet papered Coach Fransen's house. I couldn't believe you figured out how to disable those security lights."

"Some skills shouldn't be shared." She smiled at the memory. "I hope you've outgrown the need to decorate people's yards that way."

He didn't answer, his eyes darkening as he leaned closer to brush his lips against hers. Her heart knocked hard in her chest, and she leaned into the kiss.

The water in the lobby fountain trickled in the background, the scent of fresh flowers wafting on the air. A shiver ran through her when Devin's fingers tangled in her hair, one of her own hands reaching up to rest on the strength of his shoulder. Comfort, strength, acceptance. The emotions powered through her, overwhelming her with both their simplicity and the knowledge that she hadn't felt any of them this strongly since the loss of her parents.

When he pulled back and stared down at her, the love that swelled within her nearly tumbled out in words.

"Let's walk for a bit. I want to hear the real story of what's been happening since you left Sedona."

"I thought you wanted to go shopping."

"Shopping can wait." He pressed his lips to her forehead again. "I want to know who you've become since we were together last."

"I'm the same person you knew before."

"No, you've changed," Devin insisted. "We both have."

"Then maybe it's me who needs to get to know the new you."

"That works too."

Chapter 4

Fai knew he couldn't put it off any longer. Qing wasn't a patient man, and it was only a matter of time before he demanded a report on Kyle Rode's status. The fact that Rode had shown up for work the past three days was reason enough for Qing to be displeased.

Fai had already arranged for Rode to meet him. That part of his task had been ridiculously easy. After all, the man was looking for secrets, and Fai had alluded to the possibility that he had some to share.

Now Fai waited near the bus stop by the restaurant where they were to meet. Traffic rushed by, both the automotive and pedestrian variety. At precisely three minutes before the time they had agreed upon, Rode stepped off a local bus. 8:27 p.m. After nightfall.

It was a shame, really, Fai thought to himself. The man was only thirty-one years old, and his advanced degree from Oxford was proof enough of his intelligence. His aptitude in finance showed promise; it was a pity he had such a penchant for looking into things that weren't any of his business.

Spies knew the risks, Fai reminded himself. This particular British spy had come here of his own free will, and now he would pay for that choice.

Fai adopted a worried expression and moved down the sidewalk to cut Rode off before he could enter the restaurant. "This way," Fai said in a low voice, angling toward a nearby alley. "I don't want anyone to see me with you."

Without another word, both men slipped away from the crowded sidewalk and into the shadows. When they reached the back of the building, Rode turned to face him only to find the barrel of the silencer attached to Fai's gun pointed right at him.

The whisper of two shots puffed into the breeze, and Kyle Rode crumpled to the ground. Fai checked the man for a pulse and found none. Satisfied that his task was complete, he continued down the alley to where he could reemerge onto the street without drawing attention to himself.

Pushing aside the image of the man in his current state, Fai headed for a restaurant down the block. Time to get something to eat and put such unpleasantness behind him.

* * *

Devin didn't think it was possible to fall in love in less than twenty-four hours, but he had done exactly that. Grace was all he could think about. Or maybe he really had been in love with her since high school and had been in denial all these years. Before yesterday, he hadn't thought about what his future would look like beyond his professional life. Now the personal side of things was all he could think about.

Did Grace already have a job lined up once school was behind her? Would she be willing to consider a move to Washington, DC, after gradu-ation so they could see where this relationship could take them? He consid-ered for a brief moment that he was getting ahead of himself, but memories of holding her earlier reaffirmed what he already knew—he was in love with her, and he wanted her in his future.

His internship with the Central Intelligence Agency had helped pay for his undergraduate tuition and provided him independence from his parents. The agency had granted him an extension on his commitment to them and allowed him to continue on and get his MBA. Evidently a degree from Stanford could benefit them in some way. He didn't know how yet, but he imagined once he started full-time it wouldn't take long to learn of their plans for him.

He couldn't tell Grace about the internship, of course, except to share the cover story the CIA had created for him. The agency varied the locations where he worked each summer: Washington, New York, London, Hong Kong. The overseas assignments had been his favorites so far.

Clearly Grace had spent the past several years preparing for her own career. Would she be open to joining him in moving around the world as he pursued his career, or would her plans alter his to a new path that would keep him in one place?

Maybe it was the constant reminders that his best friend was getting married in four days that made him wonder what it would be like if Grace had agreed to marry him. The offer had been spontaneous, with only a hint of underlying seriousness, but now the possibilities had become firmly planted in his brain.

A knock on his hotel-room door startled him back to the present. He answered it, the face of his questions smiling back at him from the other side of the threshold. "Are you ready for dinner?"

"Yeah." He stepped into the hall just as the door across from his opened and Cody and Sean walked out.

"Hey, we were just about to come find you," Cody said.

"Why were you looking for me? We're all meeting for dinner in five minutes."

"Yeah, but we wanted to talk to you while Caleb isn't around. We're trying to decide if we should have his bachelor party here at this hotel or if we should book a room at one of the other places here on the strip."

"Bachelor party?" Grace repeated. "I thought Caleb and Molly decided to skip that."

"Every guy needs a bachelor party before he gets married," Cody insisted. He focused back on Devin. "What do you think?"

"I think you'd better be sure Caleb is on board with this before you make any plans."

"If we let him have any say, it won't happen," Sean said. "We figure you can help kidnap him for the evening. If Grace will distract Molly for a while, it should be easy to get the party started."

Devin sensed the surge of emotions welling up in the woman beside him. It was all coming back to him. The way Grace's shyness had made her seem reserved to those who didn't know her well and the satisfaction he always felt when he saw how animated she got when she was passionate about something. He suspected she was about to become very animated now.

Grace fisted her hands and planted them on her hips. "Cody, whose wedding is this?"

Cody looked at her suspiciously. "Is this a trick question?"

"Not at all. When you get married, your buddies can throw however many bachelor parties you want, but Caleb specifically said he didn't want one."

"Oh, come on, Grace. It's not like we're going to let things get out of hand. We're only talking about getting the guys together one last time before Caleb is a married man. No big deal."

"Again, Caleb and Molly said they didn't want parties. What part of that don't you understand?"

"They said they didn't want them the night before their wedding," Cody corrected. "This is four nights before."

Devin motioned toward the elevator. In an effort to play peacemaker, he said, "I think we should table this discussion for now. We're supposed to be at the restaurant in a couple minutes."

"Fine." Cody huffed out a breath and started forward. He looked over at Grace. "Will you help us if Caleb agrees to the bachelor party?"

"I'd be happy to as long as Molly is on board too," Grace said. "I just don't want us to lose sight of what this week is all about."

"Not a chance," Cody said.

Devin put his hand on Grace's back to guide her forward. "Do you really think Caleb will go for this party idea?"

"If we tell him we're keeping it low-key, I think so." Cody pressed the down button. "Remember, it was Caleb and Molly's idea for us to spend a few days together before their wedding. They want us to have a good time."

"True," Devin conceded. "And I'm sure it will be a great time for everyone once we talk over our plans with the bride and groom."

Grace gave him a nod of approval. "I completely agree."

* * *

"Are you sure you're okay with this?" Grace asked Molly, with Ellie and Elyse walking beside them. "The guys won't go through with it if you object."

"It's fine," Molly assured her. "I don't know that I trust Sean farther than I can throw him, but with Cody and Devin there, I doubt there will be any problems."

"Besides, this gives us a chance to check out the town without my brothers acting like they're my babysitters," Ellie added.

"And we can scout out cute guys," Elyse added. "Or at least Ellie and I can. You two can help."

"Grace is single too," Ellie said.

"Hardly. It's obvious Devin is head over heels for her," Elyse countered. "I feel like an idiot for flirting with him last night. No one told me you two were a couple."

"We aren't exactly," Grace said, not sure how to define her relationship with Devin. "We used to date in high school."

Molly stopped walking and turned to face Grace. "Wait. He's *that* Devin? The one you were completely in love with?"

Leave it to Molly to air all of her private feelings in front of everyone. Grace deliberately kept her voice light. "Yes, he's that Devin."

"Well, it certainly looks like the old flame has rekindled into a bonfire," Elyse said.

"Yes, it does," Molly agreed. She grabbed Grace and Elyse by their arms. "Let's go have some fun."

"Where are we off to?"

"Circus Circus. It's a family-friendly place. I figure we can't get into too much trouble there."

"One would hope," Grace said.

Molly handed each of them fifty dollars. "Here is my little gift to all of you for coming to my wedding. Try not to lose it all in one place."

As soon as they arrived, the group split into two. Molly and Elyse decided to try their luck in the traditional casino while Ellie and Grace opted for the arcade portion. Three hours later, Molly and Elyse arrived upstairs with only five dollars left between them. Ellie and Grace, on the other hand, suffered from luck of a different kind. Beside the shooting range, a pile of stuffed animals flowed from the space beside where Grace was shooting water into the mouth of a clown.

"How are you guys doing?" Molly's eyes landed on the mountain of stuffed animals, and her jaw dropped.

"You can see for yourself." Ellie pointed to the pile.

"You won all of those?"

"We kind of have a system down," Ellie said.

Grace ignored the conversation, her focus on the spray of water and the little balloon rising up until she was once again declared the winner. The game attendant came over and handed her a purple monkey.

"Thanks." Grace stepped back and relinquished her spot to a boy around ten who had been waiting behind her.

"What are we going to do with all of these stuffed animals?" Molly asked.

"It was worse a while ago. We traded in a bunch of them for the bigger versions," Grace said. Now that she looked down at the pile, she felt a little guilty that she hadn't stopped playing earlier.

Molly put her hand on a five-foot-tall teddy bear the color of sand. "Is this yours too?"

"Yeah." Grace considered for a moment. "I don't suppose you would like that for a wedding present?"

"No." Her answer was firm.

Ellie flagged down a resort employee. "Excuse me, but do you have some garbage bags we can have to carry all of these in?"

The lady looked at the pile and laughed. "Sure. I'll be right back."

Fifteen minutes later, they all stuffed themselves into a cab, the huge teddy bear lying across their laps because it wouldn't fit in the overfull trunk.

"Seriously, what are we going to do with all of these?"

"I have an idea." Grace grinned at them. "After all, we don't want the guys to think they had all the fun."

Molly pushed down on the teddy's stomach. "I'm listening."

Chapter 5

DEVIN DIDN'T KNOW HOW IT was possible to have a good time and still wish he was somewhere else. The bachelor party had already moved from the casino to a show then back to the casino, yet Grace always seemed to be on the edge of his thoughts. Part of him wanted to extend his time with his friends, but another part wished this party would end so he could spend more time with Grace.

He shook that thought from his mind, focusing once more on the people he was with. The decision to take a break for a bite to eat was a welcome one, and he settled into his seat between Cody and Sean.

"So what's going on with you and Grace?" Cody asked as soon as they had their drinks.

"What?" Devin looked up from his glass.

"Every time I see you, she's at your side."

"We've had a lot of catching up to do," Devin said, not ready to confess his feelings to his friends, especially when Grace didn't understand he was seriously still in love with her.

"Maybe you should convince her to extend her vacation here for another week," Cody said.

"That's not a bad idea." The idea took root, and Devin considered the possibilities. Admittedly, he wasn't terribly excited about spending the holidays alone, and he would have time to see his parents after they returned from Europe if he decided to delay his trip to Sedona. He was still pondering the possibilities when Sean's words cut into his thoughts.

"Grace may be hot, but from what I've heard, she's the wait-for-marriage kind of girl."

Sean's sneer told Devin he didn't approve of Grace's high moral standards, and he wasn't about to admit he shared them, not in front of a bunch of men at a bachelor party.

"I already offered to let them join in on the fun," Caleb said, shifting his attention to Devin. "We can still have a double wedding."

"That would be something." Cody lifted his drink and gestured as though toasting him. "What do you think, Devin? Is Grace the ring-on-the-finger type?"

"I think the couple we should be toasting right now is Caleb and Molly," Devin said. After lifting his soda and clinking glasses with the other men at the table, he took a sip and wondered how much longer he would have to wait before he could see Grace again.

Even though Devin hoped to slip away from the party at a reasonable hour, his friends insisted they needed him as they went from one show to another, one casino to another. Finally, at three o'clock in the morning, all four men wearily made their way from the elevator toward their rooms located at the end of the hall.

Sean staggered a step, nearly losing his balance.

Devin exchanged a look with Caleb that spoke of their mutual appreciation that neither of them had ever chosen to drink alcohol. Fatigue alone was enough to make their steps unsteady.

Devin was so focused on the men beside him that he was nearly to his room before he noticed something scattered on the floor. "What in the world?"

Stuffed animals. Everywhere. Big ones, small ones, one enormous one. A teddy bear nearly as big as he was leaned against his door. The rest of the floor was wall to wall with stuffed animals piled almost two feet deep.

"I think the girls had fun tonight." Caleb waded through them, kicking a pink flamingo into the air. It landed a few feet down the hall.

"I think we need a shovel," Cody said, one arm supporting Sean.

"You can find a shovel if you want. I'm going to bed." Devin pulled his key from his pocket and put a hand against the wall to keep his balance as he trod over the animals. He had to shift the teddy bear to the side to get to the lock, and as soon as he managed to open the door, Teddy and a handful of stuffed animals closest to his room spilled inside.

Too tired to try to push them back out, he set the giant bear inside and kicked the other toys out of the way.

"Good night," he called to the other men, who were currently doing their own balancing acts to get to their rooms.

Teddy blocked the narrow hallway by the bathroom, and Devin picked him up and dropped him on the extra bed. Then he collapsed on his bed, too exhausted to change out of his clothes. The image of Grace and the other women creating the disaster outside his room brought a smile to his face.

He pulled his phone from his pocket. He knew he shouldn't call so late, but if she hadn't wanted him to call, she wouldn't have left him all those presents, right? He hesitated only a moment before he found her number.

She answered with a groggy, "Hello?"

"I'm lying here next to the present you left me."

"What present is that?" she asked, humor chasing away some of the sleep in her voice.

"Teddy." He rolled onto his side and adjusted the phone so he could talk without holding it. "You realize I'm going to wake up thinking about you now."

"That's nice."

"It is nice." He closed his eyes. "Not as nice as if I was waking up to you."

"Sorry, Devin. I'm not that kind of girl."

"I'm not asking you to be." His breathing slowed, and he could hear the exhaustion creeping into his words. "Marry me."

"Good night, Devin."

"I really am going to marry you someday."

"Have you been drinking?" she asked.

"I don't drink. I love you, you know."

"I think you need to get some sleep."

"Good idea. We'll plan the wedding tomorrow." He rolled over and promptly fell asleep.

* * *

Grace woke up wondering if the phone call from Devin had been a dream. She could have sworn he'd said he loved her. Her insides fluttered with excitement at the thought, then moved with a wave of exasperation.

She swung her legs over the side of the bed and raked her fingers through her hair. She really needed to stop letting Devin's marriage proposals work their way into her dreams.

A text message chimed. She glanced at her bedside table, her eyes narrowing when she didn't see her cell phone. She was certain she had plugged it in to charge. She ran her hand over her bed, searching for the source of the sound. Under her pillow?

Suddenly uncertain, she read the message illuminating her screen. *I'm trapped! Stuffed animals everywhere. Come save me.*

Her laughter carried across the empty room as she typed, *Don't you like your gifts? I won the teddy bear just for you.*

Meet me downstairs in an hour? I'll take you out to eat before we go shopping.

See you then.

She plugged her phone back into the charger, her mind clearing. A couple of pressed buttons revealed what she had thought was impossible. She really had talked to Devin earlier this morning. That meant . . .

Her chest tightened, a kind of ache settling there when she let the first flutterings of possibilities creep into her mind. Had he really been serious when he'd professed his love? Or had he had some other motive to say such things to her? Or was it because he'd lost all sense of logic at 3:00 a.m.?

Afraid to dream but equally afraid not to, she headed for the shower. They had only a few more days together, she reminded herself. After the wedding, she would find out if Devin really did plan to be a more permanent part of her life.

* * *

"Let's go in here." Devin tugged on Grace's hand and headed into a jewelry store in the mall, where they had spent the past several hours. After he had managed to clear a path through the dozens of stuffed animals outside his door, he had met Grace for a morning workout. By the time they had showered and changed, their first meal of the day had been lunch, rather than breakfast, followed by this shopping trip.

She waved at the shopping bags he carried. "I thought you said you were done with your shopping."

"I'm done shopping for my family. I haven't bought you a Christmas present yet." Neither of them had mentioned the phone call last night, and Devin had come to realize Grace didn't trust his sincerity. In truth, he was only coming to grips with it himself.

"You don't have to get me anything. Until three days ago, you hadn't seen me for years."

He stopped by the doorway and looked down at her. Her words held no malice, but they stung just the same. "I still can't believe I let that much time slip by."

Devin pulled her into the store, surprised to find it empty even though Christmas was only ten days away. Maybe people in Vegas didn't shop for jewelry on Wednesday afternoons.

"May I help you?" the store clerk asked. She appeared to be in her early forties, her dark hair pulled back into a sleek ponytail, turquoise and silver adorning her ears and neck.

Opting for the subtle approach, Devin said, "We're just looking for now."

"Let me know if you have any questions."

"We will. Thanks."

Grace lowered her voice. "Devin, you are not buying me a Christmas present, especially not jewelry."

Though his instinct was to dispute her claim, he said simply, "It won't hurt to look around."

Devin took his time leading her to the display cases. They looked half-heartedly at bracelets, necklaces, and earrings. When a tray of birthstone rings caught his eye, he motioned to them. "What about one of these?"

"Devin, you are not buying me jewelry."

"What's your ring size?" Devin asked.

"I have no idea."

"I thought all women knew their ring size."

"Women who wear rings probably do."

The clerk stepped forward and opened a drawer beneath the display case. She pulled out a large ring with silver bands in various sizes hanging from it. "Here. We can find out for you."

The clerk reached for her hand and started slipping bands on her finger, finding the correct size on the second try. "Six and a half."

"I like that one. It's simple. Classic." He motioned to a ruby solitaire.

"I'm not letting you buy me a ring," Grace repeated.

"Humor me for a minute. If you were going to pick out a ring for yourself, which one would you want?"

"I don't know. I guess something like that." She tapped on the glass above a pearl ring, two small diamonds offsetting it against a platinum band.

"Can she try that on?" Devin asked.

"I think it will need to be resized." The clerk pulled the ring free and held it out. "Yes, this is a seven."

Devin took it from her and slipped it onto Grace's left hand. "It suits you."

Grace stared at it for a moment and then removed it and handed it back to the clerk. "Thanks for your help." She then took Devin's hand. "We should get back to the hotel."

"You realize you're being difficult, right?"

"Not at all." She moved toward the door, glancing back to make sure he was following her.

Devin wished he could find a way to distract Grace long enough to buy the ring for her but knew it would look suspicious if he tried. Instead, he lowered his voice slightly and spoke to the clerk.

"Do you have a business card in case I can change her mind?"

"Yes, of course." The woman retrieved a business card from a card holder on the counter, and cluing into Devin's dilemma, she turned the card over and jotted down a string of numbers.

Devin took the card from her and smiled when he saw the product code for the ring Grace liked scrawled on the back. "Thanks. You have a great day."

The clerk smiled. "You too."

* * *

Grace reined in her horse, slowing to look at the sun lowering in the distance. Orange, yellow, and purple streaked the sky, the red rocks of the desert outside of Las Vegas casting long shadows across the ground.

Ahead of her, Molly and Caleb were deep in conversation as they rode side by side. The rest of the wedding party had opted to spend the evening at another show, but Devin and Grace had both been ready to get outside.

Horseback riding in the desert wasn't what Grace had expected to do two days before her cousin's wedding, but it was the perfect distraction.

Even though she had spent most of her time in Vegas with Devin, the constant pace of doing something all the time had started to wear on her. If she had her way, after they got back to the hotel, she was going to find a nice quiet corner somewhere to hang out.

Devin slowed his horse and waited for her to catch up.

"You okay?"

"Yeah." She nudged her horse forward to pick up the pace. "I was just thinking how gorgeous this is. It's been a long time since I've done something like this."

"You know, I was thinking maybe we could stay and spend a few days here after the wedding."

Surprised, Grace shifted her focus so it was fully on him. She had hoped Devin would want to see her after the week ended, but she hadn't anticipated his wanting to extend their time here.

"I don't know. . ."

"You don't have to decide right now. When are you supposed to be flying out to see your grandfather?"

"Not until Christmas Eve."

"Perfect. Stay with me until then."

"You aren't serious." She tried to read his expression, but the sunglasses he wore prevented her from seeing his eyes. "I thought you wanted to see your parents. Besides, our hotel rooms aren't exactly cheap."

"We can cut that cost in half as soon as you marry me." The trail narrowed, forcing them to ride single file for several yards. As soon as Devin brought his horse beside her once more, he continued. "I want to spend the rest of the break with you. Staying in Las Vegas works, but if you'd rather go somewhere else, we can do that instead."

Her heart softened, and she yearned for more time with Devin. She hated the idea of his being alone at Christmas, so she made an offer she could barely believe was coming out of her mouth. "You can come with me to Colorado for Christmas."

As though he had triumphed in some hard-won battle, his face relaxed into a smile. "I'd like that. Of course, I'd like it a whole lot better if you married me first."

"Haven't we already had this conversation?" Grace asked him.

"The ending hasn't turned out the way I want yet." His grin widened. "I'm going to convince you I'm serious. You'll see."

Chapter 6

GRACE HELD HER GROUND THAT day and the two days following. Now, as she stood beside Molly and listened to wedding vows being exchanged, longing seeped into her. She supposed weddings always made single people long for what they didn't have, but she hadn't expected it to hit her this hard. Was it knowing that her friendship with her cousin would change now that Molly was married, or was it the desire for some permanence in her life to replace what she'd lost when her parents had died? Or perhaps Devin's frequent comments about marriage really were wearing on her.

Her gaze swept the room, from the bride and groom staring into each other's eyes to her aunt and uncle sitting close by. Then her eyes met Devin's, and her stomach flip-flopped. She saw an intensity there she couldn't ever remember seeing before. Something was different about him, as though he had found a new sense of determination, but Grace didn't understand the source of the change.

They still hadn't nailed down their plans for going back to Arizona, and Grace hoped Devin planned to join her in Colorado. She had given him her flight information and mentioned to her grandfather that she might be bringing a guest. She hadn't, however, mentioned any of this to Molly. She always wanted to know the whole story, and the last thing Grace wanted right now was for anyone to try to dissect her renewed relationship with Devin.

She didn't want to think about what would happen after the holidays, but with him staring at her from across the room, she was considering the possibilities. All of them left her uneasy. A long-distance relationship was the best she could hope for. Finding her heart shattered a second time, the worst. Was there anything in between?

As Molly and Caleb shared their first kiss as husband and wife, a little seed of hope blossomed within Grace. Devin might have been joking about getting married, but maybe one day, he would discover that the love she felt for him so many years ago hadn't faded. Maybe, just maybe, he would learn to love her too.

* * *

Devin held Grace in his arms, swaying to the slow song Caleb and Molly had chosen to be their last dance before leaving on their honeymoon. He took in the scent of roses lingering on Grace, a reminder of the bouquet she had carried all day, though her hands were now linked loosely around his neck.

Every time he asked Grace about marriage, she brushed him off as though it was a big joke. But he wasn't joking, and he was ready to make sure she understood his intentions whether she was ready or not.

Throughout the wedding and ensuing activities, Devin had imagined what it would be like to be in Caleb's place, to have Grace standing beside him at the altar. He couldn't remember ever wanting something more than he wanted to put a ring on Grace's finger and know that their futures would tie together. The urgency he felt to marry her wasn't logical. He knew it, but he couldn't stop himself from taking steps to make it happen.

He had a list of every bridal shop in the area and knew which ones were open after normal business hours. The pearl ring wasn't traditional for an engagement, but Devin hoped to only be engaged for a few days at most. Besides, he wanted her to wear something she liked, and he admired her choice.

"What time did you want to get on the road tomorrow?" Grace asked. "Checkout is at eleven."

"I wasn't joking about wanting to stay here longer with you," Devin told her.

The song ended, and Devin reluctantly released her. Good-byes followed as everyone wished the newlyweds the best. As soon as Caleb and Molly left, the party dispersed, and everyone but the parents of the bride and groom decided to head for one of the nearby nightclubs.

"Do you mind if we skip out on the dancing tonight?" Devin asked. "I have other plans in mind."

"I guess." She looked at him hesitantly.

"Great." He slipped his arm around her waist and guided her out of the room and to the elevator. As soon as they were inside alone, he added, "I think you'll want to change clothes for what I have in mind."

"What do you have in mind?"

He pushed the elevator button.

"Devin?"

He heard her unspoken question, but he still didn't respond.

"Devin, what did you want to do tonight?"

"I left you a little present in your room."

She stopped. "How did you get into my room to leave me a present?"

"The concierge delivered it for me."

He sensed her wariness and hoped to put her at ease despite the nerves racing through him. "Don't worry. I promise to be a gentleman."

"That's good to know, but you still haven't answered my question."

"Let me ask you a question." He mustered his courage. "What do you envision when you think of your wedding day?"

"Not a tacky wedding chapel with an officiator dressed like Elvis."

"I'm serious. What is important to you?"

The sincerity in his voice apparently surprised her enough to make her consider the question before responding. The simplicity of her answer resonated with him. "I want to stand beside a man I love, a man who loves me, and know that the rings on our fingers will stay there forever." She gave a little shrug. "I want my wedding day to be the start of my happily ever after."

He thought of how many times over the past few days he had nearly expressed his feelings for her. Had it been dozens? Hundreds? He couldn't quite manage to express the words he wanted to, but he managed to ask, "Do you love me?"

She kept her eyes on his and gave him the truth he had hoped and prayed for. "Yes. I love you."

Relief and determination merged together to create a new resolve. The words came easily now. "And I love you." He leaned down and kissed her. "So why won't you marry me?"

"Because the only reason you want to marry me is because your friends put the idea in your head." She turned the question around on him. "Why else would you be so determined to get married this weekend?"

"Because I don't want to spend another day without you by my side." He ran his hands down her arms. "I want to wake up every morning lying next to you. I want to start on our happily ever after."

She could only stare.

"Open your door."

As though in a trance, she complied. He felt her surprise when she saw the bouquet of flowers on the dresser. She crossed to it and picked up the white envelope propped in front of it, *The Bridal Shop* scripted in gray across the front.

"What is this?"

"A present." He motioned to it. "Open it."

Slowly she broke the seal to reveal a gift card. Instead of an amount, the words *One Wedding Dress* were written across the front. She turned to face him.

Devin dropped to one knee. "I know I've asked you this before, but I'm asking you again." He drew a breath and forced the words out. "Grace Harrington, will you marry me?"

* * *

Grace didn't know what to think. How many times had she dreamed about a moment like this? How many nights had she wished for someone like Devin to come into her life, a man she could love with her whole heart? Now she wasn't looking anymore. She was face to face with the man she had always loved, the man she had been afraid would never again be part of her life.

"I . . ."

"Please?" He pulled a ring box from his pocket and opened it.

Her doubts about his sincerity vanished the moment she saw the ring inside, the same piece of jewelry she and Devin had seen at the mall.

Her eyes moistened, and she found herself nodding. "Yes."

An instant later, he was on his feet once more, gathering her close. Fumbling, he finally pulled the ring free and slipped it on her finger. As soon as he had it in place, he added to his request.

"Tonight. Marry me tonight."

"What?" She pulled back so she could see his face. "That's insane. We've only been back together for a week."

"I've loved you since I was seventeen years old, and I was too stupid to recognize my feelings for what they were. As soon as I saw you again, I knew I wanted to be with you forever."

His words melted her heart but not her logic. "I felt the same way, but that doesn't mean we should jump into marriage. We won't even be in the same state for another five months."

"I know I'm being selfish, but I don't want to give you the chance to change your mind."

"I'm not going to change my mind."

"Then why wait? The dress shop is open all night. We can go shopping on our way to the wedding chapel." He leaned down and captured her mouth in a mind-numbing kiss. Rational thought ceased to exist as she leaned into him, his hands firm against her back.

This was the man she was going to marry. The newness of that fact combined with a sense of certainty, and suddenly she could see the future she had never dared hope for.

His lips trailed down her neck, and a shiver ran through her. She remembered they were alone in her hotel room and forced herself to pull back.

His eyes intense, he said, "Tonight."

It was no longer a question but a plea.

"This is insane," she said as much to herself as to him.

This time he didn't use words to convince her. He simply watched her, giving her time to process what had already been said and to come to her own decision.

She weighed the options. She could spend her last semester planning a wedding, wishing her mother was still alive to help her, or she could spend that same time married to the man she loved. Instead of using their free time to plan a wedding, they could find time to spend together.

Against all logic, she slowly nodded. "Okay."

"Okay?" He looked at her suspiciously. "As in okay, you'll marry me tonight?"

"Yes. I'll marry you tonight," she said. "But I'm holding firm on the Elvis thing. I'm not getting married in a tacky wedding chapel."

"The one Molly and Devin got married in was nice."

"Yes, it was," Grace agreed.

"Then let's go."

A little seed of doubt crept in. "What about your family and friends?"

"You're the only person I care about. Is there anyone you will regret not having there?"

She thought of her grandfather and various aunts and uncles. As much as she loved Molly's mother, her aunt Marie, the woman was likely to drive her insane if they planned a wedding together.

"I'm okay with eloping if you are."

"In that case, let's go."

Forty-five minutes later, they were in Caleb's car heading to the wedding chapel, the garment bag holding Grace's newly purchased wedding dress spread across the back seat.

Chapter 7

DEVIN STARED AT GRACE WHEN she walked into the chapel from the bride's dressing room a vision in white. The dress fit her beautifully, and her brown hair flowed freely over her shoulders.

Only hours before, Caleb had stood in this exact same spot, and Devin had envied his friend. Now his heart felt like it might burst as his dream walked toward him.

The wedding bands he had purchased when he'd bought Grace's engagement ring were tucked in his suit pocket. He knew the purchase had been reckless initially, but now he was glad he had followed the impulse.

Grace carried the same bouquet she had held when she'd stood as Molly's maid of honor, only now she didn't look as confident; she was nervous.

He prayed she wouldn't change her mind.

As though she felt his silent pleas, she continued toward him until she stood at his side. The ceremony itself was simple and straightforward, only a few minutes passing before the officiator posed the most important question either of them had ever had to answer. Devin felt a weight lift off of him when Grace offered a cautious "I do." Rings were exchanged, the platinum band feeling odd on his left hand, even though he had tried it on only two days before.

"I now pronounce you husband and wife."

Devin didn't wait to be told he could kiss his bride. He pulled her to him, his lips finding hers in a kiss that was both playful and filled with joy.

Holding her close, he hoped the joy would last a lifetime.

* * *

"I can't believe we're married." Grace sat across the table from Devin, the breakfast they had ordered from room service laid out between them. The love she felt for him seemed to have multiplied overnight, and she found herself stunned and giddy at the prospect of being Devin's wife.

"That makes two of us." He broke off a piece of a cinnamon roll. "Did you want to tell any of our friends about this before they leave, or are we going to hide out and pretend we left before they did?"

"They're going to think we're crazy."

"You're right. We can tell them later."

Her heart melted when he leaned across the table and kissed her. Never had she considered when she'd arrived in Las Vegas that she would leave here a married woman.

At least she knew her parents would have approved of Devin. That thought brought another to the surface.

"What are your parents going to think when you tell them?"

"Who knows." He shrugged. "I already told them I wasn't coming home before they leave for Paris, so we have some time to decide how to deal with them."

"Shouldn't you call them now and tell them we're married?"

"I don't want to deal with my parents right now."

"Why not?"

"They're leaving for Paris this afternoon, and you're the only person I want to think about today. Besides, we have more important things to talk about."

"Like?"

"Like where we want to spend the rest of our honeymoon." He took another bite of his pastry. "How does a few days at Lake Powell sound? My folks have a condo there that's sitting empty."

"That's practically on the way to my grandfather's ranch." Grace considered. "Maybe we could go to Lake Powell until Christmas Eve and then spend the holiday with him."

"Sounds perfect," Devin said. "Since we have Caleb's car and he won't be back in Phoenix until after New Year's, we can just drive."

"That would work," Grace said. "Did you want to leave today?"

He leaned over and gave her another kiss and then another. "We can leave tomorrow."

"It's a plan."

* * *

Qing strolled through the gardens behind his home and spoke in a lowered voice to the man beside him. "What's the latest on Shanahan?"

"The offer has been prepared, and our source assures us it will be accepted," Fai told him.

"Surveillance concerns?"

"Everything is as we hoped. No girlfriend, and his closest friends seem to be those he went to high school with."

"Time and distance will weaken those."

"I agree. His best friend got married yesterday. That will change things as well."

"How confident are you in our source about this man?"

"Very. Besides being paid well, we have made it clear what will happen if his loyalty comes into question," Fai said. "What happened to Kyle Rode is quite the motivator."

"Maybe we should have killed someone for falling out of line sooner." Qing considered. "Fear can be an effective tool."

The cold look in Qing's eyes sent a ripple of fear through Fai, and he found himself nodding. "Yes, sir, it can, indeed."

* * *

The idea that Devin probably should have asked Grace's grandfather for her hand in marriage popped up a few miles before they reached the ranch. The land stretched out before him now, the ranch house occupying a clearing surrounded by trees.

Devin could envision a shotgun hanging over the mantel, and he glanced at Grace. "How is your grandfather going to take the news that we're married? He isn't going to shoot me, is he?"

Her lips turned upward. "I don't think he'll want me to be a widow at the age of twenty-three, so I think you're safe."

Devin wasn't sure he believed her when he pulled up in front of the house and the door immediately opened. He had envisioned her grandfather as old and frail. The man standing on the porch was neither.

His hair might have been more gray than brown, but he moved with agility and probably had a full inch and thirty pounds on Devin.

Grace climbed out of the car and hurried into his embrace. "Grandpa!"

"There's my girl." He hugged her and then held her at arm's length to study her. "How are you?"

"Funny you should ask that." She turned and waved at Devin. "Things were a little crazy while I was in Las Vegas."

"How so?" His eyes narrowed when his gaze landed on Devin. "And who's this?"

"This is who I was telling you about, Devin Shanahan. This is my grandfather, Quentin Harrington." She hesitated a brief moment before adding, "Grandpa, this is my husband."

Quentin stopped halfway through the motion of extending his hand. The hesitation lasted only a moment before he finished reaching out to shake hands with Devin. The older man's expression changed from welcoming to suspicious.

"I think we should go inside out of the cold. It sounds like you two have a lot of explaining to do."

Devin tried to think of how he would feel if he were in Quentin's shoes but couldn't begin to imagine what it would be like to have a child, much less a grandchild.

He followed the older man and Grace inside to where a fire burned in a brick fireplace, a brown leather sectional facing the warmth centered there. He looked up and swallowed hard. As he had feared, a shotgun hung above the mantel.

Devin tried to find the words to form the apology he was sure he owed this man, but he couldn't quite figure out how to phrase it. Instead, he remained silent, taking Grace's hand in his as they all sat down together.

"Devin, is it?" Quentin began.

"Yes, sir."

"How long have you known my granddaughter?"

"Grandpa, you don't need to interrogate him."

"It's okay, Grace. I think he's entitled." Devin squeezed her hand and shifted his attention to her grandfather. "We've known each other since high school. We dated back then, and it wasn't until we saw each other again that we realized we've been in love this whole time."

"I see." He stroked at his gray mustache. "And what are your plans now that you're married? Are you going to live together in Arizona while Grace finishes school?"

"Actually, I'm one semester away from finishing my MBA at Stanford," Devin told him. He noticed that the mention of the prestigious school didn't impress Quentin the way it did many people. "We'll work something out to see each other as often as we can. As soon as we both graduate, we'll figure out where we want to live."

"I expect you will give Grace's opportunities equal consideration to your own." The words weren't phrased as a question, and Devin wisely didn't respond. He hadn't told Grace about his commitment to the CIA, and he certainly wasn't going to do so now. "And have you discussed children? I assume starting a family will be in your plans at some point in the future."

Devin felt his hands go clammy at that assumption. He hadn't thought that far into the future. After growing up an only child, with parents who didn't exactly know how to parent, he wasn't sure where he stood on having children of his own.

Whether it was instinct or coincidence that Grace picked that exact moment to intervene, Devin was grateful for the distraction.

"Grandpa, that's enough." She put her hand on Devin's knee. "Devin and I interrupted our honeymoon to come spend Christmas with you. The only thing you need to know is that we love each other and we're happy."

"You're right," he said grudgingly. When he turned his gaze back to Devin, his voice was firm. "But I do expect you to keep my granddaughter happy."

"I will do my best."

"That's all I can ask for."

Chapter 8

DEVIN AWOKE CHRISTMAS MORNING TO an empty bed. He reached out to find the sheets beside him cool, causing him to open his eyes and scan the room. Finding himself alone in Grace's bedroom, he rolled onto his back and stared at the ceiling.

How was it that after only a week, he already expected to have her by his side each morning? Had he really settled into married life so easily?

He expected bumps in the road, but so far their honeymoon had been nothing short of perfect. The only exception had been the interrogation by her grandfather. He supposed it would take some time before Quentin adjusted to the new reality of his granddaughter's marital status.

He climbed out of bed and pulled on a pair of sweats before going in search of Grace. He assumed he would find her in the kitchen from the scent of cinnamon filling the air. To his surprise, the kitchen was empty, despite the evidence that it had been well used since they had cleaned up last night after dinner.

Several bowls were soaking in the sink, and another occupied the counter, a cloth covering it. A pan of cinnamon rolls cooled on a rack, a small bowl of icing sitting nearby, ready to be spread.

Finding himself alone in the house, he grabbed his coat off the rack by the front door and headed outside toward the barn. His breath caught from the cold, and he bundled his coat more tightly around him.

He stepped inside the traditional barn structure, the smell of hay and animals mixing with the scent of snow. Horses munched in their stalls, and a black-and-white barn cat eyed him suspiciously. He was only a few steps inside the door when he heard voices.

"I told you you didn't have to do this," Quentin said.

"It's Christmas," Grace replied, her voice muffled by the wall separating the front section of the barn from the section where the feed was stored. "I always feed the animals for you on Christmas morning."

"What about next Christmas morning? Maybe your husband's family will want a turn having you for the holidays."

"You always told me marriage is about knowing how to balance the needs of both people," Grace countered. "What do you think of Devin?"

"Hard to say. I just met the man."

"Seems to me he held up pretty well when you were trying to scare him off."

"I suppose." The gruffness eased out of Quentin's words when he added, "I only want you to be happy."

"I am happy. I love Devin. I think I've loved him since I met him in high school."

"But you said yourself you hadn't seen him in years. How do you know he's still the person you remember? He was a boy then. He's a man now."

"He's a good man. Trust me to know what's best for me."

Through the slats of wood, Devin could see Grace give her grand-father a hug.

"And for my Christmas present, I want you to forgive me for getting married without you there."

"You drive a hard bargain."

"I learned from the best."

Devin backed out of the barn and returned to the house. If Grace's grandfather was still having a hard time with their elopement, what would his parents think? As much as he wanted to think his happiness was the most important thing to his parents, experience had taught him they weren't like Quentin. Appearances mattered. History had demonstrated that too many times over the years.

When he had selected Arizona State University for his undergraduate work, his father had been embarrassed by his choice. Instead of talking about where his son was going to school, he mentioned only that he had been accepted by Harvard. The state championships for track Devin's senior year had irritated his mother when he had been unable to accompany them on their planned cruise in the Mediterranean because of the scheduling conflict. For as long as he could remember, Devin had felt like a bragging right rather than a part of the family.

He supposed he had let superficial things matter to him as well over the years, but he liked to think he was overcoming that tendency, especially when he was around Grace and his other friends who had the consistent support of their families.

The question Quentin had posed about Devin's plans for a family circled through his mind. What kind of father would he be? Would he be like his parents, more concerned about how his children would impact his social life, or would he find joy in parenthood the way Grace's parents had done? Devin was still contemplating the possibility of his family expanding beyond Grace and him when she walked into the kitchen, her cheeks red from the cold.

Instantly, her face brightened. "Merry Christmas."

"Merry Christmas yourself." He welcomed her into his arms when she crossed to him, and he greeted her with a kiss. "I was lonely when I woke up and you were gone."

"I was helping Grandpa feed the animals." She motioned to the cinnamon rolls. "And I thought the men in my life would enjoy something special for breakfast today."

"You're too good for me. You know that, right?"

She laughed. "You just keep thinking that, and I'll pretend I believe it."

Grace reached up and kissed him again. "Thank you for making this the best Christmas I've had in a long time."

"You haven't even opened your present yet."

"I don't need any presents to be happy. I have you."

No gift wrapped under the tree could have meant more than those simple words. As he leaned down to kiss his bride once more, Devin felt like he might finally have found the true meaning of happiness.

* * *

Grace fiddled with her rings as Devin pulled into the driveway of his childhood home. The three days with her grandfather had helped smooth over any regrets about his not being at her wedding, but she and Devin weren't going to have that kind of time with his parents. A single lunch was all they had planned. She'd thought for sure Devin would at least want to stay with them to celebrate New Year's.

"Are you sure you don't want to stay a few days to visit with your family?" she asked again.

"I'm sure." His curtness caught her attention. His parents had always been civil to her in high school, but she had always felt like they'd looked down on her. Her parents hadn't been in the same social circles in town, but she'd hoped her perception wasn't based on fact. Now she wasn't so sure.

"Your parents aren't going to be happy about our marriage, are they?"

"No."

"Are you sure you want me here today? Maybe it would be better if you told them without me around."

"I want them to get used to the idea of us being together. I'm just not sure how to drop the bomb on them that this is permanent."

His tense posture was so unlike him that Grace would have done anything to help him get back to the person she was so used to being with.

"We don't have to tell them today." On impulse, she pulled the rings off her finger and put them on her right hand.

His shoulders immediately relaxed. "Are you sure you're okay with that?"

"It's fine. Like you said, maybe it will be better if they get used to the idea of me being part of your life again before they know we're married."

Devin leaned over and kissed her. "You really are too good for me."

"Maybe you're too good for me," she countered.

He took his own wedding band off his finger and tucked it into his front pocket. "Come on. Let's get this over with."

She was struck with the thought that Devin saw this time with his parents as a burden when she would give anything to have such an opportunity again with her own. She longed for her past, when her parents were part of her life, and wished Devin knew what such a relationship could be like.

He circled the car and opened her door for her. She took his hand and stood beside him. His eyebrows drew together. "What's that serious expression for?"

"I was just thinking. It's odd that you struggle to spend time with your parents when that's something I miss so much it hurts."

He fell silent for a moment. "I guess sometimes it's hard to appreciate what you've got when you always expect it to be there."

"I know what you mean."

They started up the long path leading to the front door, the Sedona red rocks setting the stage beneath the crisp blue sky. Devin's steps slowed.

"I overheard you and your grandpa talking in the barn on Christmas morning."

She turned to face him. "I never saw you out there. Why didn't you join us?"

"You were talking about us, about asking him to forgive us for getting married without him there."

"And?"

"You knew the whole time that everything would be okay between the two of you because there isn't a doubt that your grandfather wants you to be happy. It's like that is the most important thing to him."

"It is one of the most important things to him. Not just my happiness but the happiness of all of his kids and grandkids."

"My parents aren't like that."

Grace felt the hurt that hummed beneath the surface for Devin. "Maybe they just don't know how to show it."

"I used to think that." He stopped several feet short of the door and kissed her. "I'm just glad you're my family now. I hope I can learn to be like your family instead of taking after my own."

"Whatever we have to deal with, we'll face it together."

"In that case, let's see what today has in store for us." He let go of her hand to reach for the door.

With a flutter of nerves, Grace took a deep breath and stepped through the door he held open.

Chapter 9

DEVIN COULD FEEL THE WAVE of disapproval the moment his parents walked into the entryway and laid eyes on Grace. How could they be so blind to her inherent goodness? How could he have been?

Facing that familiar look he had seen so many times when he had dated Grace in high school made him wonder if his family had influenced their breakup as much as his friends had. He liked to think his mother's comment about them getting too serious at too young an age had been made out of love and concern. Seeing the expression on her face now, he suspected Grace's lack of wealth and family connections was the root of the problem.

The Sedona snobs. His parents could have invented the phrase.

They looked perfect, as always. His mother's dark hair didn't show any sign of gray, thanks to her biweekly trip to the hairdresser. The few streaks of gray in his father's hair made him look distinguished rather than old. Devin didn't have to see the labels to know his parents' clothes were the latest from Paris and Milan and their winter tans a product of their most recent trip to the Caribbean.

"Devin, how good to see you." Catherine Shanahan leaned toward her son and kissed the air beside his cheek.

"Mom, Dad. How was Paris?"

"Fine." His dad shook his hand. The fact that he didn't expound on his answer to include some criticism of the flight or hotel proved he wasn't prepared to see him with Grace.

"You both remember Grace, don't you?"

"Yes, I believe so," Catherine said. "You ran track together, didn't you?"

"That's right," Grace said without missing a beat. She smoothed over the obvious oversight of their previous relationship. "It's good to see you both again."

"Is lunch ready?" Devin asked.

As if on cue, Liwei, the longtime family cook, appeared in the doorway leading to the dining room. In his heavily accented English, Liwei bowed slightly and said, "Lunch is ready."

Devin grinned at the older man, automatically shifting into Cantonese. "Liwei, so good to see you."

Though he wanted to cross to him and give him a hug, he knew such behavior would be frowned upon. Instead, he tilted his head toward Grace. "Can you set another plate? I don't think my parents were expecting her."

"I already did." His voice was serious despite the sparkle in his eyes.

"Must you do that?" his father asked. "English is the language we speak in this house, not Chinese."

Devin didn't correct his father in his assumption that all Chinese languages were one and the same. Instead, he fell silent. He waited for his parents to lead the way into the dining room and put his hand on Grace's back to guide her forward.

As he passed Liwei, Devin whispered under his breath in Cantonese, "Is Jun here?"

"Yes. She will be serving you today."

"Good. I've missed you both."

He saw Grace's questioning glance.

After Devin helped her into her seat, he sat beside her and wondered if his parents would ever forgive him for the choices he had made. They wouldn't be happy if they knew he had committed to work for the CIA for at least the next five years, but the agency had been very clear that he wasn't to share that information with them anyway. As for his relationship with Grace, he wondered how long he could keep his marriage a secret or if he should even try.

He glanced over at the rings on Grace's right hand and debated coming clean right then.

Jun appeared in the doorway, carrying two salads, Liwei following behind her with two more. Upon seeing his longtime nanny, Devin stood. He hated that his parents had let her go when he was in college, but she had made a decent life nearby working as a maid for a number of local families.

"I've missed you," he said, again slipping out of English, this time to converse in Jun's native Mandarin. He gathered her close in a way he never could have done with his own mother. He supposed his fluency in both

Mandarin and Cantonese was a testimony to how much time he'd spent with the household servants and how little he'd spent with his parents. Ironically, of his three languages, he had found English to be the most difficult to learn as a child.

"I have missed you too, but you are going to get both of us in trouble."

"You're right." Devin reclaimed his seat. "Grace, do you remember Jun and Liwei?"

"Yes. I don't believe I've ever had egg rolls as good as the ones Liwei made us when we were in high school."

Movement in the doorway caught Devin's attention, and he looked over to see his father's secretary holding a pad of paper and a pen. Like Liwei and Jun, Maureen had been working for his parents for as long as he could remember, but her stiffly formal demeanor had kept Devin from ever connecting with her the way he had with the others.

"Excuse me, Boyd, but I wanted to let you know I'm going out to run those errands for you," she said.

"Thank you, Maureen."

Maureen turned, her heels clicking on the tile floor as she disappeared from the room and then out the front door.

"I see she hasn't changed at all," Devin said in Mandarin.

"Her visits to the beauty parlor are more frequent now. That blonde hair is most definitely out of a bottle," Jun said. Her own dark hair was streaked with gray, but she didn't seem to be concerned with the natural effects of aging. Jun looked around at everyone's eyes on them. "We'll talk later."

His mother looked from Devin to Grace and asked, "How did you two meet up again? Are you dating?"

"Not exactly." Devin reclaimed his seat, not surprised that Jun and Liwei quietly slipped out of the room. Devin supposed he could date his wife, but he wasn't sure how to phrase his answer without lying directly. Some spy he was going to make.

Grace rescued him. "We were both at Caleb's wedding a couple weeks ago. Caleb married my cousin."

"Oh, how nice. What have you been doing since high school?"

"I'm going to ASU to finish my MBA."

"I'm sure you know Devin is getting his MBA this spring from Stanford," Boyd said.

"Yes, I do," Grace said. "You must be very proud of him. He has always been such a good student."

As though Grace had authenticated his father's belief that Devin's education was superior to her own, some of the stiffness eased out of his parents, and they were able to fall into familiar small talk. Grace and Devin listened to the latest news on Devin's two older cousins, their successes in business and their travel plans.

The realization that he was the first to marry out of his generation struck him. Though his cousins were now in their early thirties, as far as he knew, neither of them was in any kind of serious relationship with anyone or anything beyond their careers.

He glanced at the woman beside him and hoped again that he could overcome his own family traditions and be a good husband to her.

Chapter 10

GRACE BLINKED AGAINST THE THREATENING tears, her arms wrapped tightly around her husband. Passengers hurried by, cell phones and boarding passes in hand, luggage rolling behind them.

How had the days flown by so quickly? Their wedding day had been two and a half weeks ago, yet it felt like yesterday that they had been in Las Vegas together. They had been selfish with their last few days in Phoenix. Caleb and Molly had returned from their honeymoon, but Grace had deliberately put off seeing her cousin or any of her friends while Devin was in town.

Her little one-bedroom apartment had become their home, and she already looked forward to his return.

As though reading her thoughts, he shifted so he could see her face. "I'll be back for the next long weekend. It'll be here before you know it."

"And we'll talk every day." She blinked hard again.

"And we'll talk every day," he repeated.

She thought of his concerns about his parents and took his left hand in hers. His wedding band was back in place, as was her own, but so far, the only person who knew of their union was her grandfather.

"When are we going to tell people we're married? As soon as Caleb finds out, your parents are bound to get wind of it. He's not the best at keeping a secret."

"I hadn't thought about that." Devin considered for a minute. "How often do you think you'll see Caleb and Molly?"

"Now that they're married, hardly ever. Their new apartment is over thirty minutes away on the north side of Phoenix."

"Are you okay with keeping this to ourselves until we tell my folks? Maybe we could see them when I come back next."

She considered the implications and looked down at her own left hand. "Does that mean you don't want me to wear my rings?"

"I want your rings to stay on your finger forever."

"Maybe I shouldn't have changed my name yet if we're going to keep this marriage quiet for now."

"I love knowing we have the same last name."

"You aren't making any sense." Grace linked her fingers with his. "In one breath you say you want to keep us a secret, and in the next, you want me to act like we're married. Which is it?"

He let out a sigh. "I need to tell my parents, don't I?"

"I don't want them to find out from someone else."

"I'll call them tonight after I get home."

"And then call me and let me know how it went," Grace said.

"I will. I love you."

"I love you too."

He leaned down and kissed her good-bye. "I'll see you in a few weeks."

Grace's heart ached the moment he stepped toward the security checkpoint.

She stood unmoving as he made his way through the line and reached the security agent, then looked back for one final wave. An instant later, he was swallowed up in the chaos of bag screenings and X-ray machines. With a sigh, she looked down at her phone. She unlocked the screen and texted Devin. *I miss you already.*

* * *

Time to get this over with. Devin had played that thought in his head a dozen times since he'd walked back into his apartment in California. He had gone through every stall tactic he could think of: grocery shopping, grabbing dinner from a local deli, starting his laundry, and talking to Grace for the second time since landing at the airport.

He mustered his courage and dialed his father's number. If he was going to be the kind of husband Grace deserved, he needed to start by admitting he had married her.

"Hi, Devin," his father answered. "Are you back at school?"

"I am. I just got home a little while ago."

"Is something wrong?"

"No, sir." He drew in a breath and blew it out. "There's something I need to tell you and Mom, something that happened over the holidays."

"What's that? Is everything okay?"

"Everything is fine. It's great, in fact." Another deep breath. "Grace and I got married."

"*What?*"

Devin could imagine his father drawing a deep breath himself, only not to steady his nerves but to prepare to explode. He hurried on before his father had the chance.

"We saw each other in Las Vegas and realized we've been in love with each other since we were together in high school. I didn't want to spend any more time without her, so I convinced her to marry me."

"You convinced her." His father's voice was tight and even. "Are you sure she didn't convince you? After all, you do have a sizable trust fund."

Devin bristled. "Grace has never cared about my money. I don't know why you would think that."

"Her parents . . ."

"Her parents are dead."

Silence hummed for a moment. "I'm sorry to hear that, but it doesn't change the facts. She comes from working folk. You don't."

Exasperated, Devin tried another direction. "I'm finishing my education so I can make something of my life. Grace is doing the same. Now we've chosen to do that together."

"You aren't even at the same school. You aren't leaving Stanford, are you?"

"No, of course not. We'll live apart for the next few months, and after graduation, we'll find jobs together."

"I can't believe you were this stupid."

"I wasn't stupid. I chose to be happy. I'm sorry I've disappointed you yet again."

"Did you at least have her sign a prenuptial agreement?"

"Nope."

"What?" The single word exploded over the line at full volume. "If you think I have worked this hard to build a future for you only to have some gold digger marry you to take half of everything you own, you have another thing coming."

"She's not a—"

"All these years of us giving you every advantage, every privilege, and now you do something this absurd. I knew when you were in high school she wasn't in our league, but you wouldn't listen."

"She's not a gold digger," Devin insisted through clenched teeth. "I love her. Why can't you be happy for me?"

"I'm your father. I know what's best for you."

"No, you don't know what's best for me. I'm a grown man."

"Oh, you are, huh? Let's see how grown up you feel when I cut off your trust fund."

The money threat was the final straw. "Dad, as soon as you can calm down, I'll be happy to talk to you again. As for now, I would like to call my wife and wish her a good night before it gets too late. We both have classes in the morning."

"This isn't the end of this."

"Good-bye, Dad." Devin hung up, his hands shaking. He sank down into the living room chair and leaned his head back. He did want to call Grace, but perhaps he would wait a few minutes until he could let some of his father's words fade away.

* * *

Grace curled up on her couch and stared at the television on the wall. The thought that Devin had been beside her as she'd watched a movie last night left a cloud of despair hanging over her. She hated not being with him.

The moment the phone rang, she snatched it off the coffee table in front of her. "How did it go?" she asked in lieu of a greeting.

"About as expected."

"I'm sorry. Were they really upset?"

"I only talked to my dad. I'm sure my mom will call at some point," Devin said heavily. "We knew they would be surprised. I'm sure after they've had some time to get used to the idea, they'll be fine. After all, even your grandpa needed time to adjust to the news."

"That's true." Not wanting to dwell on the negative, she changed the subject. "Are you all ready for classes tomorrow?"

"Yeah. It's weird to think that this is the last first day of school I'll ever have."

"Unless you decide to go for your doctorate."

"Definitely not," Devin said. "I'm not an academia type."

"You'd be good at it."

"Thanks, but I've already got a job lined up for after school, and another degree isn't in the plans."

"You already have a job?" Grace asked, surprised. "You never told me that."

"I'm still waiting for the final details, but I suspect I'll get an offer based on my summer internships."

"What company is it for?"

"It's called Willow Enterprises."

"I don't think I've heard of it. Where is it?"

"I'm not sure yet. It's actually a parent company of a lot of subsidiaries. There are a couple of locations I could end up at, but I should know in a couple months."

"Oh."

"What's wrong?"

"It just won't be easy for me to look for jobs if I don't know where you expect to be."

"Since I could end up anywhere in the world, I think you should apply for anything that looks interesting," Devin told her. "I can see if I can match my location to yours. Otherwise, we'll figure something out."

"I guess that makes sense." She paused. "Does it ever scare you, the idea of getting out of school and going out into the world?"

"Not anymore."

"What do you mean?"

"Now I have you."

Her lips curved. "I love you, you know."

"I love you too. I'll talk to you tomorrow."

"Okay." She hung up and contemplated their work situation. She had always planned to find a job in Arizona after graduation. Her temporary work with an investment firm last summer held promise for a full-time job, and she had already interviewed with a couple of other companies with local offices. If Devin already had a solid job offer, it only made sense for her to follow him, though it was odd to think of putting his career before her own. In truth, though, she didn't know how they would both feel about her career once they decided to start a family.

That thought gave her another jolt. What would it be like to have children with Devin, to see their family expand beyond the two of them? She thought of their first date, of his sweet disposition with the lost little girl. He would make a wonderful father. And if she chose to put her career on hold for a while to raise their children, surely Devin would support her in that decision.

She looked across the room at the enormous binder she had received in one of her finance classes—the study guide for her Series 7, the license she needed in order to work as a financial adviser. It had been weighing down her desk for weeks.

She had initially thought she wouldn't go that route, but now she wasn't so sure. Maybe it would be worth it to check off that box. After all, once certified, she could work as a financial adviser anywhere in the country. And it sounded like that was where she and Devin were going to start their future together: anywhere in the country.

Chapter 11

A CARD IN THE MAIL from his mother was the last thing Devin expected. Three days had passed since he had shared the news of his marriage with his father, and he had dreaded the disapproving call he'd been certain would follow from his mother. That call hadn't happened. Could it be that she had experienced a change of heart? Maybe now that he was married, his parents would come to terms with how much Grace meant to him.

He ripped open the envelope to find a simple card with a photo of Sedona red rocks on the front. When he turned to the inside, his breath backed up in his chest, hurt and anger battling inside him. The words on the otherwise blank card were written in his mother's hand and left no doubt as to her feelings on his marriage.

Your father and I expect more from you. We presume you will rectify the situation before we see you at graduation.

Paper-clipped to the back was a business card for a divorce attorney.

"Unbelievable." The word came out on a sigh of despair. How could his parents do this? Did they truly not care about his happiness? And was he going to have to choose between his family and Grace? He was afraid the yeses and nos to those questions wouldn't fall in the order he wanted if he posed them to his parents.

His phone rang, and he saw Grace's photo illuminate the screen. He let it ring a second and third time while he tried to rein in his emotions.

"Hey."

"Did I catch you at a bad time?" she asked.

"No, this is fine. How are you doing?"

"At the moment, I'm regretting I didn't try to get my MBA at Stanford. I miss you."

"I miss you too." And he did. Every time he thought of her, his life seemed brighter somehow. "It's only a few weeks until I'll see you next."

"I know, but it feels like forever. I'm already trying to get ahead on my classes so I won't have any homework when you get here."

"I need to do the same thing. Anything new and exciting in Arizona today?"

"I saw Molly and Caleb for the first time since their wedding. They looked good."

"Did you tell them about us?"

She chuckled. "Molly complimented me on the pearl ring you gave me, but it never registered that I was wearing it on my left hand."

"Did you have your wedding band on too?"

"Yep. I started to tell her, but I decided it would be more fun to tell them together when you're here. I thought maybe we could surprise them and take them out to dinner or something."

"I like that idea." Devin lay down on his bed and let the cheerfulness of Grace's voice overshadow everything else.

By the time they said their good-byes, there was only one thing to do about his mother's note. He crossed the room, picked up the card, business card and all, and dropped it into the recycling bin.

As for graduation, he was sure his parents would be in attendance, and so would Grace.

* * *

Grace shifted her weight from one foot to the other as she watched the stream of passengers passing through security. She knew it would have been easier for her to pick Devin up outside, but she didn't want to wait those few extra minutes to see her husband. She had received a text from him ten minutes ago to tell her he had landed. She pulled out her cell phone and looked down at the screen. Make that twelve minutes.

Pushing up onto her toes, she craned her neck to see past the X-ray machines and body scanners in the security area, hoping for a glimpse of Devin. Her grin was instant when she caught sight of him weaving past a businessman and then a family of four. She sensed the moment he saw her, and his already rapid pace increased.

Grace started forward and did some weaving of her own when Devin passed the security guard, and she tried to get past the people standing between them. Pulling his carryon bag behind him, Devin broke into a jog and closed the distance. The moment he reached her, he set his bag upright and pulled her against him, lifting her off her feet.

His lips found hers in a brief but dizzying kiss.

"Welcome home," Grace managed to say.

"Thanks." He kissed her again before lowering her to the floor. Grabbing the handle of his suitcase, he asked, "Where are you parked?"

"This way." Grace indicated the direction of the parking garage. "I'm so glad you're here."

"Me too." They made their way to the garage, both of them maintaining a hurried pace. "We don't have any plans tonight, do we?"

"No. I never got ahold of Molly and Caleb to see if they wanted to get together," Grace admitted. She pulled the car keys from her purse, unlocked the car, and popped the trunk.

Devin loaded his suitcase, and Grace headed for the driver's side door. She pulled it open only to have Devin put his hands on her shoulders to turn her around to face him. The intensity in his eyes surprised her, and her breath caught in her chest. The scent of his cologne teased her senses, and her breath shuddered out the instant before his lips met hers.

Grace melted against him, reveling in the sensation of having him here with her, of being in his arms once more. A car passed by, and she pulled back.

"I missed you," Devin murmured, his voice low.

"I missed you too." He leaned toward her for another kiss, and Grace shook her head. "I think we should save this for when we get home."

Another car drove by, and Devin looked around like he was just noticing where they were. "You're probably right." He jogged around to the passenger side and climbed in. As soon as he was seated beside her, he asked, "How far is it again?"

"About thirty minutes." She clicked her seat belt in place and looked at him only to find herself being kissed again. Laughing, she put a hand on his chest and nudged him away. "Behave."

"Oh, all right." Devin shifted back into his seat.

She looked over at him, amused. "Don't worry. I'll take the shortcut."

* * *

Grace spent every waking moment trying not to count down the days until she would see Devin again. Fifteen days had passed since she'd seen him for Presidents' Day weekend. Nine more until they would be together again.

The few plans she had made for Presidents' Day weekend had been pushed aside the moment they had gotten home from the airport. Except for the twenty-three-minute drive from the airport to her apartment, she had spent almost the whole time in his arms. Three crazy days of takeout food and breakfast in bed, long walks through the neighborhood, and movies late at night while cuddled together on the couch had ended too soon, and Grace was ready to be done with school so they could start their new life together.

Nine more days, she repeated to herself as she parked her car in the student lot and headed to class. This time, instead of a long weekend, they would have a whole week together, in Stanford instead of Phoenix. Spring break for her, finals week for him. The timing wasn't perfect, but they were both anxious to take whatever they could.

She worried that Devin still hadn't heard where his company was sending him. Every time she asked about his employment, he said he would explain once he received his assignment. Surely he would hear before graduation.

She wanted so badly to start planning for what would come next. She would take her Series 7 exam two days before leaving for Stanford, and she hoped she and Devin would be able to plan where they would move after her graduation six weeks after his. It didn't seem fair that his semester ended so much earlier than hers. Of course, he didn't have spring break, and their schools had very different schedules.

Devin had been thrilled with the idea of her being there in the days leading up to the end of his graduate work, especially when she offered to help him pack and clean his apartment. She knew he would likely have to go ahead of her to his new job, but she was hoping he could postpone his start date until she could go with him. She wanted to wake up each morning with him beside her. She had never realized how much it would mean to her to come home every day and find him there. Now that she'd had a taste of married life, she was excited for what was to come.

Seeing his parents at graduation worried her a bit because she was still unsure of how they felt about her. Other than saying his parents were getting used to their marriage, Devin had barely spoken of his family during their nightly calls.

She was heading into her first class of the day when a crowd around a bulletin board by the career center distracted her.

"What's going on?" she asked Heidi, one of the girls in her organizational behavior class.

"They just posted the upcoming grads who got a second interview with Anderson Enterprises. Only four people made the first cut."

Grace's heart sank. She had been among hundreds who had interviewed for those few precious positions. Working with investor wealth management fascinated her. If only four people had made the cut, she was certain her name wasn't on the list. "Who are they?"

"Check it out for yourself."

Grace edged forward and read the names. She gasped. "I got it?"

"You got the interview," Heidi said with a smile. "Now go get the job. I'm totally planning on coming to visit you in New York this fall."

"You're on." Grace looked over the posted sheet again, this time reading the details on the top.

"We'd better get to class," Heidi said. "You can set up your interview this afternoon."

"I hope I get the job."

"You'll get it. If they cut the list down that much, this final interview is only a formality."

Grace followed Heidi into class, and reality caught up with her. What if her dream job and Devin's dream job were on opposite ends of the country? He mentioned the possibility of requesting a location for his job, so she texted him. *What are the chances of your job taking you to New York?*

The response came back within seconds. *Could happen. Why?*

Second interview with Anderson Enterprises tomorrow. Nervous and excited.

Awesome! You'll be great. I see my personnel officer next week. I'll let you know.

Excitement and anticipation stirred within her. Everything was falling into place. Without even looking for it, she had found her path to her happily ever after.

* * *

"Hong Kong?" Devin repeated the news back to Jalen Cruz, his personnel officer. "I don't understand. I thought this meeting was to discuss the possibilities of where I might be assigned, not to receive my actual posting."

Jalen sat behind his desk in the small windowless office. The man was only ten years older than him, and Devin suspected Jalen was simply the messenger. "I'll admit, this is a bit unusual, but your skills uniquely qualify you for this job."

"My skills?"

"You're fluent in Mandarin and Cantonese, and you have an MBA from a top school. That's not an easy combination to find in the agency, especially for someone who doesn't have any Chinese heritage."

"So what is my job going to be?" Devin asked, still trying to process the possibilities.

"You will be going undercover to work with a capital management group. We submitted your résumé over a year ago, hoping we could get you into this position."

"Over a year ago? You've got to be kidding."

"Not at all. These types of undercover operations take years to set up. Your internships were tailor-made to enhance your résumé for this particular job." He leaned forward in his chair and lowered his voice. "For more than two decades, the Chinese intelligence service has managed to ascertain information they shouldn't have any prayer of accessing. Analysts have looked at the leaks and plugged some of them, but there is a significant number that remain unsolved. We don't know where they're coming from, and we haven't been able to identify a common denominator."

"How do I play into the picture?"

"Your mission is twofold: first, we have identified several Chinese nationals at this particular firm who we believe could be cultivated to provide us with valuable information. In this new position, you will have sufficient access to identify individuals the agency can recruit as assets."

"Wait a minute. I never planned to be an operative. I've always been slated for a support position."

"As corny as it sounds, your country needs you on this one." His expression remained serious. "The financial stability of this country hinges on our relationship with the Chinese."

"Doesn't spying on their soil create negative ramifications for that relationship?"

"Only if we're caught. The second part of your mission is to help us identify who has been leaking information to the Chinese. Chatter has picked up several indications that Hong Kong has become a hotbed for the sale of government secrets, and this firm seems to be a favorite place for Chinese intelligence to filter money to their sources. We need to know who is involved and when money transfers are occurring so we can counter any possible threats against our government as a result of these intelligence leaks."

Devin rubbed both hands over his face. "This is a lot to take in."

"I know. Believe me, we have looked at a lot of options on securing the intelligence we need on this. We had another operative we intended to send in as well. He only speaks Cantonese, so he wasn't as strong a candidate. When he got married six months ago, he was reassigned since he was no longer fully eligible to go."

"What does getting married have to do with anything?" Devin asked, suddenly wary.

"A married man wouldn't be able to socialize freely in the right circles in Hong Kong, and we didn't want to risk his wife inadvertently revealing his true purpose."

"We may have a problem. I'm married."

"What? Your file doesn't show anything in it about you being seriously involved with anyone, much less married. When did this happen?"

"Right before Christmas. I ran into my old high school girlfriend, and we eloped."

"You do realize you were supposed to notify me before this happened, right?"

"I was told I had to inform you if I had any close and continued contact with anyone who is a foreign national. Grace is American."

"Even if that's the case, you should have told me." A hint of panic laced his voice. "Does she know you're CIA?"

"No. I didn't know what I would have to do to get permission to tell her, but I knew there was some kind of procedure in place for that."

"There is a procedure in place, but I'm afraid even with the proper paperwork, your request will be denied."

"What? Why?"

"We've been working on your placement for months. We can't put someone else in your place at this point. It's too risky for anyone, even your wife, to know who you really work for."

"Can my wife come with me?"

"No. As I said, you won't be included in the same social circles if you're married. You'll have to go unaccompanied."

His heart sank. "For how long?"

"Usually this type of assignment is for at least three years."

"*Three years?* I can't do that."

"With any luck, we can get what we need within six months. A year tops."

Six months. It sounded like an eternity, but he and Grace had already managed to survive three months apart.

The internal debate continued to wage as Jalen handed Devin a thick envelope. "Your official offer from the capital group, Revival Financial, is in there, along with your airline tickets, the keys to your new apartment, and a new cell phone."

"Why do I need a new cell phone?"

"It has the ability to receive encrypted texts. It also prevents anyone from using your current phone to track you."

"What about calling home to friends and family?"

"Keep it to a minimum. The more you contact people you know at home, the more at risk you all are." He stood. "You have two weeks before you fly out. We assumed you would want to spend some time with family and friends before you leave, so your flight will come out of Phoenix. From there, you will fly to Los Angeles and stay for a couple days to be briefed on our interests in Hong Kong.

"Of course you know all of this information is top secret and can't be shared with anyone outside of our unit," he said.

"What you're telling me is that my friends and family will think I really work for Revival Financial."

"You will really work there. You'll just work for us too." He stood, and Devin followed suit, then shook the man's extended hand before he turned to leave. "And, Devin?"

"Yes?"

"Like I said, these situations don't happen often. Take advantage of it. This can make your career."

With a nod, Devin turned and headed for the door. The moment he stepped into the hallway, he closed his eyes and rubbed his hands over his face again. What was he going to tell Grace? And how was he going to survive without her?

Chapter 12

GRACE COULDN'T WAIT TO TELL Devin the news. The offer from Anderson Enterprises was in her backpack, and she could choose to work in Los Angeles, New York, Chicago, or Washington, DC. Devin had mentioned three of the four as possibilities for his new job, so things had to work out.

The financial package was more than she had hoped for, and she could already imagine house shopping with him. She made her way through the airport to the security checkpoint, grinning when she saw Devin waiting for her with a bouquet of flowers in his hands. Her footsteps quickened, and she practically ran into his embrace.

"I missed you," he said, his voice low.

"I missed you too." She saw the redness in his eyes and narrowed her own. "Have you gotten any sleep lately?"

"Had a paper I needed to finish by this morning," he admitted. "Tomorrow's a study day, so I can sleep in for a change."

He took her bag from her with one hand and kept his other firmly around her waist. "Do you have more luggage?"

"No. Just this." She managed to keep her news contained until they made it out to his car. As soon as they were settled inside, she turned to face him. "You aren't going to believe what happened."

"What?" he said, sounding as excited as she was.

"Anderson Enterprises offered me a job, and they're giving me a choice of four cities to work in."

"Grace, that's fantastic."

"Have you met with your personnel officer yet? Do you know where they want you to work?"

"They're still trying to work a few things out. How soon do you have to let Anderson know which city you want?"

"I have to tell them in three weeks. I figure you'll already be working by then."

"Probably." He kept his focus on the road, and Grace felt unease creep in.

"Is everything okay?" she asked.

"I'm just tired." He managed a smile. "I'm glad you're here though. My world doesn't feel complete when you're not with me."

"I feel the same way. I can't wait until we're both living in the same house together."

"I know what you mean."

* * *

Devin walked into his apartment to the scent of chili and an underlying aroma of lemon furniture polish. He looked around. Several white moving boxes were stacked against the far wall, neatly labeled, and his few pieces of furniture gleamed from a fresh dusting.

"Oh, you're home." Grace emerged from the kitchen and greeted him with a kiss. "How did your final go?"

"Okay." He linked his fingers around her waist. "I can't believe it. I'm done. No more school. No more studying. No more tests."

"Don't gloat too much. I still have five more weeks."

"Sorry." He leaned down and kissed her. "But I have to celebrate a little bit. This is big stuff."

"You're right. It's huge. What do you want to do to celebrate? I made chili, but we can go out if you want to."

"I'd much rather stay in." He leaned down and pressed his lips against hers. The moment her breath caught, he deepened the kiss. How many times would they be together like this before he had to leave her behind? How many days and weeks and months would it be until they could settle into a home together?

He knew he should tell her the truth, but more than anything, he needed this weekend to get his bearings. His parents would arrive tomorrow, and he wanted to present a united front when they learned he was keeping Grace in his life.

Pushing those thoughts aside, he circled Grace toward the bedroom.

She pulled back and motioned to the kitchen. "What about dinner?"

"We can eat later." He kissed her again. "Much later."

* * *

Grace's hair was still wet from the shower when the doorbell rang. The oddity of answering her husband's door struck her as she turned the knob. When she saw the stunned expressions of the couple standing on the other side of the threshold, she realized she may have made a mistake in not letting Devin answer it himself.

"Grace." Catherine's cool tone vibrated on the crisp spring air. "I didn't expect to see you here."

"Mr. and Mrs. Shanahan." Flustered, she stepped back and motioned them inside. "Please come in. I'll tell Devin you're here."

They stepped inside, and she had no sooner closed the door than Devin called out, "Hon, do you know where my white shirt is? I can't find it."

"It's hanging in the bathroom," Grace called back. She started toward the bedroom, but she had taken only two steps before Devin appeared bare chested in the doorway, shirt in hand. He was so focused on her, he didn't notice the newcomers.

"Why was my shirt in the bathroom?"

"I hung it there after I ironed it." She shifted her gaze to his parents and felt his tension rise the moment he saw them.

Devin shrugged his arms into his shirt. "Mom. Dad. What are you doing here? I thought you were going to meet me at graduation."

"We thought we would drive over with you. We didn't realize you had company," Boyd said, looking past Grace.

"Grace's spring break was last week. She stayed a couple extra days to be here for my graduation."

"I see."

Devin motioned to the couch. "Why don't you sit down and make yourselves comfortable while Grace and I finish getting ready."

Grace felt her cheeks heating beneath the Shanahans' glares.

Devin took her hand and pulled her into the bedroom, closing the door between them and his parents.

"I'm so sorry," Devin whispered. "I had no idea they were going to show up here."

"I thought you talked to them," Grace said uneasily. "Do they even know we're married?"

"Yeah, they know."

The tone of his voice and his parents' reaction added up, and Grace managed to put the complete picture together. "They don't want you to stay married to me."

"They're still getting used to the idea of their only child getting married at all. It's not you. They've never liked any girl I've dated."

"I'm not exactly someone you're dating. Not anymore."

"No. You're the woman I love." He put his hands on her arms, and reluctantly Grace lifted her eyes to meet his. "They'll adjust eventually. As for today, we'll suffer through it together, okay?"

"Okay."

* * *

Devin prayed for calm when he led Grace out of their bedroom, both of them dressed and ready to go. Surely his parents would remember today was an occasion he had been striving toward for years and was one of the few goals he had set for himself that they had wholeheartedly approved of.

"I thought I made myself clear," his mother said the moment they stepped into the living room. "This is not a time in your life you should be tying yourself down with marriage."

"Maybe Grace and I should meet you at graduation. I believe you already have your tickets."

"We're not finished discussing this."

"I never said we were," Devin replied coolly. "However, I'm ready to walk across the stage and receive my diploma. Everything else you want to discuss will have to wait until after I have accomplished that."

Devin pulled his car keys from his pocket. "Please lock the door when you leave."

Taking Grace's hand in his, he pulled her out the door toward his car.

"You aren't just going to leave them like that, are you?"

"Yep." He opened her door for her. "For once, I'm going to do what I need to and I'm not going to let them get in the way of it."

She studied him for a brief moment before sliding into the car. Once she got in and he was settled beside her, she looked at him. "I don't want to make this day anything less than perfect for you. I'm so sorry being here has caused issues with your parents."

"Please, Grace. I don't want to talk about them right now."

"Okay. How about we talk about how you're going to walk away from here today with a degree in your hand with Stanford University scripted across the top." The cheerfulness in her voice was forced, but he appreciated the effort. "How would you like it framed? Black? Wood? Gold? Silver?"

Some of his tension eased out of him, and he started the car. "You don't have to frame my diploma."

"Of course I do. This is huge." She slipped her shoes off and tucked her feet up under her.

"You're getting awfully comfortable for a five-minute drive."

"Habit," she admitted.

Devin glanced in his rearview mirror, hoping to see his parents preparing to follow him. His hands clutched on the wheel when he saw his apartment door still closed, his parents nowhere in sight.

Chapter 13

"MAYBE YOU SHOULD CALL THEM again," Grace suggested. She hadn't seen Devin's parents at graduation, although the crowd had been large enough that she hoped she had simply overlooked them. They had returned to Devin's apartment two hours earlier, and thus far, they hadn't seen or heard from them.

Devin dropped onto the couch. "They're already gone."

"Gone where?"

"Grace, I know they didn't come to my graduation." Devin looked up at her, his expression weary. "My guess is they waited until we were out of sight and then went straight to the airport."

She sat down and curled up beside him. "I'm sure they at least went to watch you graduate. That's why they came to California."

"Did you see them there?" Devin asked.

"No, but . . ."

"Their tickets would have put them in your section. There's no way you would have missed them."

"I'm sorry, Devin. I wish I knew what I could do to make this better."

"There's nothing that can fix this. My relationship with my parents was broken long before you came along."

"Do you still want to go out to dinner?"

"Sorry. I'm not really in the mood." He pulled out his phone. "Do you mind if we order in?"

"That's fine."

She watched him pull up a contact on his phone and dial. He spoke in a Chinese dialect, and she tried to figure out which one. As soon as he hung up, she asked, "Cantonese?"

"Very good." He put his hand on hers and rubbed his thumb over the back of her hand. "Do you know that my parents had Jun and Liwei working for them for more than twenty years, and they still don't know that they had to learn to talk to each other."

"Why did they have to learn to talk to each other?"

"Jun's native language is Mandarin. Liwei's is Cantonese. My parents don't seem to even know there's a difference."

"I thought it odd when we visited them how much it annoyed them when you didn't speak in English."

"I think it brings up bad memories." Grace watched him expectantly, and he continued. "My first words were in Mandarin. When one of my mother's friends realized I was speaking to Jun, not just babbling, my mom was embarrassed that I didn't speak English yet."

"Do you realize how cool it is that you can speak a foreign language at all, much less be fluent in two that are so difficult?"

"I can speak them," Devin corrected. "My reading isn't exactly fluent."

"I still think it's pretty amazing." When Devin stiffened, Grace drew her eyebrows together. "What's wrong?"

"You may not think it's amazing when I tell you my news."

"What news?"

"I got my assignment from my personnel officer."

Grace was afraid to ask for details. If he had neglected to tell her earlier, it couldn't be good. "And?"

"I'm being sent to Hong Kong."

Her jaw dropped. "Hong Kong?"

"It's not as bad as it sounds. I should only be there for six months."

"Six months."

When she fell silent, Devin let a minute pass before he prompted her. "Grace?"

"Just trying to wrap my mind around all of this." Grace considered the ramifications of his announcement. "Is there any way you can get it changed to somewhere here in the US?"

"I already tried. Six months was the shortest I could get them down to." He rushed on before she could comment further. "The company paid my tuition for undergrad, so I have a contract with them. I have to work for them for five years."

"Maybe I can delay my start date with Anderson Enterprises for a few months and come with you," Grace said. "We can probably store our stuff at my grandpa's house."

"I wish that would work, but the company was pretty adamant that I not bring you with me. Besides, I'll be traveling all the time. I'd feel lousy knowing you were home alone, especially knowing that you would be giving up on taking your dream job. You can't expect Anderson to hold your position for that long."

She pulled her hand free. "So you're telling me we're going to be apart for six more months."

"I'm afraid so." He reached for her hand again, but she stood before he could take hold.

"This is a nightmare." She raked her fingers through her hair. "What kind of marriage is this?"

"I know this isn't what we had planned." Devin stood as well. "I'm sorry things worked out this way. I honestly didn't see it coming, but it's only for a few months."

"That's what you said when we got married a few months ago."

"Grace, I love you more than anything. We're going to make this work."

Her eyes dark, she folded her arms and looked up at him. "How?"

The question clearly caught him off guard. "I don't know exactly." He walked a few steps away, then turned back to her. "We can still call every night, FaceTime, Skype, whatever."

"But we won't see each other for six months."

"Like I said, I'll be traveling a lot. Maybe we can meet somewhere every couple months. London would be about halfway if you take a job in Washington."

"Is that where you want me to take a job?"

"I think that's where I'll be posted next."

"You think?"

"Tell you what. I'll talk to my personnel officer this week to see if they can guarantee my next posting in one of the cities Anderson Enterprises offered you. That way you can set up house and be settled in when I get back." He put his hands on her arms to hold her in place. "Besides, we already knew we were going to be apart for the next month or so until you graduate."

"I really hate this," Grace said.

"I know." He gathered her close, and reluctantly she lifted her arms to encircle his waist. "I do have about ten days I can spend with you in Phoenix before I fly out."

"That's one bit of good news." She sighed. "You're lucky I love you so much."

His voice lowered to a whisper. "Yes, I am."

* * *

Devin pulled into the parking garage, his hands gripping the steering wheel. How was he supposed to live like this? He had arrived in Phoenix four days earlier, and every time Grace left for a class, he rushed off to meet his new CIA handler. Chee Quon had arrived in Phoenix the day after Devin, and each day they met to go over procedures and objectives.

The information he gained each day fascinated him, but he hated deceiving Grace. He never actually lied to her, but he was becoming a master at misleading her. She assumed he stayed at home each day while she was gone, and he let her. Or on the few occasions when he knew she would beat him to her apartment, he deliberately ran an errand so he would have a reason to be gone.

She never asked if he had gone anywhere else, and he didn't tell.

The burden of his secrets weighed on him as he made his way into the office building next door, which housed a variety of businesses, from doctors' offices to financial planners and insurance companies, and allowed him to come and go without looking out of place. He took the stairs rather than the elevator, climbing the six flights necessary to reach his destination.

The office he entered looked vacant, and Devin suspected it would be vacant again after he and Chee left for Hong Kong, on separate flights, of course.

The furnishings inside were sparse, only a long folding table and a couple of office chairs. As he did every day, Devin flipped the lock behind him before joining Chee at the table, where he had papers spread before him.

Chee didn't greet him. He simply slid a stack of photos toward him. As always, his words were precise and articulate, his Chinese accent noticeable. "Today we need to look over the employees at the brokerage house who we expect you to come in contact with. Fai Meng has been on our radar for almost two years, but we haven't been able to get anyone close to him."

"Before we start on that, there's something else we need to discuss." Devin straightened his shoulders and forced himself to speak his mind. "I need to tell my wife what's really going on."

"That's not possible," Chee said. "I'm sorry, but keeping your involvement with us secret is as much for your protection as for hers."

New fears shot through him. "What do you mean it's for her protection? Do you really think this could put her in danger?"

"Not if you stick with your cover story." Chee leaned back in his chair and took a moment before speaking, as though translating his thoughts before putting them into words. "The challenges come when a spouse says or does something that could compromise you. Keeping her in the dark is the best protection for both of you."

"What about when I come back to the US? Can I tell her then?"

"Most likely your request would be approved at that time." He lifted a shopping bag from the floor and set it on the table. Reaching inside, he retrieved a gift-wrapped box about half the size of a shoe box. "I did, however, receive permission for you to give your wife this."

"What is it?"

"A new cell phone. Like the one we gave you, it has a blocker on the GPS signal so no one can track her without having our access code. This will allow you to speak to her without worrying that someone may try to find you through her."

"How do I explain why I'm giving her a new phone?"

"Tell her you got it for her so you can have unlimited international calling."

Devin nodded. "That should work."

"Let me see your phone. I'll show you how to reset the blocker in the event anyone ever manages to trace your signal." Chee held out his hand and took the phone Devin offered. After a brief demonstration, he handed the phone back to him and motioned to the photos between them. "We still have a lot to cover and not much more time together."

"I thought you were going to be seeing me regularly in Hong Kong."

"Yes, but our interactions will be extremely limited. As I explained yesterday, my cover is working for your apartment building. Drops will be left in the safe in your apartment. When I come in to clean, I'll pick them up and leave whatever information I need to pass on. Once we leave the United States, however, we'll never know when it's safe to speak openly. Whatever questions you have, this is the time to ask them."

Resigned to keeping Grace in the dark, Devin scooted forward in his seat and prepared to get to work.

Chapter 14

GRACE COULD FEEL THE TEARS threatening, and she blinked hard against them. Why was she being so emotional? She had gone through this numerous times over the past few months. "I really hate good-byes."

"I know. We've had way too many this year." Devin stopped short of the security line and turned to face her. "Next year will be different. I promise."

"I hope so." She fought against the despair she felt. She wanted to enjoy these last few moments with Devin. "You'll let me know as soon as you find out when you can meet me in London."

"I will. And you let me know if you need help looking for an apartment in New York. I can at least help search online with you."

"Call me as soon as you land."

"It'll be the middle of the night for you."

"I don't care. I want to know you made it okay." She reached up to press her lips to his. She had expected the kiss to be brief, but Devin drew her in in a way he rarely did in public. Something was different, and everything in her dreaded the moment he would leave her arms and walk away.

The intensity in his eyes revealed Devin was struggling with this good-bye as much as she was. "I love you," he said.

"I love you too. Be safe."

The muscles in his jaw tightened briefly. "I will. You too."

His chest rose when he drew a deep breath, and then, as though gathering his courage, he let it out and stepped out of her embrace. Without another word, his fingers curled around the handle of his carry-on and he stepped into the flow of other travelers heading for security.

As she always did, she watched him make his way through the line to the TSA agents. He pressed his fingers to his eyes briefly, but at the moment he normally turned back for a final wave, he hesitated for a fraction of a second. Then, as though fighting his own internal battle, his shoulders straightened and he continued forward, never looking back.

* * *

The few tears that escaped in the security line were the last Devin could permit to surface. He couldn't do the job his country needed him to do if he let himself forget why he was going to Hong Kong, why he was sacrificing the next few months away from his wife.

As Grace had requested, he called her the moment he landed. He had intended to keep the call brief, a simple exchange of I love yous and I miss yous, but as soon as he heard her voice, he hadn't been able to resist stretching out the conversation. An account of his travels, the latest lecture she had attended at school. They chatted the entire twenty minutes he had waited for his luggage, finally saying good-bye when he'd caught a cab to his new apartment in a high-rise a short distance from a tram station.

When he entered the lobby, he felt like he was walking into a hotel. He approached the long front desk and the man who stood behind it.

"May I help you?" the man asked in English.

Since the other man clearly had a command of English, Devin responded in the same language. "Yes, I'm Devin Shanahan. I believe I'm in apartment 4A."

"Yes, sir." Anticipating his arrival, the man picked up a folder and retrieved several papers from within. "I need your signature here and here."

Devin skimmed the documents written in English, signed in the designated spots, and pushed the papers back toward the clerk.

The man took the papers and gave Devin a folder.

"The information about the building is in here, as well as a list of local businesses and the tram schedule."

"Thank you." Devin took a step back before saying, "I didn't catch your name."

"Yang. My card is in the folder. Please let me know if you need anything."

"Thank you, Yang. It's good to meet you." Devin turned and headed for the elevator, the stainless-steel doors opening with a quiet hum.

When he reached his apartment, he opened the door to a small, well-organized space. The one-bedroom apartment would have been considered a studio had it not been for the sliding panel that separated the living area from the corner housing the bed. The kitchen was little more than a counter with a faucet and microwave and a half-sized refrigerator and a few cabinets containing basic kitchenware.

Streamlined and modern, the rest of the furniture consisted of a white couch facing a flat-screen television mounted to the wall and a tiny kitchen table with two small chairs. The bedroom didn't have a dresser, but the closet contained a combination of hanging bars and shelves.

Though exhausted from nearly a day of traveling, Devin hauled his suitcases into the bedroom and unpacked. Clothing folded and hung, toiletries put away in the bathroom, computer on the kitchen table, and a framed photograph of Grace on his bedside table. Circling the room, he wondered how long it would take him to feel like this was home.

A single glance at Grace's smiling face answered the question for him. Never. How could it ever feel like home unless she was here too?

* * *

Grace nearly cried when she unlocked her new apartment and saw what was behind the door. Tears of exhaustion had already been simmering from the exertion of hauling three suitcases up four flights of stairs, but now that she was faced with her final destination, her mood took yet another downward turn.

For the past month since Devin had left for Hong Kong, she had tried to distract herself by making plans for her new home. This was not what she'd had in mind.

The sun beamed through the tiny window on the far wall, the only window in the room, dust motes dancing in the light. She had expected the three-hundred-square-foot studio to be small, but she hadn't anticipated the brick wall to her left that looked like it might come tumbling down at any minute or the black-and-white chipped-marble flooring that appeared to be straight out of the 1920s.

A cockroach scampered across the floor and under the stove.

"What have I gotten myself into?" She wrestled her suitcases inside and closed the door behind her, then looked for the closet so she could stash her suitcases out of the way. But there wasn't a closet.

Another cockroach crossed the kitchen floor, and Grace gritted her teeth. What was she supposed to do about her six-legged uninvited guests?

Furniture was another issue she would have to deal with. Thanks to her grandfather's help, all of her and Devin's furnishings were now stored in the old detached garage by his house. Devin had convinced her she wouldn't want to pay for parking in New York City, and he obviously didn't want to ship his car to Hong Kong, so they had both sold their vehicles before their moves.

Her grandpa had offered to ship her furniture to her as soon as she decided what she needed in her new place. Looking around, she didn't know how any of it was going to fit. Her queen-sized bed alone would fill the room.

She looked around again, trying to find something good in the outdated kitchen appliances and the two narrow cabinets above the small counter. Looking up, she found one positive. The high ceilings would give her the chance to go vertical. She had a feeling that the moment her shipment arrived, she would be living with pillars of boxes reaching the ceiling.

One thing was sure: as soon as she and Devin were living in the same city, they were going to move into someplace nicer. Once they were able to combine their incomes, they could find something with a little more light and space.

She made her way across the room to the doll-size bathroom. A silverfish eyed her from inside the shower stall. Grace committed homicide by turning on the water and drowning the invader as she washed it down the drain.

Determined to make this space work, she crossed back to the door, set her suitcases along the wall, and dug her purse out of her backpack. Then she headed for the stairs with a mental list of the first things she needed to buy: a sleeping bag and an insect bomb. Groceries could wait until tomorrow. Tonight she was going to rid herself of the bugs and enjoy eating dinner somewhere that had Wi-Fi. It was time to do some furniture shopping on the Internet.

Chapter 15

DEVIN LOOKED IN THE MIRROR and straightened his tie. On the surface, he looked like what his parents had always expected him to be: rich, successful, stylish. His closet was full of tailored suits and ridiculously expensive shoes. Silk neckties, a designer watch. All props to make him fit in with his peers working in high finance.

If he could look only as deep as his reflection, he could almost believe he really was an up-and-coming financier. His time in the office made him feel like exactly that most of the time. Then he would hear someone talking about shifting market resources or the arrival of some government official, and he would remember why he was really here.

His CIA contact had met with him only twice so far—once in the airport men's room when Devin had first arrived and again on the elevator in Devin's building when Devin was heading to work. Each time, Chee had slipped him a flash drive with instructions on what information was currently a priority.

His first task had been relatively straightforward: copy the company directory and gather as much information as possible about the other employees at Revival. More recently, he had begun analyzing accounts he had access to for ties to the Chinese government.

Since his last meeting had occurred over two weeks ago, he found himself anticipating the next time their paths would cross. He tried to put that part of his job aside and live his cover story completely. All except for one thing. He looked down at his watch, and an alarm went off on his phone a moment before he picked it up.

He hit the button to FaceTime with Grace, his mood brightening as soon as her face lit up the screen. "Hey, gorgeous."

"Aren't you the charmer?" she asked with a smile. "How are you doing? How did the party go last night?"

"Kind of boring, actually. A bunch of people in suits talking about global markets and interest rates."

"Sounds like my international finance class."

"There was plenty of international and finance being discussed." He guided the discussion away from him. "How are you doing? Are you all settled into the apartment?"

"As much as possible. I swear, it's the size of a shoe box."

"If it's that bad, I can dip into my trust fund to help you get something bigger."

"No."

"Why not?"

"Your parents already think I married you for your money," Grace reminded him. "I'm not going to give them the opportunity to think they're right."

"It wouldn't be like that, and we both know it."

"It's only for a few months."

"With any luck, by the time I get there, we'll have enough money saved to start looking for something bigger."

"I was actually wondering if we might want to see if we could transfer to somewhere a little less crowded."

"I gather you aren't loving New York so far."

"It's not that I don't like New York. I just miss having some space." She brushed a strand of hair from her face. "Are you going to be working here when you get back stateside?"

"That was what I was told, but I might be able to request a change. Why? Where would you want to live?"

"I was doing some research last night. I thought Northern Virginia might be a nice area. If I transfer, that's where my office would be, and it's not far from Washington, DC."

Devin considered her suggestion. In truth, if he could get reassigned to the DC area, they could stay there indefinitely since he would be so close to CIA headquarters. "I'll ask my boss about it."

"Sounds good."

They chatted a few more minutes about their jobs and the novelty of being in new cities on opposite sides of the world. When he finally signed off so he could leave for work, he wondered how to best approach the topic of a transfer to DC. After all, since arriving in Hong Kong, he had barely spoken to anyone within the agency.

He pocketed his phone and slid a few files into his briefcase. After he snapped it shut, he headed for the door. Time to pretend he wasn't a spy while wishing he could go back to being the husband Grace wanted him to be.

* * *

It couldn't be right. She stared down at the little plus sign glaring back at her. Positive. Positively pregnant.

Her heart fluttered with emotions, a flood of thoughts rushing through her mind. She was having a baby. Devin's baby. Fear and uncertainty slowly gave way to anticipation.

Our baby.

What would Devin think? They hadn't really talked about starting a family. She'd expected they would have children, but when and how many hadn't entered the conversation. Both of them had been so consumed with finding ways to spend time together while finishing their degrees that those life decisions had been put aside until their life together really began.

Ideas of how she could share the news with her husband brought a smile to her face. A pair of baby booties as a gift when she saw him in London in a few weeks? Or maybe an ultrasound picture in a card? Surely she could get in to see a doctor before her trip.

The real question was whether she would be able to stand keeping this news to herself for so long. She and Devin still spoke nearly every day. Six o'clock every night, which equated to seven o'clock in the morning for him.

She had gotten into the habit of waiting for his call at work or in various restaurants near the subway station before going home for fear she would miss their daily connection. Now she understood why the smell of bacon and coffee had left her feeling queasy the past few days.

Lost in her thoughts, she startled when the alarm on her cell phone went off, a reminder that she needed to walk out the door in ten minutes.

She finished getting dressed and crossed to the kitchen, rummaging through one of the narrow kitchen cabinets until she found some crackers. She put them in a plastic sandwich bag and dropped them into her purse.

Another glance at her phone revealed her tardiness, and she hurried toward the stairs. Jogging down four flights left her breathless, but the effort paid off, and she managed to make it onto the subway platform mere seconds before her train arrived.

All the seats were occupied, and she grabbed on to the bar beside her to keep her balance when the train began its forward motion.

A baby, she thought to herself again. Looking around the crowded train, she couldn't help but contrast it with where she had come from. The open spaces of Arizona and Colorado seemed a distant memory.

The subway stopped, and another wave of people poured on. Someone jostled her with no words of apology or concern. A seed of doubt crept into her mind. Was New York City really where she wanted to raise a child? And would Washington, DC, be any better?

* * *

Devin had eaten dinner out every night for three weeks straight. Restaurants, pubs, even an evening at a comedy club. The venue changed from day to day, but he now understood why the agency had wanted someone single. The people he worked with at Revival Financial worked hard all day and socialized well into the night.

Making a connection with Fai Meng had taken some time. He worked on a different floor from Devin, and Devin hadn't wanted to appear as though he was seeking out a friendship. Instead he had watched and observed, the way Chee had instructed him. Once he had identified whom Fai socialized with, Devin had casually started expanding his network of associations to include those mutual acquaintances. Last night his patience had finally paid off, and he had ended up at dinner with Fai and three of his friends.

The wiry man carried an air of suspicion with him, and Devin couldn't help but wonder why the agency had keyed in on him. He didn't look like someone who would be easy to convince to help feed information to a foreign government.

Two of his dining companions were women, and Devin found himself trying to put up invisible walls when Meilin, the one seated closest to him, started flirting. The image of Elyse sitting beside him at the comedy club in Las Vegas sprang to mind. Then, as now, the only woman he was interested in beyond a casual conversation was Grace.

He thought of his daily conversations with her. Something about her seemed different, but he couldn't put his finger on what. Maybe it was the struggle of being apart for so long. Since marrying, they had never gone this long without seeing each other.

Meilin leaned a little closer, and Devin knew he had to make a choice. Though he doubted his CIA superiors would be pleased with his decision, he looked at his watch and pushed away from the table.

Speaking in Cantonese, he said, "I'd better get going. I have some research to do on the London market before work tomorrow. I'll see you later."

When Devin stepped back from the table, he thought he saw a flash of surprise on Fai's face. Or was it annoyance? With him, it was hard to tell. Hoping he hadn't damaged their fragile relationship, he headed for the door and the crowded sidewalks beyond.

Chapter 16

GRACE SAT IN THE EXAMINATION room, ultrasound equipment parked to her right and a chart displaying the growth of a fetus hanging to her left.

The door opened, and a woman in her midthirties entered, her black hair pulled back into a sleek ponytail, and Grace guessed her to be only about five foot two.

"Mrs. Shanahan, I'm Dr. Benson." She extended her hand.

"Nice to meet you." Grace waited for the news, finding that she was now more worried to find out she wasn't pregnant than to receive the confirmation that she was. "Did the blood test results come back?"

"They did. You are most definitely pregnant." Dr. Benson motioned to the machine. "Go ahead and lie back on the table. I'm going to do an ultrasound so we'll have some initial measurements, and we'll be able to give you a more accurate due date."

Grace did as she was asked, the doctor chatting with her about Grace's new career, her living situation, and how she was adjusting to life in New York.

As they talked, Grace stared at the monitor, black, white, and gray images shifting on the screen as the doctor began the ultrasound. Grace didn't know how the woman could identify anything based on what she saw. She also didn't notice the silence that had come over the room until Dr. Benson spoke again.

"You said your husband is working overseas?"

"That's right."

Something in the doctor's demeanor had changed, and fear lodged inside Grace. "Is everything okay?"

"Everything is fine," Dr. Benson assured her. "How long is your husband expected to be gone?"

"About four and a half more months."

"So he'll be back before you deliver."

Grace nodded.

"That's good. You'll want him to be here when you get your Christmas present."

"Christmas present?" Grace asked.

"Your due date is December 23, but I imagine you'll deliver earlier than that." She motioned to the monitor, using the cursor as a pointer. "Right here is baby A's heartbeat."

Grace stared at the rapid movement on the screen with a sense of awe.

Dr. Benson moved the cursor to the left. "And this is baby B's heartbeat."

Grace's eyes widened. "Twins?"

"Twins."

"Are you sure?" Grace tried to make out the two little heartbeats, but without the doctor pointing them out, everything still looked like a blur.

"I'm sure." She made several clicks and measured two gray blobs. She then hit the print button and, a moment later, handed Grace a narrow strip of five attached photos. Thankfully, each one was labeled so Grace could sort of make out what she was looking at.

"Keep in mind that twins are prone to come early. Ideally we would like you to make it to December 2, but there are things we can do to make sure the babies' lungs develop in the event that they come prematurely." Dr. Benson continued. "While we will do everything we can to make sure you make it to thirty-seven weeks, I strongly recommend you prepare for their arrival much earlier."

"What about travel? I was planning to meet my husband in London in a couple weeks."

"You should be fine with that. I would recommend taking a day off work when you get home to give yourself some recovery time though." She pulled out a lab-request form and filled it out. "I want you to start taking prenatal vitamins every day, and you'll need to go to the lab for blood work."

The doctor went on to explain some of the possible complications and instructed her on diet, exercise, and the frequency of her checkups.

By the time Grace left the office, her head was spinning. Excited and terrified at the prospect of having two babies instead of one, she wondered how Devin was going to take the news.

* * *

Devin walked into his apartment and closed the door behind him. He was two steps inside before he realized he wasn't alone. His heartbeat quickened, and his head whipped around until he found the intruder.

"Chee. What are you doing in here?" He looked around nervously.

"What is this?" Chee held up a computer printout.

"I don't know. What is it?"

"Airline reservations for London in two weeks. I never heard about you going to London."

"It doesn't have anything to do with work. I promised Grace I would meet her there for a long weekend. I already put in for a couple days off work."

"Devin, you can't go."

Nothing would have hit him harder. "Excuse me?"

"You heard me. You can't go flying around the world meeting up with some woman."

"She isn't 'some woman.' She's my wife."

"You aren't married, remember? Not while you're living here."

Devin set his jaw. "Let's not forget that I didn't ask for this. I wasn't told I was being groomed for this job until I had already been married for three months."

"But you didn't tell the agency you were getting married until it was too late."

Devin recognized the truth of the statement, but the other man's posture told him something he hadn't considered before. "We both know if I had asked the agency about getting married, they would have denied my request. I'm supposed to be fighting for freedom, not sacrificing all of my own."

"You can't go to London," Chee repeated. He held out his other hand. In it rested a pea-sized listening device.

"Is that . . . ?" His voice trailed off.

Chee nodded. "I deactivated it when I came in."

"How did you find it? And who put it here?"

"I do a sweep of your apartment every week. I'm not sure who put it here. I'll have headquarters run a search of the building's security footage to see if we can identify who could have come up here. Unfortunately, the security cameras are only on the main level."

The ramifications of the device being found in his apartment struck a chord of fear and apprehension. "If this is here, then I've been compromised."

"Not necessarily."

"Someone bugged my apartment." Devin motioned toward the device. "That isn't something people do if they aren't suspicious."

"It's possible they suspect something, but so far, everything you've been feeding us has been from your observations or from files you were granted access to. More likely, they see you as someone they might cultivate as an asset of their own."

"What?" Devin couldn't be hearing him right. "You think some intelligence agency wants me to be a spy? If they don't know who I really work for, I have nothing to offer."

"Unless they're going to convince you to apply for the CIA. Like I said, your language skills make you a valuable asset. You also fit the profile. Young, ambitious, no strong family ties."

"Is that why the CIA recruited me?"

"You applied for the internship, remember?" Chee said. "Your language skills and aptitude tests are why you were hired."

Devin thought over the last few days, replaying his conversations with Grace, all of them here in his apartment. "They must know about Grace."

"What?"

"I talk to her every morning, sitting right there at my kitchen table. We FaceTime, so whoever planted this would be able to hear our entire conversation."

"Her phone is encrypted, remember? Even if someone did hear the conversation, they can't find her." Chee spoke the words as though trying to convince himself as much as Devin. "What do you talk about? Did you say anything about your work here or give her information that might compromise you?"

"Not me." His heart sank. "But she mentioned her apartment in New York and how she thought she might want to move somewhere else so we could have more space. She brought it up again a couple days ago."

"Did either of you mention your marriage?"

"I don't think so. At least not in the last couple weeks."

"New York is a big city. No one is going to be able to find Grace without knowing her last name, and she hasn't lived there long enough to be locatable anyway."

What he said made sense, but that didn't chase away the sick feeling in Devin's stomach. "What do I do now?"

"The same thing you do every day. I'm going to reactivate the listening device before I leave. You'll open the door and act as though you are receiving a delivery so the sound of the door doesn't sound out of place."

"Why would you want someone to be able to spy on me?"

"Because someone who is CIA would be able to find this. Someone who isn't would never know it was here," Chee said. "Also, from now on, when you speak to Grace, make sure you call her on the phone instead of FaceTiming her. That will allow you to control what is overheard."

"Won't whoever is listening notice the change?"

"Probably. When you talk to Grace, make a point of telling her that you're having trouble with your phone and you couldn't get FaceTime to work."

"I'll cancel my trip, but I want someone to make sure Grace is safe."

"I'll take care of it, but the best way to keep her safe is to make the people listening think she's no longer in your life."

"You want me to break up with my wife?"

"Make it sound like you're breaking up with her. Tell her a lie about why you can't come to London. That will set the tone for an upcoming split. We'll follow that with a fake conversation of you breaking up with her."

"So I need to find somewhere else to go when I call her," Devin said, seeing where Chee was going with his plan.

"Exactly. I'll look into some locations that could work. In the meantime, you need to sound like you're distancing yourself from Grace."

Devin hated the idea, but it was a much better alternative to putting her in danger. "I understand."

Chee placed the listening device on the back edge of the mirror that hung on the living room wall. After activating the device, he made his way quietly to the front door and motioned for Devin to follow.

As they had agreed, Chee knocked on the inside of the door. Devin then opened it and pretended to receive a delivery. As soon as Devin was alone, he looked around his apartment, a sense of violation coming over him. Who had been here? And why did they care what happened within these walls?

Chapter 17

GRACE CAREFULLY PLACED TWO PAIRS of white booties in a gift box, setting one of the ultrasound photos on top before folding the tissue paper over it and closing the lid. She could already imagine watching Devin open it, seeing that moment when his confusion gave way to understanding. In the scenario she had conjured up in her mind, he always went from stunned to excited in a heartbeat. She hoped reality mirrored her dreams.

Her phone rang, and she drew a steadying breath. She knew it would take all her willpower to keep from telling him everything. Keeping her pregnancy a secret over the past few weeks had been hard enough, but twins? She felt like she might burst with excitement.

She grabbed her phone, surprised to see him making a regular phone call instead of choosing to FaceTime with her. "Hey, there. How are you?"

"Actually, I've had better days."

"What's wrong? You sound exhausted."

"Grace, I'm so sorry, but I'm not going to be able to meet you in London."

She wasn't sure what she had expected him to say, but that was not it. "You can't be serious. We've been looking forward to this for weeks."

"I know. I got called into my boss's office yesterday and found out I have a big presentation we have to prep for. They aren't approving any leave for at least a few weeks."

"We haven't seen each other for over two months." If he couldn't get away, maybe they could change their plans and still make things work. "What if I come to you? If I can get a couple extra days off, I can come to Hong Kong instead of London."

"I wouldn't feel comfortable having you fly over here by yourself."

"I'm a big girl," Grace said, even though she really was nervous about traveling where she didn't speak the language. "I'm sure I can figure out how to get there."

"Honey, I appreciate the thought, but I'm going to be working ridiculous hours. I don't want you to come visit only to be home alone all the time."

She let out a sigh. She understood his logic, but she didn't have to like it. "I really hate this."

"I know. I'm not crazy about the situation either."

"I never thought being with you would be this complicated."

"Sometimes things get worse before they get better."

"They're definitely worse at the moment," Grace grumbled. Trying to fight away her disappointment, she said, "I'm sorry. I just miss you."

"I know. I feel the same way." Before she could say anything further, he added, "I have to get going but I'll talk to you later, okay?"

"Okay. I love you."

"Talk to you tomorrow."

Grace heard the click when he hung up, and she held out her phone, staring at it. Not once since their marriage had he ended a call without saying "I love you." Uneasy, she slipped her phone into her purse. He was just busy, she assured herself. The disappointment of not being able to see each other must be affecting him as much as it was her.

Those thoughts rattled through her brain, but they didn't chase away the doubt that had been planted. Was Devin really too busy to see her, or was he putting her off because he didn't *want* to see her?

She rubbed a hand over her swelling abdomen, the little bump beneath her skirt that was still unnoticeable to everyone but her. *It's just hormones.* She loved Devin, and he loved her. In four more months, they would be together, and then they could focus on finding a new home where they could welcome the newest members of their family.

* * *

Devin rubbed a hand over his face, his stomach muscles clenching as he fought against tears. Censoring his words when talking to Grace had been hard enough, but being afraid to express his love for her left a hole in his heart.

He had hardly slept last night, constantly opening his eyes and looking around the room to make sure he was alone. Visions of some Chinese intelligence operative standing over him with a gun continued to push into his mind, and nothing he did succeeded in squelching the fear that gripped him.

Running alongside those images was the constant replay of his conversations with Grace over the past week. What had they said that could have compromised her safety or his? The topic of her relocating from New York had been a constant lately, along with whether he would be able to move to the DC area with her. He was rather certain they hadn't spoken of their marital status, but that didn't stop the niggling doubt from plaguing him.

He forced himself to finish getting ready for work, overthinking each step for fear he might change his routine now that he knew someone was listening. How had he become a target? And what did anyone think they could gain from him?

His brain felt like it was about to explode by the time he walked into his office. Every person he passed, everyone he greeted felt like a threat, and he had to draw deep into his limited acting talents to behave normally. As the day wore on, slowly the adrenaline from his fear wore off, giving way to exhaustion.

The lines on the marketing report in front of him had been blurring together for the past half hour, and though he had tried to concentrate, when a knock came on his office door, he welcomed the distraction. He looked up to see Fai standing on the other side of his desk.

Devin stood. "Fai. What can I do for you?"

"I was looking at the London market today and saw a drop in commodities. Does your research indicate a long-term shift, or do you think this is an anomaly?"

"Personally, I think that will depend on whether the US's long-term interest rates go up. I think today's shift is a result of speculation on whether or not that's going to happen."

They discussed the economics of the ripple effect of the major world financial markets until Fai guided the conversation to more personal topics.

"Meilin was asking about you after you left last night. She thought perhaps you had a girlfriend."

Recognizing the comment as a possible test, Devin skirted the truth while keeping his story consistent with what happened within the walls of his apartment.

"Actually, I did leave someone behind in the US."

"Are things serious?"

"They were heading that way, but I have to admit that having a long-distance relationship is a lot harder than I thought it would be."

"Will she come here to Hong Kong?"

"I don't think so. She doesn't speak the language, which would make it hard for her here."

Fai turned to go. "I'll let you get back to work." He paused at the door. "Several people from my department are going to the opening of a new art exhibit on Tuesday. Perhaps I will see you there."

Devin nodded and watched the older man leave the room. As soon as he was alone, he leaned back in his chair and forced himself to take calm, steady breaths. Had Fai simply been making conversation, or had he been fishing for information?

Again the question simmered in his brain. Why would anyone target him? Beyond his language abilities, he didn't know enough about anything in the intelligence community to warrant the attention of the Chinese, and he couldn't think of anything he had done to draw attention to himself.

He remembered Jalen's comment about how the CIA had put his application in a number of months before. Perhaps it wasn't him who had made a mistake. Perhaps something in the CIA's processes had compromised him before he'd even started. If that was the case, what was he even doing here? Whether it was in New York City or Washington, DC, he would much rather be on the other side of the world with Grace.

* * *

Fai handed Qing the transcripts from Devin Shanahan's conversations in his apartment.

"Did you find anything of significance?"

"Possibly," Fai said. "Every morning at the same time, Devin calls a woman in the United States."

"Who is she?" Qing asked.

"We believe she is the woman he left behind, but all we know is her name is Grace."

"Did you trace her phone?"

"Her phone is encrypted."

"And his phone?"

"Encrypted as well."

Qing scanned over the transcripts. "It appears this woman may be of use to us."

"How do we find her? All we know is that she lives in New York and works for Anderson Enterprises."

"See if you can find anything through her work. I'll request a trace on Devin's other communications. Perhaps she also talks to him on his work phone or sends him e-mails."

"What do you plan to do when we find her?"

"I plan to see how much she knows about Mr. Shanahan's real reason for being here. And if necessary, we will use her to get exactly what we need."

Fai bowed his head. "I understand."

Chapter 18

SHE COULDN'T STAND IT ANYMORE. Despite setting off insect bombs twice in the past week, every day when she got up and flipped on the lights, cockroaches scurried across the floor and kitchen counters.

The futon couch that doubled as her bed thus far seemed to be immune to the infestation, but she suspected it was only a matter of time. The truth was, the futon mattress was far less comfortable than advertised online, and her back ached from the lack of support.

She needed a real bed and a real apartment. And a real exterminator.

Devin still hadn't confirmed whether he would be able to work in his company's DC office when he returned home, but it wouldn't hurt for her to ask her HR department if that option was still available to her.

She crossed her legs on her couch and pulled her computer onto her lap. She had yet to sign up for Wi-Fi, but the couple next door had an open network she was able to use if she situated herself just right.

On a whim, she checked her company's website for available job openings. Her heart lifted when she saw that both Washington, DC, and Los Angeles had listings she was qualified for.

She then typed in Revival Financial and did a similar search.

She was disappointed when she didn't find anything available in either location. Curious to see if there were any other locations where both companies had job openings, she continued looking through the company's website. When she happened upon the page that identified all of their office locations, Grace froze. She read over the page four times, certain she must be missing something.

A few more open web pages confirmed what she had first seen, but she couldn't believe it. She found the contact number and called the company directly.

A woman answered, her voice businesslike. "Revival Financial. How may I direct your call?"

"I'm trying to locate the address for your office in Washington, DC."

"I'm sorry, ma'am, but we don't have an office in DC."

"What about Los Angeles?"

"No, ma'am. Our offices are located in Hong Kong, Tokyo, London, Frankfurt, Paris, and New York."

"And you don't have any subsidiaries located elsewhere?"

"No, ma'am."

Grace's heart sank. "Thank you for your help."

She hung up. Devin had been so certain that his company had offices in both DC and LA. After more than two months with the company, how was it that he didn't know his assumption was wrong? Or had he been lying to her all this time? And why would he?

All throughout high school, he had been one of the most honest people she'd known. Had something happened to change that? And did he really intend for them to be together as husband and wife when he returned to the United States? Was he even planning to move back to the US?

A wave of nausea threatened. She looked at the clock and did the calculations. Nine o'clock on a Saturday morning meant it would be ten o'clock on Saturday night in Hong Kong. She gripped her phone in her hand. She and Devin had agreed on when they would talk to make sure they weren't interrupting the other's work or sleep.

At the moment, she didn't care what he was doing. She needed answers, and she needed them now.

She dialed his number, her free hand falling to rest on her stomach. If nothing else, Devin needed to know about the babies and have time to prepare for fatherhood.

The phone rang five times and rolled to a generic voice-mail account. Her stomach churned uncomfortably, but whether it was from stress or hormones she didn't know.

She crossed the room to the kitchen counter and sent the last of the roaches scattering. Opening one of the cabinets, she fished out a box of saltine crackers and pulled out a handful. Three crackers and a glass of water later, she dialed again.

This time Devin answered on the third ring, the sound of music playing in the background. "Grace. Is everything okay?"

"Not exactly."

"What's wrong?"

Where to start? Grace thought of the canceled trip to London, the deception regarding his job, the surprise she had planned when she told him of their pregnancy that he had totally ruined.

"Are you okay?" he asked before she could formulate an answer.

A deep breath. "Other than some morning sickness, I'm fine."

"Morning sickness?" he repeated. "Are you sure that's what it is?"

"I'm positive."

"Is it something to worry about?"

"It'll pass eventually."

"I hope you feel better soon."

That was it? She had just told him she was pregnant, and he brushed her off like she'd said she had a cold? Or did he somehow already know she was expecting? And if so, how had he figured it out, and why hadn't he said something sooner?

Grace paced five steps and turned when she reached the far side of the room. Was he really not going to say anything else?

She would come back to that. She drew another deep breath. "You said you might be able to transfer to DC when you got back."

"Yeah," he responded, obvious confusion in his voice. "So?"

"Your company doesn't have an office in Washington, DC."

Music came over the line but nothing else.

"Devin, you've been lying to me. Why?"

More silence. Thirty seconds passed before he finally spoke. "I really can't talk right now. Can I call you later?"

"It sounds like I don't have a choice."

"I'm sorry, Grace," he said, but she wasn't sure what he was apologizing for—cutting off the call or lying in the first place. "You're okay, though, right?"

"Other than not knowing where we stand, I'm perfect."

"I'll call you in a few days. Things are pretty crazy here right now."

"On a Saturday night. Right."

"Bye, Grace."

The phone disconnected, and she stared down at it. She managed to blink twice before the tears started. Her husband was lying to her, and he didn't care that she was pregnant. What would he have said if she'd told him they were having twins? She was having twins, she corrected. At the moment, Devin was barely part of her life. The question was whether he wanted to be part of it in the future.

Another cockroach skittered into view, and she wiped at the tears on her cheeks. The next time she talked to Devin, she was going to make it clear. She couldn't live like this anymore.

* * *

Devin took a moment to compose himself before he returned to the table in the bar where he had joined Fai and several of their coworkers from Revival. He'd hated lying to Grace before, but that was nothing compared to this. Knowing he had lost her trust was killing him inside.

The background noise had made it hard to hear her, even after he'd walked across the room so he wouldn't be so close to the band playing in the corner. At least she hadn't seemed too concerned about whatever sickness she had caught. Maybe it was better they weren't still planning to meet in London after all. The last thing either of them needed was to finally see each other and have one of them feeling lousy.

At the moment, he had the feeling lousy part perfected. He needed Grace, and this job was destroying everything he cared about.

He pocketed his phone, his chest tight and burning from the tension running through him. At least the music was loud enough that he wouldn't have to make much conversation. He wondered how soon he could make an excuse to leave.

Bolin, the man directly across from him, had become a friendly acquaintance over the past two months. They were around the same age, and like Devin, he hadn't been with Revival long. Tain, the man sitting beside Fai, was ten years Devin's senior and tended more toward the serious side.

"Is everything okay?" Fai asked when Devin reclaimed his seat between him and Meilin.

"Fine." He had barely sat down when the waiter arrived with their latest round of drinks.

Devin picked up the nonalcoholic orange-and-strawberry juice placed in front of him, and Meilin put her hand on his arm. Devin reminded himself not to pull away. He couldn't let things get too friendly, but he needed to look like he was single, or at least appear that he wasn't married. And at the same time, he promised himself he would find a way to talk to Grace tomorrow.

He would have to give Chee an ultimatum. If he was compromised anyway, it was time to let him go back to the States, back to Grace. And it was time he was allowed to tell his wife what he really did for a living.

Bolin commented on an upcoming trip to Beijing, and Devin reminded himself of why he was here. Gathering information. He took a sip of his drink and reminded himself to act casually as the conversation continued to flow, everyone raising their voices to compete with the music.

Half an hour was all he could take before he decided it was time to make his exit. He moved slightly to his left, preparing to reach for his wallet. The room blurred for a moment, and Devin blinked to focus.

He managed to pull out a few bills to pay for his part. He opened his mouth to say good-bye, and a wave of dizziness hit him.

"Are you okay?" Fai asked.

"Just a little dizzy." Devin gripped the edge of the table and managed to stand. "I'll see you all later."

Chapter 19

GRACE'S EYES WERE STILL SWOLLEN but finally dry when her phone rang again. She wasn't sure how much time had passed, but at least the crying jag had seemed to overshadow her morning sickness for the time being.

She grabbed her phone, not sure if she was ready to talk to Devin again but knowing, too, that speaking with him was the only thing that was going to make her feel better.

"Hi, Grace. It's your grandpa."

"Hi, Grandpa. How are you?" she said, relieved and disappointed at the same time.

"Can't complain. How's my little girl?"

"Pregnant."

"What? Did you just say you're pregnant?"

Grace couldn't believe she had blurted out the truth. Maybe it was the emotional exhaustion, or maybe she needed to share the news with someone who didn't have the word *doctor* before their name. "That's right. You're going to be a great-grandpa."

"Well, honey, congratulations. How are you feeling?"

"Tired, nauseated."

"Your grandma was the same way with your daddy. It'll pass."

"That's what I hear." Grace settled onto her couch, and a little ripple of excitement surfaced as she prepared to share the rest of the news. "There is something else I should tell you."

"What's that?"

"I'm having twins."

"Twins? I don't know whether to congratulate you or offer my sympathy."

Grace chuckled. "Let's stick with congratulations for now. You can save the sympathy for when I'm dealing with sleepless nights."

"At least Devin will be back when that happens."

"I hope so." Her mood darkened at the mention of his name.

"Is something wrong?"

"It's just hard being away from Devin for so long. With our days and nights opposite, communicating isn't as easy as it used to be."

"Hang in there, kiddo. This too shall pass."

"Promise?"

"I promise." He paused, then said, "Before I let you go, I hoped to ask a favor."

"What's that?"

"The financial planner who has been handling my investments is retiring. I hoped you might be willing to take over for him." He pressed on quickly. "If you think it would be too much for you, I'll understand, especially now that you have two babies on the way."

"I'd love to handle it for you. Managing investments is what I enjoy the most."

"Before you agree, there's something else I should tell you."

"What's that?"

"I sold the ranch."

"What? You've lived there for as long as I can remember."

"That's true, but I found a place I want to live more. The workable land is about the same size, but there's also a dozen bungalows on the edge of the property that overlook the river and can be rented out."

"Where is it?"

"Vail, a few miles from the ski resort."

"So you work the land during the summer months and rent to skiers during the winter. Smart."

"That's what my investment adviser said too right before he announced his retirement."

Grace thought over her schedule. "The Fourth of July is coming up. Maybe I can fly home for a few days, and we can look over everything then."

"As much as I would love to see you, you don't have to come all this way to look at spreadsheets. I can have everything sent to you."

"I know, but I was planning to take the time off anyway, and I'm ready to get out of the city for a while. Besides, I would love to see the new property."

"You just let me know when to pick you up from the airport, and I'll be there."

* * *

Devin's stomach roiled, and his heart hammered in his chest. Groggy and disoriented, he pushed his hands onto the mattress and managed to sit up. His eyes opened a slit, and impossibly, his heartbeat quickened further. This wasn't his bed but rather a futon mat.

The apartment was only half the size of his own. A man with brown hair sat at the table across the room, a laptop open in front of him.

"Where am I?" Devin asked in English.

"You're still in Hong Kong."

"Who are you?"

"You can call me Ghost." He shifted in his seat so he was facing Devin. "What's the last thing you remember?"

"I remember having drinks with some people from work. I got up to leave . . ." Devin's voice trailed off. "I don't know what happened after that." He tried to bring forward the memories of the night, but nothing came. "What did happen after that?"

A knock sounded at the door before Ghost could respond.

Ghost rose and crossed the few feet to answer the door. Chee entered quickly, relief appearing on his face the moment he saw Devin.

"You're okay," Chee said more to himself than to Devin.

"Can one of you tell me what's going on?"

"You were drugged," Ghost told him.

"What?" Devin looked around the apartment again. "How did I end up here?"

Chee sat at the table while Ghost leaned against the wall. "When I found the bug in your apartment, I requested some extra help for you. Ghost has been trailing you for the past several days."

Ghost spoke now. "I was outside the bar when your friends walked out with you. It was obvious you weren't yourself. Two of the men were helping you call a taxi."

"And I ended up here how?"

"Ghost convinced them that you were old friends. Seeing that you were ill, he insisted on taking you home."

"Who drugged me, then?" Devin asked. "If it had been the people I was with, they never would have let you take me."

"I didn't give them a choice," Ghost said. "Let's just say that you weren't the only person drugged."

"You drugged my coworkers?"

"Only the two who were putting you into the car." Ghost held up his cell phone to show Devin their pictures. Both men were lying in a narrow alley.

"That's Bolin and Tain."

"Who else were you with?" Chee asked.

"Fai, Meilin, and Huan."

"One of them must have your cell phone."

"My cell phone?" Devin patted his pockets to find it gone. "If they have my phone, they can find Grace."

"We'll make sure she stays safe."

"Grace?" Ghost asked.

"His wife," Chee said.

Ghost sat in his seat and leaned forward. "It sounds like you need to start from the beginning."

* * *

Grace watched the seconds tick slowly by. Why was it that whenever she wanted time to pass by quickly, it seemed to do the opposite?

The night custodial staff had already come through to empty the garbage cans and vacuum. Her presence didn't seem to deter them from their jobs, nor did they seem to worry why she was still here. A handful of other employees were also still at their desks despite the late hour. Of course, most of them were involved with international funds and had reason to keep odd hours.

Trying to distract herself from her fatigue, she looked over the paperwork she had received from human resources. Transfer possibilities, maternity leave request forms, insurance information.

Another glance at the clock. Five more minutes. Butterflies fluttered inside her. What would she discover when she made this call? She was afraid to know and equally afraid not to.

Unable to concentrate, she cleaned the papers off her desk and tucked them into a file in her drawer. After shutting off her computer, she picked up the phone and dialed, keying in the calling card number she had purchased at lunch to cover the overseas charges.

The female voice that answered spoke in a foreign tongue, presumably Cantonese.

"Devin Shanahan, please."

"Devin Shanahan?" the woman repeated. Grace couldn't tell if she was questioning her or confirming what she had said. In accented English, she finally said, "One moment."

The phone clicked once, and then began ringing once more. Three rings later, Devin's recorded voice came over the line when he announced his name. The next words were automated and incomprehensible to her. A beep followed.

Grace debated briefly whether to leave a message but decided against it. Devin had said he would be traveling the next few days, and she had the answer to at least one of her questions—he hadn't lied about where he worked. So why had he told her he could transfer to cities that weren't available to him?

A new possibility surfaced, and she felt suddenly foolish for doubting him. Perhaps it hadn't been transfer possibilities he had been looking at but rather a switch in companies in order to allow her to follow her career opportunities.

Exhausted but feeling a little more secure in her marriage, Grace stood and gathered her purse. It was time to go get some sleep. By the week's end, she would be able to talk to Devin, and they would plan their future without letting any misunderstandings come between them again.

Chapter 20

"You want me to do what?" Devin asked in English. Chee had already explained himself in Cantonese, but Devin must have misunderstood.

"You need to go back to work tomorrow."

"You can't be serious." Devin looked over at Ghost. "He can't be serious."

"He's very serious," Ghost responded. "And he's right."

"You think one of my coworkers drugged me, and now you want me to go back to work to let them try again? We already know I'm on someone's radar, or we wouldn't have found a listening device in my apartment or be here now."

"Exactly. What we don't know is how you got on anyone's radar, especially since this is your first assignment," Ghost said.

"We believe your job here in Hong Kong might have more to do with the Chinese wanting you here and less to do with us taking advantage of an opportunity," Chee said.

Devin held up his hand as he processed Chee's words. "You think the Chinese deliberately arranged for me to get a job in Hong Kong so they could recruit me as a spy? Is that what you're saying?"

"Yes," Ghost said.

"Why?"

"We don't know, which is why you need to go back to work."

"And how do I explain why I missed work today?"

"I called in for you this morning and said you were sick." Nothing seemed to rattle this guy.

"Even if I agree, what purpose would it serve?"

"I told you before taking this assignment that the Chinese have developed a way to crack through a number of intelligence projects," Chee said.

"We've seen a decrease in the past three years, which makes us think they may have lost their source. If they recruit you, we'll be able to find out the method they are using to hack into our systems."

"If they've already lost their source, does it matter what method they were using?" Devin asked. "I have to be honest. After waking up without knowing where I was, I'm not exactly anxious to stick around in Hong Kong, especially considering that my wife is still in the States."

"The Chinese are going to find someone to give them what they want. This window of opportunity to discover what they're doing may never open to us again."

"And I may not be so lucky next time someone decides to come after me. I'm sorry, but all I want to do is go home."

"Devin, I promised to keep Grace safe, but I can't do that if you go to New York. For all we know, you could be followed there."

"Why would someone follow me there?"

"Because if they can get to Grace, they can get to you," Chee said solemnly. "The one thing that could cause you to turn your back on your country is your wife's safety."

Devin rubbed a hand over his face. Chee was right. If he knew Grace's life was in jeopardy, there wasn't anything he wouldn't do to save her.

"Go to work tomorrow," Ghost said simply. "If anyone asks why you weren't at work today, tell them you had a rough weekend and that you and your girlfriend broke up."

Chee nodded in agreement. "If the Chinese don't make a play to recruit you, at least when you go home, they won't know to look for Grace."

His heart heavy, Devin dropped his head into his hands. "Tell me what you want me to do after that."

* * *

Grace turned in her leave slip first thing Monday morning. She followed that up with a request to meet with her human resources officer. Regardless of Devin's plans, she needed to explore her options. Raising two babies in her current living situation wasn't one she was willing to entertain. She either had to find something farther out of the city and commute or transfer to another city altogether.

The thought of having her babies and leaving them in someone else's care left an uncomfortable tightness in her chest, which she hadn't expected. Though she hadn't consciously thought about what she wanted when she started a family, she now realized that being a working mom wasn't it, at least not in the traditional sense. Rather, she wanted what her mother had been given: the chance to stay home and raise her family. Her father had given her that gift, but Grace had no idea if such a possibility even existed with Devin.

He was coming back in three more months, assuming he really did want to stay married to her. She forced that thought aside but couldn't quite put it to rest completely.

His reaction to her pregnancy continued to confuse her. She could have sworn he hadn't even registered what she had told him. Maybe shock had prevented him from expressing his true emotions. After all, he hadn't been expecting to talk to her at all, and the background noise indicated he wasn't at home. If only she could talk to him now and air out all her questions.

All weekend she had tried to make sense of everything Devin had told her about his job, but she still couldn't get everything to add up. She had seen his airline itinerary to Hong Kong, but she couldn't remember ever seeing anything else work related.

Another thought surfaced, a more direct way to find out exactly what was happening with her husband. She headed for her cubicle. It looked like it was going to be a much longer day than she had originally intended.

* * *

Devin followed Chee and Ghost's instructions to the letter, and he hated every minute of it. He went back to work day after day. He confided in several coworkers that he and his longtime girlfriend had broken up and that his cell phone had been stolen Saturday night. He didn't change his routine of going to and leaving work and accepted invitations for dinner most evenings. And he didn't call Grace.

Though the stress of not knowing whom he could trust ate him up, not being able to call Grace was killing him, and it had only been a week. Of all of Ghost's instructions, that was the one he had intended to ignore. He would have ignored it, except that he had never memorized her phone number. Ghost and Chee must have anticipated that fact, or he doubted they would have provided him a new phone.

His own phone number had changed too, so he couldn't even wait for Grace to call him.

Chee had promised him a chance to call Grace next week, but even that seemed like an eternity away. And he'd have to use a burn phone so no one could trace it back to him.

The listening device in his apartment was still in place, but other than a couple of business calls, he was certain he was a very boring subject. Regardless of the reasons he was under surveillance, Devin felt eyes on him everywhere he went. Every morning when he went to work, he reminded himself to look natural, and every day, he felt like he had a target on his back and that someone was going to take a shot at him.

Three more months. Then this assignment would be over, and he would be back home where he could explain everything to Grace. He only hoped she could forgive the lies and the silence currently stretching out between them.

* * *

Grace was halfway to the airport before she realized she'd left her cell phone in her apartment. She checked her backpack a second time. Wallet, laptop, the passport she didn't need, an extra pair of socks, a granola bar, lip balm. She blew out a breath in frustration. No cell phone.

Leaning forward, she spoke to her cab driver. "Can you go back, please? I forgot something in my apartment."

In thickly accented English, he replied, "Yes, miss."

Grace looked at the clock on the dashboard and calculated how long it would take to get back to her apartment and then make the trip to JFK airport. If she hurried, she should still be able to make it with a few minutes to spare. Thank goodness she had chosen to leave early.

Of course, if she would have simply remembered everything, she wouldn't have needed to leave early.

Three cabs and several other cars blocked the area in front of her building. A black SUV took the only available spot only moments before they reached it.

Her driver pulled slowly past her building, finally parking two buildings down. "I'm sorry, but this is as close as I can get you unless you want me to circle around again."

With the thick morning traffic, Grace suspected she could walk the distance in half the time it would take to drive it. "I'll walk."

She looked at her suitcase and computer bag on the seat next to her. Carrying everything with her would take too long, so she chose to take only the items with the highest value. The cabbie might look trustworthy enough, but that didn't mean she needed to tempt fate and leave him with her wallet and laptop.

She slid one arm through the strap of her backpack, stepped from the car, and started toward her building, a little annoyed when she saw three Chinese men climb out of the SUV that had taken the last parking space. All three of them looked to be in perfect health. Surely a pregnant woman should have been entitled to the better spot.

In a perfect world, she thought to herself. The men's nationality made her think of her husband and the many questions she had about what had happened between them.

Devin had said he would talk to her in a couple days. That had been six days ago.

She had forced herself to be patient, but yesterday she had finally had enough and tried calling him at his office. Seven times.

The first time, he had answered, but she couldn't hear him say anything. Realizing it was a bad connection, she had hung up and called again. And again. Each of the subsequent times she'd called, the phone had rung five times and gone to voice mail.

Walking quickly, Grace made her way down the sidewalk, weaving through the foot traffic. She had lived in New York long enough now to not be surprised when the men in front of her didn't look back to see her or think to hold the door for the person behind them.

If anything, the men appeared to be in a bigger rush than she was. Their dark suits and deliberate movements made her think they could have come straight out of a spy movie.

By the time she reached the door and walked into the lobby, the men were nowhere to be found. She headed for the stairwell and rushed up the first flight. By the second flight, her steps had slowed. Deciding slow and steady would serve her better than exhausting herself before her trip, she kept her hand on the rail and made her way to the fourth floor.

Not for the first time, she considered the one positive of her apartment: her door was right across from the stairs. She pushed the stairwell door open, took one step into the hall, and froze.

Her front door hung open, and she could hear voices inside . . . speaking in a foreign language. Was that Chinese?

Questions raced through her mind. Who were these men? Why were they in her apartment? What did they want? Were they looking for her specifically?

Another horrific thought shot through her. Was Devin okay? Had these men come looking for her to deliver bad news?

Logic surfaced, and she retreated back into the stairwell. If they had come to tell her something was wrong with Devin, they would have waited for her to answer her door rather than break in.

At a loss as to their true motives, she considered her options until she heard two of their voices coming toward her.

Afraid the men might be heading back downstairs, she went the other direction. She had just passed the landing halfway to the fifth floor when the door on the fourth floor opened. She couldn't understand the men, but she could sense their frustration.

Grace froze, afraid to make any sound.

A discussion ensued below her, and ultimately two men headed back down the stairs.

The stairwell now empty, she continued to the fifth floor. She didn't have her phone so she couldn't call for help. To get to her cab, she would have to walk out the front entrance, where the men's car was parked. She also had no idea where they were now, except for the one who was still in her apartment.

The weight of her backpack offered her another possibility for communication. Lowering it to the floor, she pulled her laptop free and powered it on. She slipped the backpack onto her shoulder once more and walked slowly down the hall while watching her laptop screen. When she didn't find what she was looking for, she climbed to the sixth floor and once again walked the hall.

This time her silent prayers were answered in the form of an unsecured Internet connection.

She accessed the New York Police Department's website and sent a message. *Apartment break-in happening now. Three Chinese men, midthirties, dark suits, driving a black SUV.* She then gave her address and submitted the message.

Chapter 21

GRACE WAITED FORTY-FIVE MINUTES before she finally ventured down the stairwell on the opposite side of the building from her apartment. She had no idea if the police had ever arrived or if the men in her apartment were still in the building. What she did know was that she was tired of waiting around and praying that she wouldn't be found.

She reached the first floor and cracked the door open wide enough to peek into the lobby. She didn't see a police car out front, nor was the black SUV still present.

The likelihood of the cab still waiting for her hovered somewhere between slim and none. She wondered vaguely if the cabbie had filed a complaint once he'd realized she wasn't coming back. Grace emerged from the stairwell and turned away from the front entrance. The side door led into an alley she normally avoided at all costs. Today, she was grateful for its seclusion.

Her heart was pounding as she turned toward the back of the building and used the maze of alleys to hide herself from view until she reached the next block. She raised a hand to hail a cab, grateful that she had to wait only a minute before one pulled up to the curb.

"Where to, miss?"

Grace looked at the clock on the dash. Her flight was scheduled to leave in less than an hour. Even if she could get to JFK in the next twenty minutes, she'd never clear security in time, and unfortunately, her ticket didn't allow for changes. The image of the men in her apartment was enough to prompt her to alter her plans. "Grand Central Station, but I need to stop at a bank along the way."

The driver nodded and put the car in gear. He pulled into traffic, and Grace turned to look over her shoulder. She didn't see any familiar faces behind her and hoped that would remain the case for the rest of her travels. She didn't know who the men were, but she wanted to know why they were looking for her.

* * *

Feeling very much like a fugitive with no one readily available whom she could trust, Grace made her way to the bank of pay phones in Grand Central Station. The withdrawal she had made from the bank would give her traveling cash, but now she had to decide what to do with it. Her first call to the police department did little to ease her concerns.

The officer who took the call confirmed that they had apprehended a man in her apartment. The only thing of hers they'd found in his possession was her cell phone, but instead of charging him, they'd let him go. The Chinese national had diplomatic immunity. Other than a report being filed with the State Department, nothing would happen to him.

Not sure if and when she would be able to return, she called information and asked for the number for her company so she could let her boss know she might be gone longer than anticipated.

"Anderson Enterprises, how may I direct your call?"

"Helen Keswick, please."

"One moment." The moment stretched out until the receptionist came back on the line. "I'm sorry, but she is in a meeting. May I leave a message?"

"This is Grace Shanahan. I wanted to let her know I've had a family emergency and I may need to take a few extra days off."

"Oh, Grace. I was just looking for you."

"I beg your pardon?" Grace thought of the hundreds of people who worked in her office. She doubted the receptionist even knew her name, so why would she recognize her now?

"A couple of people were looking for you a few minutes ago. I offered to take a message, but they left."

Grace closed her eyes. "Thanks for letting me know."

"One more thing."

"What's that?"

"The police were here looking for you too. Are you in some kind of trouble?"

"No. They were probably following up on a report I sent in. Thanks for your help."

Grace hung up. The men at her apartment really were looking for her. The same question continued to flood her mind: why?

Her imagination, fueled by the various television shows she had watched over the years, helped her consider how best to disappear from New York without being followed.

She picked up the pay phone once more, this time calling a number from memory.

"Grandpa?"

"Grace? Is that you? I thought you were supposed to be on a plane right now."

"I was. I had some trouble getting to my flight." She thought over the various flight schedules between Phoenix and Grand Junction and considered the passport in her backpack that still identified her under her maiden name. If someone was looking for her by name, maybe it was time to go back to being Grace Harrington. "When were you planning on driving up to the new place?"

"I close tomorrow morning. I plan to head up afterward."

"Can you pick me up at the airport on your way? I should be able to get there by noon."

"Is everything okay?"

"We'll talk when I get there."

"Okay. I'll see you tomorrow," he said, obviously concerned. "You take care."

"I will. I love you, Grandpa."

"I love you too."

She wanted to make one more call, but the time difference made it impossible. Instead, she found a quiet corner and accessed Grand Central Station's free Wi-Fi. After logging into her e-mail account, she stared at the blank message and debated what to write. She opted for the truth.

Devin,

I don't know what is going on, but some Chinese nationals broke into my apartment today, and I'm afraid to go back there. They stole my phone, so I lost all of my contacts. Please e-mail me back and give me your phone number. I'm worried about you.

Love,

Grace

She read through the simple message, debating if she should give him more information on where she planned to go next. Her newfound paranoia kept her from revealing any more than what she had already written, so she pressed send. Once he e-mailed her back, they could talk on the phone, and maybe Devin could explain why those men had been looking for her.

* * *

"She got away."

"I already heard. Chanming was discovered at her apartment."

"What do you want us to do now?"

"Keep an eye on her workplace. She may try to stay somewhere else, but work will be her one constant."

"We had her phone until the police confiscated it. Unfortunately, that means we won't be able to trace her location anymore."

"If we can't trace her, neither can the CIA." He considered. "Make sure there isn't any way for the woman to contact Mr. Shanahan. If we can intercept any messages between them, he'll never know for sure if we are the ones keeping her from him."

"And if we do find the woman?"

"She will be our guest. Our sources tell us she is the key to getting what we want."

"I'll keep you informed."

"See that you do." He nodded. "And tell Liko it's time to make a move. We can't wait any longer. We've already missed too many opportunities."

"I'll send the message." He bowed and left the room.

* * *

Devin saw Chee sitting in his apartment and sent him a questioning glance before tapping a finger to his ear.

"I disabled it." Chee motioned to the seat beside him. "There's something you need to know." He drew a breath before giving him the news. "Grace is gone."

"What?" Devin couldn't breathe. He couldn't feel. "Define 'gone.'"

"She's missing," Chee clarified.

Devin dropped onto his couch. "Missing but alive?"

"Yes, she's alive."

"Are you sure?"

Chee nodded. "A couple of our Chinese friends showed up at her apartment yesterday. Apparently the police received a message that her place had been broken into. When the cops arrived, they found an intelligence operative still inside."

"Did he say why he was there?"

"Unfortunately, he has diplomatic immunity and isn't talking. The State Department is having him deported, but we aren't going to get any information from him."

"You said there was more than one. Could the other one have found Grace?"

"The message the police received came from Grace's building. Around the same time the cops got to the apartment complex, two Asian men showed up at Grace's work looking for her. We think she must have seen them coming and taken off."

"How would she know they were a threat? She doesn't even know who I really work for."

"I don't know. All I know is that the man they apprehended had Grace's cell phone, but she was nowhere to be found." Chee hastily added, "We were able to track her movements as far as Grand Central Station, and we know she stopped at the bank and withdrew over a thousand dollars."

"Travel money. She's trying to get home."

"I just told you she wasn't at her apartment."

"Not that home. Home to Colorado." Devin stood and headed for his room. "I have to make sure she's okay."

Chee followed. "Devin, that's exactly what these people want you to do. They're pressing buttons to see what will work. The best thing you can do is stay here. Act like you don't have any idea anything happened."

He pulled his suitcase out of the closet and tossed it on the bed. "You told me she would be safe, and she's not. How can I trust you to keep her safe now?"

"We'll make sure she's okay," Chee promised. "You stick with the story that she's not part of your life. It's the only way to make sure she stays safe."

"If I had known what I was getting myself into, I never would have agreed to this." Devin dropped onto his bed beside the now-open suitcase. He blinked against his emotions and looked up at the man across the room. "My wife means everything to me."

"I understand." Chee fell silent for a moment. "I'll ask headquarters to do a search of the various transportation possibilities out of New York and the surrounding areas. They'll make sure she gets to where she's going safely."

"Thank you."

"As for you, get some sleep. You look like you've been run over by a truck."

"At this point, I think that would be less painful." Devin watched Chee cross the room and reactivate the listening device. A moment later, the door opened and closed. Obediently, Devin walked across the room to make sure it sounded like he had just arrived. Then he shoved his suitcase back into his closet, dropped into bed, and wondered how many nightmares he would have to battle in his sleep tonight.

Chapter 22

GRACE HADN'T KNOWN IT WAS possible to be this tired. Exhaustion had ceased to describe her weariness when she landed in Arizona. Yesterday she had taken a shuttle from Grand Central Station to La Guardia and finally taken an evening flight to Phoenix.

Nine hours in the airport trying to get comfortable sleeping on the floor had been woefully insufficient, and boarding her plane to Grand Junction had ultimately been a relief. She supposed she would have ended up with a backache even if she hadn't been fifteen weeks pregnant, but her growing abdomen hadn't helped matters, and she worried that the stress of the past day and her lack of sleep would adversely affect her babies. Thankfully, the seat next to her had been empty, and she had managed to sleep on the hour-and-a-half flight.

Her stomach grumbled, and she popped a handful of almonds into her mouth. She refused to think about how much money she had spent at airport restaurants and snack bars in an attempt to get the nourishment she and her babies needed.

Wearily, she made her way outside. As promised, her grandfather was waiting in his old pickup truck when she stepped out of the airport. The truck bed was full, and he was pulling a trailer, a tarp tied over the contents to keep them protected from the elements.

He saw her coming and climbed out, circling to the passenger side to greet her.

All of the weariness, fear, and emotional turmoil spilled out the moment Grace's arms encircled him.

His voice was gruff when he asked, "Hey, what's this for?"

She couldn't speak, her throat closing up, her tears fighting to get free.

He pulled back and looked at her, one of his calloused hands brushing a tear from her cheek. He looked around. "Where are your bags?"

"This is all I have," she managed to say, nodding at her backpack.

Without another word, he pulled open her door and waited for her to get in. As soon as he climbed behind the wheel, he reached across her, opened the glove box, and fished out a packet of tissues. He handed it to her and started the engine.

"Go ahead and get the tears out. When you're done, you can tell me what's going on."

Leave it to her grandfather to give her the no-nonsense approach. With permission to let go of her emotions, her tears subsided, and she took a deep breath. "A lot has happened over the last couple days."

"We have better than a two-hour drive ahead of us. Might as well start at the beginning."

"I'm not sure what the beginning is."

"How about you tell me why you missed your plane yesterday."

"I guess that all started when I left my cell phone at home," Grace said. As she relayed the events of yesterday, she felt more and more like she was living in some kind of alternate reality. Yet two questions still remained: Why were those men looking for her? And why hadn't she heard from Devin for the past seven days?

* * *

Devin declined Fai's dinner invitation on Saturday night. The last thing he wanted was to go out to dinner with a bunch of coworkers, especially since he still hadn't received any confirmation from Chee or Ghost that Grace was okay. Not knowing where she was had every nerve in his body humming.

He knew Chee would disapprove of his decision to stay home tonight, but he couldn't do this anymore. He wanted out, and he wanted out now.

Devin had played along with Chee's plans all week, but he knew he couldn't keep it up. He hadn't signed up for undercover work, and now it was time for him to make it clear to his superiors that he was done being their puppet. He certainly didn't have any interest in sitting around like bait.

If no one had made a move on him in the past few days, it was unlikely anyone was going to.

Perhaps someone intent on robbing him had drugged his drink. If Ghost hadn't come along when he had, Devin's wallet might have disappeared along with his phone, but at least he wouldn't have this overwhelming sense of dread that the Chinese government was watching his every move.

He sat at the kitchen table to eat the leftovers he had warmed up from dinner the night before. He had taken only two bites when a knock sounded at the door.

Devin stood and debated briefly whether he should disable the listening device. Realizing that whoever was listening would notice if the room went silent after a knock sounded, he ignored that instinct and crossed to the door.

He expected to find Chee on the other side, but instead he found Fai. "Fai. What are you doing here? I thought you went out with everyone else tonight."

"May I come in?"

Though his instincts told him to deny the request, Devin nodded. "Sure." He stepped aside and waited for Fai to pass. He offered him a seat with a wave of his hand, and as soon as they both settled onto the couch, Devin asked, "What can I do for you?"

"I believe there is much we can do for each other," Fai said. "I have a business proposition for you."

"The markets are all closed. I would have thought you would want to take a break from work for the weekend."

"This business has nothing to do with the markets." Fai's eyes met his with an intensity Devin hadn't previously noticed. "You are uniquely suited for this particular situation."

"What situation is that?"

"I have friends who are interested in a certain flow of information," he said. "I understand you have a unique access to information."

"What are you talking about? You have just as much access to information as I do."

Fai reached into his suit jacket pocket and drew out two sheets of paper folded lengthwise.

"Does this look familiar?" He set the top paper on the coffee table and smoothed it out.

Devin leaned forward and looked at it. A copy of his job offer lay before him, his signature at the bottom.

"Where did you get this?" Devin asked. "And why do you have it?"

Fai's only response was to smooth out the second paper he held beside the first. Again a photocopy of a job offer lay before him, and again his signature was at the bottom. This time, however, the seal of the Central Intelligence Agency was emblazoned on top.

"Is this a joke?"

"As you can see, the signatures match," Fai said calmly. "And as you can see, I know where your allegiance lies."

Devin reminded himself that he had been expecting this, waiting for it even. That reminder didn't manage to calm his pounding heart. "What exactly is it that you want from me? If you believe that document is real, you could take it to the authorities and have me deported."

"I know it's real." The corners of his lips curved up ever so slightly, but rather than resembling a smile, the motion looked purely evil. "And if you want to see your precious Grace again, you're going to help me."

Ghost was right. Grace was his heart, and his one true vulnerability.

"I don't know how you heard about Grace, but you should know we broke up last week. I haven't seen or heard from her since then, nor do I expect to."

"I know what you said, but we both know that isn't the truth." He leaned back on the couch and pulled out a thin cigarette. As though he was very much at home in Devin's apartment, he pulled out a silver lighter and lit the tip. He blew out a stream of smoke before he continued. "Grace tried calling you a few days ago, and an e-mail followed the day after that. The contents made it sound like you are still very much a couple."

"I never got an e-mail from her." Devin forced his muscles to remain relaxed. "I don't know what you're talking about."

"We intercepted it. I've been screening your e-mail for weeks."

"Then you should know that I don't have any women e-mail me except those we work with." Devin stood. "And why would you be screening my e-mails? Isn't that against the law here? Or is it only in the United States that people are entitled to privacy?"

"When you work in intelligence, there is no privacy." He took a drag on his cigarette and blew out another stream of smoke. "It's all an illusion."

"I don't know what your game is, but I think it's time for you to leave."

Fai didn't move. "I believe we were discussing your wife."

Devin felt his face pale.

"My government has been watching you for a long time."

The implied threats against Grace rattled Devin to the core. How could this man possibly know of his marriage when most of his friends and extended family didn't even know about it? He reminded himself to respond. "Why would anyone want to watch me? I have nothing to offer you or anyone else. I'm a financial analyst. That's it."

"And a spy."

"I only finished graduate school a few months ago. What is it you think makes me so valuable to you?"

"You are more connected than you know." Another drag. Another puff of smoke. "I understand your father has a business trip to Tokyo in a few weeks."

"My father?"

Fai stood and crossed to the dinner table. He extinguished his cigarette by dropping it into Devin's water glass. "Grace is safe for now. I believe she will remain that way if you take some time with your father. I'm sure it will be very informative for us both."

"I don't understand."

"You don't have to." He took a step toward the door. "And, of course, you know that I expect this conversation to remain between us. Your wife's life depends on it."

He pulled open the door, stepped into the hall, and closed the door with a quiet click.

Devin dropped onto the couch and stared at the empty room. Was Chee lying to him about Grace being safe? Or was Fai lying about her being in danger? Why would Fai care about his father's business trip? And what was he supposed to do now? He couldn't spy on his own country, but what would happen to Grace if he didn't? What would happen to his father if he did?

Dropping his head into his hands, he offered a silent prayer to whatever god was listening to help him know what to do and to keep Grace safe and protected no matter what.

Chapter 23

GRACE OPENED HER EYES WHEN the truck stopped and the engine turned off. The two-story structure in front of her sprawled across the clearing, the windows strategically placed so the occupants within could enjoy the mountain views. To the right, a long wooden stable fashioned in the same wood as the house stretched along the base of the valley, a split-rail corral attached to one side of it. "This is it?"

"What do you think?" Quentin asked in response.

"It's enormous. How can you afford something like this?"

"I actually went in with a couple of partners. I put up half, and they put up the other half. In exchange for managing the place, I get to live here."

Red flags went up in her mind. "How did you set up the partnership?"

"Don't worry. I learned plenty from listening to you complain about your classes over the years. We set everything up as a business, and I had my attorney look over the partnership agreement. I also have the option to buy out my investors after the first five years."

"That's great, but I imagine you would have to make a pretty hefty profit to pull that off."

"I thought I could get my brilliant MBA granddaughter to help me figure out exactly what my options are," he said.

"I suppose I could take a look."

"Come on. Let's get you settled in." He climbed out of the truck and circled around to open her door. He took her by the elbow and helped her down, his eyes lowering to her growing abdomen. "I have to admit, I didn't expect you to look pregnant already."

"I guess it happens earlier when you're carrying twins." Grace followed him inside and looked around in wonder. High wood-beamed ceilings soared above her, and her grandfather's long leather couches were already situated opposite the open fireplace.

He motioned to a hallway off to the left. "The master bedroom is through there, but there's a second master bedroom upstairs I thought you would want to claim."

"How did you get your furniture here already? You said you just closed on the old house this morning."

"I hired a couple of guys to help me bring it up earlier this week. The stuff in the truck and trailer is what didn't fit in the first load." He turned to the wide stairwell to the right of the entryway. "Let me show you your room."

Grace followed him upstairs. She looked past the stack of boxes right inside the door with her name on them, appreciating the tall windows and the light streaming onto the hardwood floor. A queen-sized bed was centered on the far wall, the oak frame matching the dresser on the opposite wall. Two leather rocking recliners occupied the space by the corner window, an antique side table she recognized as her great-grandmother's situated between them.

Still in awe of the open room, she moved forward and discovered a wide doorway leading to the master bathroom. She passed by the two walk-in closets, where more boxes were stacked, and stared at the gleaming granite counters, the large bathtub, and the separate shower stall.

She moved back into the bedroom and lowered her backpack onto the bed. "Are you sure you don't want this room for yourself? It's huge!"

"Mine's just as big. The only difference is I have one closet instead of two." He winked at her. "I think I can live with just one."

"This is wonderful. I love it."

"You should be able to find some clean clothes and towels in these boxes. Let me make sure you can get into them." He moved some of the boxes so they weren't stacked more than two high. "Why don't you take some time to freshen up, maybe catch a nap. We'll talk some more once you've rested."

"Thanks, Grandpa." She moved into his embrace.

"Welcome home."

* * *

Devin paced his room, he checked his e-mail, he replayed his conversation with Fai. He needed a way to find out if Grace was really in jeopardy, but he didn't know what it could be. For all he knew, Fai and whomever he was working for could be trying to use him to find Grace so they could indeed exploit his weakness.

He barely managed to sleep Saturday night, and by six o'clock Sunday morning he was dressed and out the door.

He didn't have a specific destination in mind, but within an hour, he was out of the city and on a ferry to Lamma Island. He knew a little about Lamma, the low-key getaway of only about fifteen thousand residents, in comparison to the city's seven million. He leaned on the railing of the ferry, his mind still mulling over Fai's words.

Why would anyone care about his father's travels? Admittedly, he knew little about his father's business, except that he always seemed to be flying somewhere. He called himself a consultant, and Devin had seen him poring over spreadsheets and thick contract proposals over the years. Yet every time Devin asked him about his work, his father told him his work was confidential. He also kept his home office under lock and key.

The memory of that locked office raised a sense of trepidation. Could his father somehow be involved in working with classified material? Could he be connected to the intelligence community in some way?

Devin leaned on the rail and watched the water churn by. After a moment, he felt a presence beside him, and the familiar voice caught him by surprise.

"What did Fai Meng say when he visited last night?"

Devin turned to see Ghost standing beside him. "I'm starting to understand where you got your name. It's like you appear out of thin air."

Ghost didn't change his position, his eyes remaining on the water. "What did Fai want?" he repeated.

Devin mirrored his pose, his mind spinning. Could he trust this man beside him? Someone was lying to him about Grace, and yet he knew he needed help to find her.

"Has anyone managed to find Grace?"

"No." Ghost hesitated before he asked, "Do we need to make that a priority?"

"Yes."

"Did he tell you what he wants from you?"

Devin wanted to confide in someone, but the threats from last night pounded too loudly in his brain. Instead of answering Ghost's question, he said simply, "Find Grace."

* * *

Grace awoke with a start, images of the men invading her apartment fresh in her mind. She looked around the unfamiliar bedroom, fear melting away and being replaced by a sense of home she hadn't experienced since Devin had left for Hong Kong.

She swung her legs over the side of her bed and considered what she wanted for her future, or at least her future until Devin returned. New York had lost its appeal the moment she'd seen her apartment. Her job also hadn't turned out to be anything like she had expected, and her dreams of working with people to plan for their futures had never materialized. Instead, her days had been filled with research and reports for other people in the company. Rarely did she have the opportunity to meet with clients of any kind.

She crossed to the window and took in the breathtaking views. Two bungalows were visible along the edge of the clearing not far from the stables. Undoubtedly, her grandfather would be much happier now that he no longer had cattle to tend and could focus on his beloved horses.

An idea began to form as she thought of his shifting business interests. Perhaps she needed to consider some changes that went beyond a new address.

She looked down at the rumpled clothes she had traveled in. Desperate for a shower and a change of clothes, she headed for the closet where her grandfather had stored the boxes she and Devin had sent him. Though she had painstakingly labeled each box, they had unfortunately been arranged with the majority of the labels facing the wall instead of her.

With a sigh, she lifted a flap of the box closest to her, disappointed to find a bunch of old school papers. She had kept more random papers and correspondence than she probably needed, but it had been easier during finals week to pack everything and ship it than to sort through it all first. Now she was about to pay for that decision.

She moved to the next box, this time revealing various kitchen items. When she had exhausted the first row, she reached for a box in the next row, intent on sliding it toward her. It was heavier than she'd expected, and the cardboard ripped, sending the contents spilling across the closet floor.

"Great," she muttered to herself. She picked up the first few pieces of computer paper and realized these weren't her papers but rather were Devin's. She didn't pay attention to the first few, assuming he had saved some of the research he had conducted while in graduate school. She was halfway done cleaning when an envelope caught her eye.

The return address read simply *Office of Personnel, Washington, DC.*

Curious, she pulled the contents free. At first, she felt like she was invading his privacy. Then she reminded herself that she was married to the man.

One way or another, she needed answers.

She read the top sheet of paper, the letterhead matching the envelope. The text was simple and straightforward, detailing Devin's travel arrangements for his internship in London last summer. The next sheet bore the letterhead of a different company and repeated much of the same information.

Confused about why he would be sent the same information twice, she scanned the first letter again. Why would the letterhead be so simple, without any mention of the organization that sent it?

Her conversation with Devin's company came back to her, and her questions resurfaced. If that company didn't have an office in Washington, DC, why did he say that was one of the cities he could be assigned to?

The memory of the men in her apartment resurfaced too, only this time she tried to remember only the details and not the violation and fear. She would have sworn she was in the middle of some kind of James Bond movie. Could it be that her husband had a similar career? Was he lying to her because of some super-secret profession he wasn't allowed to tell her about?

She shook her head at the absurdity of the idea. There was another reason for those men to be looking for her and for Devin to be less than forthcoming with her about his job options.

Remembering her original reason for digging through boxes, she finished gathering the spilled papers and continued her search for clean clothing. Three boxes later, she discovered what she was looking for. The old flannel shirt and sweat pants weren't exactly what she would normally choose to wear in July, but at this point, she decided she would take whatever she could fit into.

She sorted through the box of clothing and shook her head. There was no doubt about it. She needed to go shopping.

Chapter 24

DEVIN CAUGHT A GLIMPSE OF Ghost on the tram Monday morning. It was so brief he wasn't sure it was really him until Devin reached into his suit pocket for his cell phone and found a business card nestled there. He pulled it out, looking at it discreetly, along with his cell phone.

The card was in the Roman alphabet—an address followed by 6:00 p.m.

Their brief meeting had taken place only twenty-four hours earlier. Could he already have information on Grace? Or was he preparing to lie to him to get what he wanted?

He wasn't sure what was worse, knowing he would have to wait all day to find out what Ghost had uncovered or the thought of seeing Fai today. As though his thoughts materialized instantly, Devin walked in the door and noticed Fai across the lobby.

Fai nodded in greeting and crossed to him. "How was your weekend?"

"Quiet," Devin said, reminding himself to relax. "How about yours?"

"We missed you Saturday night." He fell into step beside Devin as both men headed for the elevator.

Devin didn't respond. How could he?

As though Saturday night had never happened, Fai continued, "A few of us are getting together tomorrow night for dinner. You should come."

Though everything in him screamed that he decline, the possibility of Grace being in danger wouldn't let him follow that instinct. "That sounds good. Let me know the details, and I'll be there."

"Excellent." They stepped into the elevator together, and Devin was grateful they weren't alone. The possibility of being cornered by the man at work wasn't something he was prepared to deal with. They rode in silence until they reached Devin's floor.

He stepped off and hoped he sounded normal. "See you later."

Without looking back, he made his way to his office and immediately logged on to his computer. Though he rarely checked his personal e-mail at work, today he opened a new tab and quickly checked it in the hope that Grace had tried to contact him that way. When he saw the only new e-mails were junk mail, he knew what he had to do.

Though he hadn't communicated with his parents since the weekend of his graduation, he drafted an e-mail to his father.

Haven't talked to you in a while. Any chance your travels will bring you to my part of the world anytime soon? I'd love to meet up with you if we can arrange it.

After signing and sending the e-mail, he logged off. Maybe if he set up the meeting with his dad, he could find some answers, like why someone would threaten Grace to get him to see his father.

* * *

Devin walked into the restaurant at exactly two minutes until six. He wasn't sure what to say when he approached the hostess, but he was saved from coming up with a response when she said, "I only have seats at the bar."

"That's fine." Devin followed her to a seat at the far end. He was three seats away before he saw Ghost sitting in the chair on the end.

Devin slid into the empty seat beside him and took the menu the hostess handed him. He opened it, staring at it even though his attention was on the man beside him.

"She's safe," Ghost said quietly.

Relief swept through him. "Where?"

"We aren't sure, but we tracked her to Phoenix, then on to Colorado."

"She must be at her grandfather's ranch."

"We believe she is with her grandfather, but he sold his place yesterday. We aren't sure where he went."

"How can you be sure she's safe?"

"Because we checked the airport security feed and saw her get into the car with her grandfather. His truck was full of furniture, and he was pulling a trailer. Looks to us like he was moving and she went with him."

Another wave of relief swept through him but was paired with urgency. "You have to find her."

"If we find her, we might lead someone to her." Ghost took a bite of his dinner.

A waiter approached, and Devin ordered his meal at random.

As soon as the waiter left, Ghost spoke quietly once more. "Until we know why you're being targeted, we won't be able to keep her safe." He took another bite. "What did Fai want?"

"He wants me to meet with my father in Tokyo in a few weeks."

"Your father?"

"My father," Devin confirmed. Sickness threatened to rise up in him at the thought of the dangers facing him as well as his family. "Why in the world would the Chinese care about my dad? He's a businessman. That's it."

"Tell him you'll do it." Ghost pulled out his wallet and dropped some bills beside his plate.

Before the man could push back from the bar, Devin said, "Even though we believe Grace is safe, there has to be some way to let her know I'm okay. She has to be worried sick."

"I'll see what I can do." He fell silent and then added, "Give me something I can send her that only she would recognize as coming from you. We can't risk another security breach."

Devin lowered his voice. "You do think I've been compromised."

"I'll be close by." He stood and walked out without looking back.

* * *

"Do you think he'll cooperate?"

"He'll cooperate," Qing insisted. "You were right about the girl. I think he'll do anything to keep her safe."

"Has anyone been able to locate her?"

"Not yet. We traced her to Grand Central Station in New York, but we haven't been able to figure out where she went from there. We couldn't locate any reservations for Grace Shanahan on any bus, train, or plane within a week of her disappearance."

"What about rental cars?"

"We checked those too. Either she is still in New York, or she is traveling under another name."

"At this point, it doesn't matter where she is as long as Devin doesn't know either. If he believes she could be in danger, he'll fall in line."

"How long do you think you can use her safety as a motivator?"

"As soon as we have him in place, we can put her back in his life. Having her with him will make it easier to monitor her and to keep him in line."

"And if we can't find her?"

"We won't need to. Eventually Devin will lead us right to her."

* * *

Grace washed two dinner dishes and set them on the table. She was filling their water glasses when her grandfather walked through the back door with the three hamburger patties he had just grilled.

"Those smell good."

"Hope so." He set the plate of burgers on the table and took his seat. As soon as they started eating, he asked, "Have you called the police back to find out what's going on with their investigation?"

"No. I received an e-mail from them when I was in the airport in Phoenix. They don't have any clues as to who the other men were or why they were at my apartment."

"You know, they could show up again when you go back to New York."

That thought had been circling around in her mind since she had spoken to the police department. She considered her tiny apartment, the roaches, the crowded sidewalks, the cubicle in her office, and the busywork she processed every day.

"I'm not going back."

"What?"

"How would you feel about me staying here and working as your business manager?" Grace asked. "I can help set up your website and handle your bookings. I can also take over managing your financial assets."

"I'd love that, but I'm afraid I wouldn't be able to pay you much."

"All I really need is room and board and enough to cover the cost of health insurance."

"I'm sure we can do a bit better than that. For one thing, I never took you off my health insurance. You can stay on it until you turn twenty-six." He paused and seemed to consider her proposal. Then he gave a resolved nod. "If you want, you can take over the office in the front of the house. Maybe in your spare time, you can design websites or do some financial planning. You used to dabble in that during college."

"That's not a bad idea."

"Are you sure this is what you really want?"

She thought through her options again. "More than anything, I want to be with Devin again, but until he's done with this job in Hong Kong, I'm kind of in limbo."

"You said you haven't talked to him since last week. Maybe you should call him," Quentin said.

"I don't have his number anymore. I had it programmed in my cell phone, but the guys who broke into my apartment stole it," Grace said. "The police said I can come in and claim it, but quite honestly, I'm afraid to go back. I feel like I've walked into some kind of spy movie."

Her grandfather remained silent, and Grace let herself voice her suspicions. "Do you think it's possible Devin is a spy?"

"That's a stretch."

Though she knew her assumption sounded ridiculous on the surface, she laid out the facts. "When I called his office in Hong Kong, they put me through to his voice mail, but other than that, he's been really secretive about a lot of things."

"Like?"

"He always insisted on calling me. The couple of times I did call him, even when it was late at night for him, he was always busy and said he had to call me back."

"Maybe he was busy."

"And these Chinese guys who showed up at my apartment and work—why would they be looking for me unless it has something to do with Devin? The only person from China I've ever met was Devin's nanny." She stood to pace the room. "And how did they find my apartment in the first place? I only sublet it for six months. The lease isn't even in my name, yet the guys who showed up at my work asked for me by name."

"Okay, I'll admit, this does sound pretty fishy," Quentin admitted. "Unfortunately, the only way you're going to get answers is to talk to Devin."

"Yes, but he isn't taking my calls. I left a message for him at work and on his cell phone, but I haven't talked to him since last weekend." She swallowed hard and forced herself to voice her fears. "I'm starting to wonder if maybe he doesn't want to talk to me. His parents weren't happy when they found out about our marriage. Maybe Devin decided he doesn't want to be married to me anymore."

"I saw the way he looked at you at Christmas. I can't believe he wouldn't fight for what you have together." The certainty in his voice helped push away Grace's doubts. "You're welcome to borrow my phone to call his work again. You said you found that number on the Internet?"

"Yes, but within a day, my apartment was invaded," she said. "I hate to say it, but I'm feeling pretty paranoid. How do I know whoever showed up at my apartment wouldn't somehow trace my call back here?"

"Let me ask you this—if he comes back to the US and finds you aren't in New York, where would he look for you?"

"He'd either ask Molly where I am, or he would go to your ranch."

"I can ask the new owner to tell me if someone comes looking for you."

"What if someone shows up looking for me and it's not Devin?"

"I'll have them take a phone number from them and then they can call and let us know. If you want to be really careful, you can get one of those disposable cell phones to use to call him back when he does show up."

"This is all so complicated."

"You can also let Molly know where you are."

"I don't know about that."

"Why wouldn't you want your cousin to know where you're living? I thought you two were close."

"We are, but she's also a reporter. I'm afraid she'll start digging and get us all into trouble," Grace said. "Besides, Molly doesn't even know Devin and I are married."

"How did she miss that?"

"She moved across town after she got married, and I was spending all of my free time with Devin or trying to get ahead on homework so I wouldn't have any when we were together," Grace said. "With Devin not talking to me at the moment, I don't think I can handle her speculation. I already worry enough on my own."

"I'm sure he was just caught up with work and by the time he tried to call you, you'd already lost your phone."

"He could still e-mail me."

"I don't know, honey." He patted her hand with a twinkle in his eye. "Maybe he really is a spy."

"How in the world did I get into this mess?" Grace asked. "I'm too paranoid to reach out to him again, but I'm going crazy not knowing if he's okay."

"I'm sure he's fine. You would have heard something if that wasn't the case." He took a sip of his water. "It sounds like leaving a message with the new owners of my ranch is your best bet."

"I think you're right."

"And since you're going to stay here, I think it's time we find you a doctor. You have a few months yet before Devin should be showing up."

"I hate not being able to talk to him."

"I know, but this will all be over soon enough. For now, let's get this place up and running and see what we can do about making sure you take proper care of yourself and those babies."

Grace laid her hand on her stomach. *Three more months*, she told herself, refusing to believe Devin had abandoned her. Three more months and he would come looking for her, and they could finally be a family.

Chapter 25

DEVIN SAT AT HIS KITCHEN table, the same place he used to sit each morning when talking to Grace. His phone in hand and a ball of lead in his stomach, he dialed the number and tensed the moment his father's voice came over the line.

"Hello?"

"Dad, it's Devin."

"Well, hello there." A combination of surprise and cynicism sounded in his voice. "I got your e-mail and was wondering when you'd get around to calling."

"Sorry. With the move and work, things have been pretty crazy." The memory of the way his parents had left graduation weekend surfaced despite his efforts to suppress it. He reminded himself he had a job to do. "I was thinking of taking a week off in the next month or so. I thought maybe if you were traveling, we could meet somewhere. London. Paris. Wherever."

"Actually, I'll be in Tokyo next week."

"That would work out great. When do you get there?"

"I fly in Tuesday, and I fly out a week later. I have meetings the first few days, but I should be free over the weekend."

"Okay. I'll look into flights today."

His dad hesitated briefly before asking, "Will you be alone?"

"Yes," Devin forced himself to say. "It's just me these days."

"Good. It will be good to catch up."

"Yeah, it will," Devin said, wishing he believed his own words.

* * *

Grace didn't know how her grandfather managed to do it all, but in the space of a week, he had worked miracles.

He e-mailed her letter of resignation to a friend in Indiana, who then forwarded it on to her boss. The precaution to keep her location hidden seemed ridiculous in the daytime hours, but late at night, she wondered if she was being careful enough.

He also bought her a new cell phone under his plan, again keeping her name hidden. Tomorrow she would have her first appointment with her new doctor, and since the insurance information was still under her maiden name, she felt safe about going in.

Using her grandpa's truck, she had gone into town and managed to replace most of her wardrobe.

Thankfully, her first trimester was behind her and so was her morning sickness. If it weren't for her constant concern for Devin, she would be feeling great.

The first guests at Oasis Ranch would arrive in two weeks, and she knew her grandfather was getting antsy to get his new business started. She could admit that the numbers looked promising for this venture. She also appreciated that it wouldn't be so physically taxing on her grandfather, who had been struggling to keep up with the heavy demands of raising cattle.

She looked over the upcoming bookings for a few minutes before checking her e-mail for the sixteenth time today. Grace considered today an improvement. Yesterday she had checked it twenty-one times by now.

Three new messages. The first two were confirmation e-mails for payments she had made to buy out the rest of her apartment lease in New York and settle her utility bill. The third appeared to be an advertisement from a hotel website.

She nearly deleted it without opening it, but she decided it wouldn't hurt to see how the competition was advertising their locations.

She clicked on the e-mail, and her eyes widened. This wasn't an advertisement for just any hotel. This was the hotel where she and Devin had stayed for Molly and Caleb's wedding and their own wedding night.

She blinked several times before her eyes looked beyond the photo of the hotel to the advertisement below. Honeymoon suite special $1,219.

She read the price again. That couldn't be right. Devin had insisted on upgrading their rooms to the honeymoon suite the night they'd been married, but she was certain it hadn't been nearly that much. She looked over the advertisement again and opened a new tab. She went to the hotel's website and looked up the various rooms. She found the honeymoon suite and clicked on it to retrieve the price. $429.

"What in the world?" She clicked over to the e-mail again and read the price. "Twelve nineteen," she said aloud, only now the numbers had new meaning. Twelve nineteen. December 19. The day she and Devin had gotten married. Could this be a message from Devin? And if so, what did it mean? And why was he being so cryptic?

She thought of the odd job offer she'd found in his things and the inconsistencies in what he had told her over the past many months. As implausible as it was, she didn't see any other explanation. She was married to a spy.

* * *

Devin doubled back four times before he finally made his way to the safe house. Ghost must have had some kind of surveillance equipment in place because the moment he approached the apartment door, it swung open.

"Were you followed?" he asked as soon as Devin was safely inside.

"No, and I left my regular cell phone at home like you told me."

Ghost motioned him inside. He anticipated Devin's next question and said, "We sent the e-mail to Grace and verified that she did open it."

"I hope she understood."

"I'm sure she did. One of my colleagues monitored the activity for her IP address. Right after she opened her e-mail, she did a search of the hotel's honeymoon suite. She obviously realized the price was wrong."

Devin took a seat at the table in the small kitchenette and faced the unlikely truth. Someone was leaking information about him from the CIA, and he didn't know whom he could trust. He looked up at the man across from him. Though Ghost appeared to be only a few years older than him, he carried a sense of confidence and wisdom. Devin hoped trustworthiness was another trait inherent in the man.

"I've been replaying that first conversation with Fai in my head," Devin began.

"When he showed up at your apartment?"

Devin nodded. "He said a couple of things I think are important."

"Such as?" Ghost prompted.

"He had a copy of my employment contract with the CIA."

"What?" Ghost stood and paced to the window before turning back to face him. "Any idea where he got it?"

"None. The only thing that makes sense is that someone within the agency leaked it to him."

"I agree." Ghost raked his fingers through his hair, which seemed out of character for the normally calm man. "Your file is highly classified. Only a few people would have access to it."

"I've only met with a handful of people from the agency. You, Chee, Jalen, the people who interviewed me. I'm not sure who else on the inside would have access."

"Except for me, everyone else probably had access to your personnel file."

"I might be able to help you narrow it down a bit further."

"How so?"

"Fai also knows I'm married. Only you, Chee, and Jalen know that."

"You can trust me and Chee."

"I hope so."

"Chee is the person who reached out to me and insisted you needed a guardian. He wouldn't have done that if he was involved. I'll start using my resources to see who else would have access to both pieces of information. Unfortunately, if Jalen followed proper protocol, he would have informed the agency of your marital status as soon as he found out about it." Ghost lowered himself back into his chair. "I assume you had something else you wanted to tell me."

Devin pulled out his emergency cell phone.

"I went out to dinner with Fai last week. Here's a photo of what he gave me." Devin showed him the picture of the modified flash drive. "I was afraid to bring it with me in case it has some kind of tracking device on it."

"Smart."

"He wants me to plug it into my dad's laptop. He said it would only take a minute or so to copy the hard drive."

"This drive is probably encrypted to keep you from being able to edit what you give him."

"That's my guess." Devin ran his fingers through his hair. "I still don't know why my father is of any interest to him and whoever he's working for."

"We're still trying to piece together how your father fits into the mix, but we have confirmed that Fai Meng has ties to Chinese intelligence."

"Great."

"When do you leave for Tokyo?"

"Next Friday."

Ghost got up and crossed to a tall wooden cabinet. He pulled open the door to reveal shelves of various electronic equipment and reached into a plastic organizer and fished out a flash drive that looked similar to the one Fai had given him.

"Take this. Before you copy your father's hard drive for Fai, I want you to make a copy for us."

"What do you expect to find?"

"Answers." Ghost dropped the drive into Devin's outstretched hand. "The sooner, the better."

* * *

Grace sat across the kitchen table from her grandfather, the sandwiches she had made them for lunch remaining untouched.

"Are you sure this is a message from Devin?" Grandpa asked, holding up the printout Grace had given him of the hotel advertisement.

"It's the only thing that makes sense."

"None of this is making any sense to me," he admitted. "Chinese diplomats in your apartment, Devin lying to you, and now this ad from the hotel you stayed at. Normal people don't communicate like this."

"Which is why I think Devin really is working in some kind of intelligence job."

"What do you think this message means?"

"I think it's his way of saying he's okay and that he still loves me."

"And?" He took a bite of a pickle. "What do you think he expects you to do now? You've been here two weeks, but no one has shown up looking for you at the old place."

"Maybe he can't come to the US right now, and that's why he sent me the e-mail," Grace said, hoping she was right. "He's supposed to be in Hong Kong through September."

"That may be cutting it close for when these babies are coming."

"I'm not due until late December."

"And you said yourself the doctor told you to be ready for them as early as September," he reminded her. He took a bite of his sandwich, chewing slowly. "Have you considered going to visit Devin's parents? Leaving a message with the folks at the old ranch is one thing, but maybe you should give Devin an easier time of finding you."

"I'm not sure they'll pass a message on to him. They want me out of his life, and the last thing they're going to do is help us stay together."

"I guess that's true considering how they acted at Devin's graduation," he said. "Maybe you need to leave a message with Molly. You said yourself that's probably who he would contact to find you."

"You're right. I'll have to think about how I can talk to her without making it easy for anyone to find me through her." She held up a hand. "And, yes, I know I'm being paranoid, but I think that's another thing Devin wanted me to understand when he sent me this." She motioned to the printout that now lay on the table between them. "I think he wants me to know that I need to be careful."

"That may be. And on that note, there's something else I wanted to talk to you about."

"What's that?"

"I think it's time I hire someone to come in and help with the house-work and the cooking."

"Grandpa, I'm perfectly fine with cooking. The doctor just said I need to be careful with things like vacuuming and mopping."

"And I don't want to take any chances with you or those babies," he insisted. "Although I was hoping you could help me find someone. I have my hands pretty full getting ready for our first guests this weekend."

"I really don't think it's necessary." She saw the look on her grand-father's face that told her he had his mind made up. "But if you want me to help find someone, I'm happy to do whatever I can."

"Good." He took another bite and leaned back in his seat. "Now, any idea what you're going to name these babies?"

Grace let out a sigh. "Not a clue."

Chapter 26

DEVIN COULDN'T REMEMBER THE LAST time he'd visited his dad on a business trip. Two hours at their hotel was all it took for him to remember why he never traveled with his father.

Though they were supposed to meet for a late dinner on Friday night, he had yet to see or hear anything from his dad beyond a message at the front desk that said he was running behind schedule.

Devin had hoped his father would offer to let him share his hotel room, but that would have made things too easy. His luck wasn't running toward easy. Instead, here he sat in his own hotel room waiting for his dad to call.

He tried watching television, but he ended up pacing the narrow room from one end to the other. He hated everything about this. Spying on his dad, lying about his relationship with Grace, trying to figure out who was working with him and who was working against him.

The very possibility of his father being involved in the intelligence business sent chills through him. His whole life he had known his father to be a workaholic and a frequent traveler, but never had he thought to look beyond the obvious. Now he only hoped that any involvement on his dad's side would put them on the same team.

The hotel room phone rang, and Devin forced himself to let it ring a second time before he pounced on it. "Hello?"

"Devin. Sorry, but I just got out of my last meeting."

"Do you want me to meet you in your room, and we can order room service?"

"No, thanks. I already ate."

"Oh." His heart sank. He had hoped to get this spy business out of the way early so he could unearth the answers to the many questions burning through him.

"I thought we could meet for breakfast in the morning."

Devin tried not to think about the fact that his father apparently wasn't in any hurry to see him. Reminding himself to be patient, he asked, "What time is good for you?"

"I'll meet you in the hotel restaurant around eight."

"Sounds good. I'll see you then." Devin hung up and paced across the room. He looked at his watch and headed for the door. Time to get some food and find something to distract him from his real purpose for being here. What had ever made him think he could work in the spy business?

* * *

Grace walked out of Dr. Gilmore's office with a sense of relief. Her new doctor indicated that her babies were growing well, and so far he didn't see any indications that she would have complications. Though she was barely four months pregnant, her stomach was now too large to hide beneath baggy clothes.

She had made a point to tell the doctor she didn't want to know the sex of her babies when he had performed the ultrasound. Though she was beyond curious to know what she was having, she simply couldn't bring herself to find out without Devin with her. Maybe she was being foolish, or maybe she was being optimistic. Either way, the important thing was that everything looked good so far.

Her doctor, a man in his forties who specialized in high-risk pregnancies, seemed to understand her need for reassurance. She was grateful he had been able to give it to her.

She knew from meeting with her previous physician that many things could change throughout her pregnancy, but knowing that the stress of the past few weeks hadn't caused any negative effect on her children was exactly what she'd needed to hear today.

What she hadn't wanted to hear was her doctor's instructions to start taking it easy. Beyond the many household chores on her banned list, he also didn't want her lifting anything over ten pounds. So much for sorting through all the boxes in her closet.

She hated knowing she wouldn't be able to do much physical labor to help her grandfather with the ranch, especially since the first guests were arriving today. He had hired help for many aspects of the new business, but profit margins would be so much healthier if she could take on some of the tasks he planned to pay for. Bringing in household help would take yet another chunk of profits away from her grandfather's new venture.

Torn between wanting to help and wanting to do everything she could to protect the two lives growing inside her, Grace drove back to the ranch. The babies won the internal battle with barely a fight.

She pulled into the drive and noticed a car parked next to the bungalow closest to the house. Apparently their first guests had arrived while she'd been in town. She climbed out of her grandfather's truck and started toward the house when she heard a familiar voice.

"Grace Harrington? Is that you?"

Grace turned, surprised to see Caleb's friend, Sean Tanner, walking toward her. She hadn't seen him at all since the night of Caleb and Molly's wedding. The night of her wedding.

"Sean. What are you doing here?"

"I was about to ask you the same question." His eyes dropped to her swollen abdomen. Surprise and speculation flickered over his face when his gaze lowered to the rings on her left hand. "It seems a lot has changed since I saw you last."

"Yes, it has," Grace agreed. "I gather you're staying here for the weekend."

"Yeah. I needed to get out of the heat for a few days."

"Tired of 115-degree days in Phoenix?"

"You know it." He motioned to her. "What about you? How long are you in town for?"

"Actually, I'm here for a while. My grandfather owns this place."

"No way. Your grandfather is Quentin Harrington?"

"Yeah." Her eyebrows drew together at his familiarity. "Do you know him?"

"All my life. He and my grandpa have been friends since high school. My dad is one of the investors in this place."

"Really?" Grace thought about the partnership agreement she had looked over just last week. She had never put it together that Clayton Tanner was the same Clayton Tanner who owned car dealerships all over the Phoenix area.

He motioned to her wedding ring. "So who's the lucky guy? Last time I saw you, sparks were flying between you and Devin Shanahan."

"Actually, my husband is overseas right now. That's why I'm staying here with my grandfather for the next couple months."

"I thought I heard you'd moved to New York."

"I did. The big-company thing wasn't for me," Grace said. "I'm actually starting my own financial planning business here in Colorado."

"That's great." Sean motioned to his bungalow. "I guess I'd better finish unloading. My brother and I are heading out to the lake this afternoon to do some fishing."

"Have fun. Let me know if you need anything."

"I will." He took a step back. "And Grace?"

"Yeah."

"Congratulations on your new family. Your husband's a lucky guy."

"Thanks." She started for the house, a hollow feeling settling in the pit of her stomach. How lucky could he be if their only means of communication was through a cryptic e-mail?

* * *

Devin fought the urge to fidget as he waited for his father Saturday morning. He had arrived at the restaurant five minutes before eight. That had been thirty minutes ago.

He stood when his father finally appeared at the entrance. As usual, he was dressed in a tailored suit, his shirt freshly pressed. The royal blue handkerchief in his pocket matched his tie, and Devin suspected his haircut and manicure were recent.

"Good to see you, son." Boyd reached out and shook Devin's hand as though they were business associates rather than family.

"You too." Devin waited for his father to take a seat before reclaiming his own. "How has your trip been so far?"

"Busy." Boyd opened his menu briefly, took a quick study, and set it aside. The moment he did, a waiter appeared. After they ordered, his father asked, "How have things been with you? How is the job?"

"The job is good. I'm learning a lot, and it's been great to immerse myself in Cantonese again."

"And the girl? Have you taken care of everything where she is concerned?"

"Things are still in progress, but I expect everything will be sorted out in the next few months."

"Good." He gave a satisfied nod. "Glad to hear it."

Devin fought against the myriad emotions that threatened to surface. He had a job to do, and he couldn't let his father's narrow-mindedness get in the way. When he was sure he could speak calmly, he asked, "What do you have planned for today? Do you have time to do some sightseeing with me?"

"I have some meetings this morning, and I need to call Maureen before it gets too late in the US."

"I'm surprised you didn't bring your secretary with you."

"It wasn't necessary for such a short trip." He glanced at his watch. "Why don't we meet back here around one, and we can spend some time in the city. I could use a little downtime after the week I've had."

"That sounds good." Devin hesitated when their food was served but then asked, "How are Liwei and Jun? I haven't spoken to either of them lately."

"Liwei is busy getting ready for some dinner party your mother has planned for next week, but I haven't seen Jun lately."

"Have you ever considered bringing Jun back on full-time? It seems she's there a lot anyway helping out."

"We really don't have the need."

"It just seems odd not having her living at home anymore."

"Things change," he said. "Tell me about your place in Hong Kong. I hope it's bigger than where you lived for your internship."

"Much." Devin changed the subject. "How's work going? You have a client here in Tokyo?"

"Tokyo is a convenient place to meet in this part of the world," he said. "Your mother asked if you'll be home for Christmas."

"That's five months away. I haven't thought that far ahead."

After they finished eating, Devin walked his father back to his hotel room. He wasn't surprised when his father dismissed him at the door, promising to call when he returned to the hotel.

Devin took note of his father's room number and made his way back to the lobby. He found a quiet spot in a corner where he could watch the door without being in plain sight. Twenty minutes later, his father left, and Devin returned to his father's room.

He looked up and down the hall. Once he was sure he was alone, he slid the keycard Ghost had given him into the electronic lock. The seconds ticked by, every one feeling like an eternity. Finally the red light turned green, and Devin pulled the door handle, relieved when it opened.

He slipped inside the dark room, waiting for a moment to make sure he was really alone before flipping on the light.

His search of the room took only three minutes and revealed what he had assumed. His father had taken his laptop with him.

Chapter 27

Every time Devin thought he might get a moment alone with his father's laptop, his dad did something to make sure it didn't happen. The man even took it with him to the bathroom rather than leave it alone with Devin for two minutes.

Two minutes was all he needed, but at this rate, he didn't know how he was going to get even a few seconds with it.

He was running out of time, and the implied threats against Grace continued to haunt him despite Ghost's assurances. Devin had extended his trip to Tokyo so he would fly out on the same day as his father, but tonight was his last opportunity to complete his mission.

With his father once again at a meeting, his laptop in tow, Devin retreated to his room and pulled out the secure phone he used to contact Ghost.

"Any luck?" Ghost asked the moment he answered.

"No. I don't know what to do." Devin explained the events of the weekend and his lack of success. "How am I supposed to plug a flash drive into my dad's computer if he doesn't trust me to be alone with it for even a few minutes?"

"I hate to tell you this, but you may have to resort to drugging him."

"Excuse me?"

"You heard me. Where are you having dinner tonight?"

"We aren't. He has a business dinner. I'm not supposed to see him until tomorrow morning when we're headed to the airport."

"We're going to have to change that," Ghost said simply.

"How?"

"You need to run into your father tonight."

Devin heard the confidence in Ghost's voice, and his own boosted up a notch. "Sounds like you have a plan."

"Always."

* * *

Grace didn't know what she was going to do. She stared at the numbers on her computer screen, but no matter how hard she tried, she didn't know how she was going to make ends meet on the minimal salary her grandfather could afford to pay her.

Even with her insurance and room and board provided, the simple truth was that she had spent the majority of her funds buying her way out of her contract in New York, and what little she had remaining was quickly disappearing in the form of maternity clothes and copays.

She also desperately needed her own car. She wasn't terribly picky when it came to what she drove, but living in Colorado, four-wheel drive was a must.

She didn't want to think about what it would cost to buy diapers and clothing for two babies, much less the larger items, such as car seats and cribs. After looking over her grandfather's financials, she knew he didn't have any extra money to spare right now either. The majority of his liquid cash needed to stay in reserve for unexpected repairs and working capital.

Though her grandfather had insisted she hire someone to help with housework, they had ultimately compromised with settling for a weekly cleaning service, at least until the business was a little more established. If only she could get her own business up and running, but finding clients required her to meet people. So far, the only people she had met in town were her doctor and a few of her grandfather's employees—not exactly the kind of people who had a lot of money lying around to invest.

She needed another source of income, but who would be willing to hire someone for only a few months? Once the babies came, she didn't want to be tied to an office job.

A knock sounded at the door, and she closed her laptop before crossing to answer it.

"Sean. I thought you were leaving today."

"I am, but I wanted to talk to you for a few minutes before I head out."

"Sure. Come on in." Grace motioned him inside and led the way to the living room. "Please, sit down."

Sean sat on the couch across from her. "I don't know if your grandfather talked to you much about it, but my dad is trying to diversify his financial holdings."

Grace shook her head. "Grandpa didn't mention it."

"His investment in this ranch was one venture, but he's still looking for a few more solid options."

"It's always good to diversify, but what does that have to do with me?"

"My dad's financial analyst with his company does a great job keeping on top of the dealerships, but expanding beyond the car business isn't his strength." Sean leaned forward and rested his elbows on his thighs. "I thought you might be interested in doing some financial planning for him."

"Are you serious?"

"Very. He approached me about doing some investing for him, but I have my hands full with my own business."

"You started a business?"

"Yes. Internet security." Sean's face lit up. "We only have three people working for us so far, but we've already landed a couple big clients."

"That's great. I'm happy for you."

"So what do you say about working for my dad?"

"I'm definitely interested." She rested her hand on her stomach. "Do you think he would be okay with me working from home? After all, I really don't need to go into an office to do my research."

"I'm sure he'll be fine with it." Sean stood and handed her a business card. "Give him a call. I already mentioned you might consider it, so he's expecting to hear from you."

"Thanks, Sean. I really appreciate it." She took the card and stood as well.

"Happy to help." He started toward the door. "And who knows. If my business keeps going the way I hope it will, I may have some business to throw your way too."

"I hope it works out for both of us."

"Me too." Sean stopped. "You know, I was thinking about coming up again next weekend. One of the benefits of owning my own plane. If you're up for it, you can fly down to Arizona with me and my brother today, and I can bring you back next week. That would give you time to meet with my father and work up his basic financial plan."

"I don't know . . ." Grace hesitated. The thought of getting on a small airplane left her with an uneasy feeling, and her instincts told her to stay here in Colorado where no one could find her.

But logic swayed her the other direction. The truth was that if she went to Arizona she could see or at least call Molly to make sure she could get a message to Devin when he came back stateside. She wavered for a moment before the practical side of her caused her to shake her head. "That's really nice of you to offer, but I'm afraid paying for a hotel room for a week is a bit out of my budget right now."

"Nonsense. My folks have tons of room at their place in Sedona. You can stay with them," Sean insisted.

"Sedona? I thought your parents lived in Phoenix."

"Not during the summer. It's too hot." Sean took a step toward the door. "My brother and I aren't flying out for another hour or so. That's plenty of time to pack."

What he proposed made sense. If she could lock down even one solid client, she could finally start moving forward in life again instead of relying on her grandfather to take care of her. "Let me talk to my grandfather. Can you stop by before you leave so I can let you know then if I'm able to go with you?"

"Sure. See you in an hour."

Grace showed him out and felt a surge of excitement and apprehension. Should she play it safe and avoid every place she and Devin had been together? Or should she start living her life again and trust that everything would work out? She looked at the office to her left. It was time to start living.

* * *

Devin tried to appear relaxed as he contemplated what he had to do. The needle concealed between his first two fingers made his presence in the lobby that much more surreal.

How had he come to this? Clearly something about his father had put him in this situation, but he still couldn't make any sense of the possibilities.

Though he had anticipated a long wait, for once his father arrived back at the hotel at a reasonable hour. Devin remained where he was, a seating area with several partitions hiding him from view as his father passed by.

Devin stood and started forward, using his long stride to close the distance between them. He was a dozen yards behind him when another man approached and greeted his father in Japanese. Devin's jaw nearly dropped open when his dad responded in the same language.

Boyd Shanahan spoke Japanese? Was this really the same man who didn't acknowledge the difference between Mandarin and Cantonese? The same person who insisted on speaking English wherever he went regardless of the native language of the countries he traveled in?

Devin pulled his phone from his pocket, pretending to look down at it to give him a reason to have stopped his forward progress. The conversation between the two men was brief, and the Japanese man returned the way he had come.

Once he was sure his father was heading for the elevators, Devin once again started walking.

"Hey, Dad." Devin stepped beside his father as he pushed the up button. "I didn't know you were getting back so early."

"Devin. What are you doing down here? I thought you were ordering room service tonight."

"I went to the hotel gym to work out." The elevator door chimed open, and Devin waited for his father to enter before him. For once, luck was with him, and he found himself alone with his father.

"I've been meaning to ask you if you'll be coming back this way any more this year." Devin hesitated only briefly before he lifted his hand and patted his dad's shoulder.

"I'll go to Paris this fall . . ." The last word slurred, and Devin reached out to support his dad's weight.

"Dad? Are you okay?" Devin spoke with concern, guilt weighing on him as he watched his father's eyes go glassy and then flutter closed.

When the elevator doors opened on his dad's floor, Devin dragged his now unconscious father into the hall. When they reached the room, he lowered his dad to the floor and checked his pockets until he found the room key. Once he unlocked the door, Devin pulled his father inside.

Going through the routine of a dutiful son first, he set his dad's computer bag aside and dragged him to his bed. Once his father was settled and Devin was certain his breathing was still steady, Devin retrieved the laptop from its bag.

He sat on the floor by the door so if, by some chance, his father regained consciousness, Devin wouldn't be visible.

After powering on the laptop, he inserted the flash drive Ghost had given him. Two minutes later, the red light flashed to green, and he repeated the process with the drive Fai had given him.

After he turned the computer off and replaced it in its case, he set the laptop bag on the desk and debated what to do next. If his father really had passed out, would he call a doctor? Should he wait with him until he woke up?

According to Ghost, the drug mimicked a sleeping pill and his father would likely sleep a full six to eight hours.

With that in mind, Devin removed his father's shoes and suit jacket and placed them both neatly in the closet.

A knock sounded at the door, and Devin's hand lifted to his rapidly beating heart. Who would be coming to his father's hotel room? Supposedly his dad's work had concluded at his meeting this evening.

Quietly, he closed the closet door, a million thoughts racing through his mind.

For all he knew, someone from the hotel staff might have seen him dragging his father into his room and come to check on his condition.

Another knock sounded. Devin debated whether to answer, but before he could move, he heard the distinctive click of the lock opening.

He ducked into the bathroom and took position behind the door to keep from being seen.

The outside door opened a split second later, and footsteps approached. Devin had to remind himself to keep his breathing slow and steady to avoid being heard.

The new arrival walked past the bathroom, the footsteps barely audible.

Devin expected some kind of reaction when the intruder saw his father passed out on the bed, but the faint footsteps continued on. It took a moment for Devin to compute when and where the footsteps stopped. Could it be that whoever was here was after the same thing Devin was? When he heard the sound of the zipper on his father's computer bag, he was faced with another choice. Did he protect the information he had just stolen? Or did he let someone else gain access to what he still didn't understand the importance of?

His cell phone chimed and made the choice for him.

Unarmed and no longer having the element of surprise, Devin quickly scanned the bathroom. He tore down the shower curtain rod and wielded it like a sword as he emerged from the bathroom. The intruder had already started toward him, and Devin was surprised to see the man was of European descent rather than Japanese as he had expected.

"Who are you?" Devin demanded in English. "And what are you doing in here?"

Seeing Devin's makeshift weapon, the man backtracked farther into the room to put distance between them. The instant he was out of Devin's reach, his hand disappeared beneath the hem of his shirt.

Sheer terror flooded Devin, along with an intense survival instinct, when the man came up with a gun. Devin surged forward and swung the rod. The hollow metal tube connected with the man's arms, but the weapon didn't drop from his hand as Devin had hoped.

The man groaned in pain, then lifted the weapon again. Devin blocked the motion by sweeping the rod low with as much force as he could muster, this time hitting the man's knees hard. He tumbled backward, simultaneously squeezing the trigger.

Devin felt the bullet whiz by him, and somewhere in the back of his mind, he heard the thump as it lodged into the wall.

"You have no idea what you've gotten yourself into," the man said. The accent was thick and identified him as eastern European, but Devin was more worried about why he was shooting at him than where the man was from.

Questions burned on Devin's tongue, but with the man's gun hand lifting once more, he didn't bother to voice them. Instead, he swung the rod again, this time aiming for the man's head. An instant before it made contact, the man lifted his left arm and blocked it. Despite his cry of pain, he managed to grab the end of it and wrench it away from Devin.

Devin backpedaled, his eyes searching for anything else he could use as a shield or a weapon.

The gun lifted once more, a door crashed open, and a gunshot rang through the air.

Chapter 28

DEVIN'S HEART FELT LIKE IT had stopped beating, his fear was so consuming. Then he managed to focus on the scene in front of him and the man who now lay sprawled on his father's hotel room floor. Devin turned to see Ghost standing behind him, a gun in his hand.

"What . . . ?" Devin stammered the word and took a deep breath before trying to speak again. "What are you doing here?"

Ghost pushed past him, retrieved the fallen weapon, and checked the man for a pulse. He stood and faced Devin. "I guess you didn't see my text."

"I heard it come in." Devin waved a hand in the direction of the man on the floor. "Unfortunately, so did he." He drew another deep breath. "Is he . . . ?"

"Dead? Yeah."

Devin crossed to stand beside his dad, a wave of relief crashing over him when he confirmed that his father hadn't been caught in the crossfire. He looked up at Ghost again and waved at the dead man. "Who is he?"

"Albert Wendell. He's been on our watch list since a security breach in London last year." Ghost leaned down once more and riffled through the man's pockets. For the first time, Devin realized Ghost wore fitted gloves. When Ghost stood once more, he held a sheathed knife, a car key, and a flash drive.

As Devin stared on, Ghost continued. "I was monitoring the security camera in the hall when I caught a glimpse of him at the door."

"And you texted a warning?"

"Yes."

"Any idea of what he was doing here?"

He held up the flash drive. "Since he had this, my guess is he was after the same thing we are."

Devin looked over at his dad, who was still blissfully unaware of what had transpired. "What is my dad into?"

"We're about to find out." Ghost pocketed the items he held and retrieved his cell phone. After typing a message, he asked Devin, "Did you already copy your dad's hard drive?"

"Yes." Devin pulled both flash drives from his pocket and handed Ghost's to him. "I want to see what's on there."

"I'll make a copy for you as soon as I access the information and upload it onto the guardian server."

"Are you sure you want to upload the information? Isn't that risky?"

"This system has failsafe procedures that would make your head spin. It's secure."

"What about him?" Devin motioned to Albert and then looked over at his father. "And how do we explain everything to my dad?"

"I have a cleanup crew heading over here now. They should be in and out long before your dad wakes up."

"A cleanup crew? As in people who will come in here and dispose of the body?"

"And make everything look exactly as it did before he arrived." Ghost put a hand on Devin's shoulder. "Trust me. I know what I'm doing."

"At this point, I don't think I have a choice but to trust you." Devin's body trembled as he exhaled.

"Go to your room. Your dad will be fine." Ghost pointed to the door. "I'll stay here until everything is put back together."

"How do I explain to my father why he passed out?"

"He'll be confused when he wakes up, but stick to the plan. In the morning, you tell him he wasn't feeling well and you helped him back to his room. After he fell asleep, you left."

Tension settled somewhere deep in his gut, but Devin forced himself to comply. "Will I see you before I leave?"

"You won't see me, but I'll see you," Ghost said. "Be careful tomorrow."

"I will." Devin took one last look at his father and then headed for the door. The questions continued to whirl, but maybe now that they had a copy of his dad's hard drive, they would finally get some answers.

* * *

Grace was grateful when Sean helped her out of the plane in Sedona and she once again had her feet on solid ground. Though she didn't particularly care for flying, she most certainly preferred larger planes over the little four-seater Sean flew. Although she could admit she much preferred the hour-and-a-half flight to the six-hour drive it would normally take between Vail and Sedona.

"Come on." Sean started toward the parking lot. "The car is parked over here."

Grace was grateful Sean had someone at the airport to take care of his plane so she wouldn't have to wait around for him. With the sun already lowering in the sky, she was ready to find something to eat and a place to lie down.

"Any idea what Mom has planned for dinner?" Scott asked Sean when he stepped beside them.

"She said something about making lasagna. I guess they're having a few friends over for dinner."

Feeling awkward about staying with Sean's family, Grace asked, "Are you sure your parents are okay with me staying with them?"

"Yeah. Dad thought it was a great idea. He's basically on vacation this week, so it will be much easier than usual to find out how he really wants to invest his money." Sean opened the front door for her and waited for her to get in. "Besides, you'll enjoy the scenery of their place."

Grace wished a change of scenery was all she needed to put her life back on track. Without comment, she clipped her seat belt in place and tried to get comfortable. Twenty minutes later, they arrived at a large cabin in Oak Creek Canyon, with a half dozen cars parked in the driveway and along the street.

"I guess Mom understated the size of her dinner party," Sean said. He climbed out of the car and grabbed his bag and Grace's suitcase. "Come on. I'll show you your room, and then we can get something to eat."

Grace followed him inside, the chatter of conversation carrying to the door. The scent of lasagna and garlic bread wafted through the air.

"It's this way." Sean led her down a hall to the right. He passed two doors before he pushed one open and set her suitcase inside. "Here you go."

She peeked inside to see a modest-sized bedroom furnished with a queen-sized bed and a tall dresser. She had hoped to find a desk as well so she could work in her room, but at least she and her growing stomach wouldn't have to manage a twin bed.

"The bathroom is across the hall, and there should be clean towels in the closet."

"Thanks."

"Let's get some dinner. You must be starving."

They made their way to the center of the house, where more than a dozen people were scattered throughout the living room and kitchen. Sean greeted a few as they walked by but didn't stop until he reached his father. The tall, balding man stood near the corner of the room chatting with a couple who appeared to be in their seventies.

"Dad."

"Sean. Glad you made it." Clayton moved forward and hugged his son. "You know Susan and Dick, don't you?"

"Yes, of course. So good to see you again." Sean motioned to Grace. "This is Grace Harrington. She's my dad's new financial planner."

"It's good to see you again, Grace." Clayton extended his hand. "And I appreciate your willingness to come work here at the house this week."

"I'm glad the timing worked out."

"How did you get into financial planning, Grace?" Susan asked.

"I started with a brokerage firm in New York after I got my MBA, but I decided I preferred to work more closely with my clients."

Dick turned to Clayton. "You'll have to let us know how things work out with Grace. My portfolio didn't do nearly as well as I'd expected last year."

"Looks like you may have a bigger client list than you planned," Sean's dad said.

Despite the excitement rippling through her at the prospect, she managed to keep her voice professional. "I promise to do my best for all of my clients."

"That's what I like to hear."

Sean escorted her into the kitchen. "Looks like dinner is ready."

They joined the others in the buffet line, some guests finding seats at the table in the open kitchen and others moving onto the wide deck. Grace and Sean were nearly to the front of the line when she saw a familiar face.

"Miss Grace." Jun stood behind the counter that separated the kitchen from the living area, a serving spoon in her hand. She bowed her head slightly. "It is good to see you."

"It's good to see you too." Grace smiled warmly, a feeling of hope fluttering inside her. Devin's parents might not want her in his life, but Jun had always put Devin's happiness above everything else. "I hope we can talk later."

"Yes." She bowed her head again. "I will find you before I leave."

"Please do." Grace picked up her plate and accepted the offerings of salad, lasagna, and bread.

"How do you know her?" Sean asked as they moved toward the deck.

"Believe it or not, she's Devin's old nanny. She lived with his family until a few years ago."

"Small world."

"I'm starting to realize just how true those words are."

Chapter 29

DEVIN HAD HARDLY SLEPT. THE thought that a man had tried to kill him overshadowed his own actions in his nightmares, but he couldn't quite shake the guilt he felt for drugging his father. Thankfully, when they had ridden to the airport that morning, his father had actually thanked him for his help the night before and apologized for not being able to spend more time with him.

Devin wasn't sure what to think of his father's lack of concern over losing consciousness in the elevator. Had it not been for Ghost's message that his father's room was clear, Devin would have thought his dad knew what had really happened. That message had arrived around three in the morning. It had also contained the instruction for him to make the hand-off to Fai when the time came.

That was another thing Devin wasn't looking forward to. Now that he'd let Fai think he'd manipulated him, what would he be asked to do next? Though it was a struggle, Devin tried to put that thought out of his mind on the flight from Tokyo to Hong Kong. He knew Ghost was somewhere on the plane with him, but he hadn't caught sight of him despite watching the various people who had boarded. Still, knowing someone was there to watch out for him helped him relax enough to sleep for most of the five-hour trip.

By the time he got off the plane, all he wanted was to get back to his apartment and pretend he lived a normal life. Unfortunately, reality wasn't following his plans. Fai stood waiting for him a few yards past the security checkpoint.

Devin assumed he would know what was on his father's laptop before he was faced with handing over the copy to Fai. He hated the idea of passing it off without knowing the damage the information might cause for him, his father, and his country.

"How was your trip?" Fai asked the moment Devin cleared the guard stand.

"Fine." Devin fell into step beside him. "I didn't expect to see you here."

"I knew you needed a ride from the airport."

Devin didn't respond. The last thing he wanted was to get in a car with Fai, but he couldn't see a way around it.

"Did you check any luggage?" Fai asked.

"No." Devin followed him to his car and loaded his suitcase in the back seat, keeping his computer bag in hand.

As soon as they were in the car, Fai put the key in the ignition and said, "I believe you brought something back for me."

"Yes, but before I give it to you, I want proof that Grace is okay."

He put the car in gear and didn't look at Devin as he backed out of his parking space. "Exactly what kind of proof do you want?"

"I don't know." Devin hadn't planned to make demands, but the idea that he could be handing over valuable information terrified him. It didn't matter that he had been told to do it by his superiors. "Let me see her or at least talk to her."

"The best thing you can do for her is to leave her alone. She doesn't know we have people nearby, and I'm sure you prefer she go about her life without knowing what is at stake."

"A photo, then," Devin improvised. He hoped more than anything that what he asked would be beyond Fai's capability to provide, but he had to be sure. "Surely you can at least give me that much."

"Yes. I can get you that much, but first I need the information."

Devin reminded himself once more that giving the drive to Fai was part of Chee and Ghost's plan to trace the leak they had been working so hard to uncover. Reluctantly he unzipped a small pocket of his backpack and pulled out the flash drive.

Fai kept one hand on the wheel and stretched out the other one. Devin dropped the drive into it, and the corner of Fai's lips curved up. "See? That wasn't so hard, was it?"

Devin didn't respond. Instead, he watched the road as they made their way from the airport to his apartment. When they reached the front of his building, Devin climbed out and retrieved his suitcase. Before he could close the back door, Fai said, "I'll make sure I have that other information you wanted by next week."

With a nod, Devin turned and retreated inside. He prayed the information he had just handed over was nothing more than boring memos and contracts, but deep down, he knew there was more to it than that. Making his way upstairs, he prayed this would be over soon.

* * *

The guests had started to depart, and Grace searched for Jun among the kitchen staff. She caught a glimpse of the woman's black and gray hair as she disappeared out a side door, a bag of trash in her hand.

Grace followed her, catching up to Jun near the front of the house where the older woman was returning from the outside trash can.

"Jun," she called out. "I was looking for you."

"I was hoping to find time to speak with you. How is Devin?" Jun asked. "I haven't heard from him in months."

Grace hesitated. She hadn't trusted anyone except her grandfather with her suspicions, and she wasn't sure she was willing to do so now.

"You do know where he is, don't you?" Jun asked. "Devin is like my own child. I will do anything I can for him. I'm worried he has been silent for so long."

"I'm worried about him too," Grace admitted. She offered what little truth she could. "His work is very complicated right now. It's hard for him to communicate with me."

Jun looked down at Grace's stomach. "But you are about to have his child. He must be calling you to see how you both are."

"I haven't talked to him since I told him." Grace saw Jun's surprise. "We were supposed to meet in London a few weeks ago, but he had to cancel. Then things happened, and we lost touch."

"That doesn't sound like my Devin."

"I know, but I told him I was having morning sickness, and he acted like I had a cold."

Jun shook her head and muttered something to herself in Mandarin. "That boy doesn't have a clue, does he?"

"What do you mean?"

"Devin is an only child, and he's never been around anyone having babies. I'm not sure he knows what morning sickness is."

Grace stared at her, stunned. How many times had she replayed her conversation with Devin, furious one moment that he had been so callous and then wondering in the next if he'd truly heard what she had said.

"What can I do to help?" Jun asked.

"If Devin comes looking for me, will you give him my number so he can call me? My old phone was stolen."

"Of course." She grew quiet. "I can't be sure I'll be here though. I haven't been able to find much work lately, and my rent went up this month. I may have to move to a bigger city if things don't change soon."

"What kind of work are you hoping to do?"

"Something that will allow me to keep a roof over my head. Nanny, housekeeper, kitchen help."

"I may have another option. You would have to move though."

"I can move."

"I need to make a phone call. Can you give me a minute?"

Jun nodded. "I will go help clean up."

"I'll find you before you leave," Grace promised.

They both walked back inside, Jun heading for the kitchen and Grace retreating to her temporary bedroom. She dialed her grandfather's number.

"Hi, Grace. Is everything okay?"

"It is. In fact, it may be better than okay."

"What's going on?"

"How would you feel about having a live-in housekeeper, one who would also be able to help with the bungalows?"

"If it's the right person, I'd consider the idea. You have someone in mind?"

"I think so. Devin's childhood nanny is looking for work. I ran into her at a dinner party. She's been working odd jobs, serving at parties and doing housework."

"Have you already talked to her about this?"

"I mentioned the possibility of a job but didn't give her specifics. I thought if you were okay with it, she could stay in the room by the nursery, at least until we can afford to pay her enough for her to get her own place."

"You're the one who would have to supervise her."

"I know."

"That also means that if it doesn't work out, you'll be responsible for letting her go."

Grace considered that possibility. "How about if I offer her a temporary position? We can make it for six months and renegotiate from there."

"Not a bad idea. That would help you get through your pregnancy and Devin getting home."

"Exactly."

"Go ahead and make an offer."

They discussed the terms Grace could present to Jun.

As soon as Grace hung up, she went in search of Devin's former nanny once more. This time she found her drying stemware in the kitchen.

"Jun, can I talk to you for a minute?"

Jun looked over at the woman who stood beside her as though silently asking permission.

"Go ahead. You can take a five-minute break."

Not sure where else she would be able to find somewhere private, Grace led the way into her room. "That job I was telling you about is available if you're interested."

"Yes, I'm interested. What kind of work is it? And where?"

"It would be at a resort in Colorado." Grace explained the job offer, including the living situation. "I'm sorry it's not that much money, but at least you wouldn't have to worry about rent."

"The money is fine," Jun said. "But if I come with you to Colorado, who will give Devin your number? You seemed concerned that you haven't heard from him either."

"Actually, I have an idea. Would you be willing to e-mail him before you move to Colorado? You can make sure he has your phone number so he can contact you. Once he does, you can give him my number."

"I'm happy to do that. We have to make sure he is there when the baby is born."

Grace didn't dispute her assumption that she was carrying only one baby. She simply nodded. "I agree."

Chapter 30

DEVIN FELT LIKE HE WAS dying a slow death in the days between returning from Tokyo and meeting with Ghost. Six long days passed before Chee left him a coded message telling him to meet at the safe house the following day. It took every ounce of patience in him to follow the correct protocols to make sure he wasn't being followed on his way to the meeting.

Work at the firm had ceased to hold any appeal for him, although Fai had made it easy to pretend everything was normal. Devin had hardly seen him since being dropped off at his apartment. He hoped that meant Fai really didn't have any access to Grace and he was looking for a way to fabricate proof.

"What was on my dad's computer?" Devin asked the moment he closed the door to the safe house behind him.

"More than we ever thought possible." Ghost motioned him to the table where a laptop lay open, a cord running from it to a desktop computer. "Take a look."

Devin sat down, and his heart sank. Two documents were displayed side by side, both contracts for sensitive government projects, both containing names of the various contractors who would work in the specific capacities the hosting agencies needed.

"Is this what I think it is?" Devin asked.

"If you think it's the base security plans for six army installations and the helicopter specs for the Marine Corps' next order, then yes, it's what you think it is."

"How would my father have these? He lives in Sedona, Arizona. We don't have military bases around there, much less government contractors."

"There are dozens of contracts on here, the majority of which contain classified information."

"Again, how would he gain access to it? Does he work in intelligence?"

"No. The CIA would have uncovered that when they did your background check."

"If he doesn't work for our side, does that mean . . . ?" Devin didn't want to voice the possibility that his father could be a traitor to his country, but it didn't keep the thought from forming.

"I don't think he's a spy if that's what you're worried about."

"It's very much what I'm worried about." Devin scrolled down the first document, searching for any clues. "I thought all my father did was consulting work."

"I think that's exactly what he does. What none of us realized is that he's consulting for firms in the business of working for the government on top-secret projects."

"My father is helping companies get these contracts?"

"Yep." Ghost fell silent, then finally asked, "Who else would have had access to your dad's computer?"

"After seeing how closely he guarded it this weekend, I'm not sure. At home his office is always locked. Even his secretary doesn't have access to the office unless he's there."

"Who is his secretary?"

"Maureen Adams."

"How long has she worked for him?"

"I don't know. Maybe twenty years."

"And she still works for him?"

"Yes. He mentioned her this weekend."

"Then it's not likely she's the source for the Chinese. From what we've ascertained, whoever was passing along the information lost access about three years ago. That means we can rule out your mother as well."

"And Liwei," Devin said. "You're sure it was three years ago when the flow of information stopped?"

"Yes. We had a couple of leaks, but nothing like we had before then." Ghost studied Devin, apparently sensing a new awareness in him.

"Who is it, Devin?" Ghost asked. When Devin didn't answer, he asked again. "Someone stopped working for your dad three years ago. Who was it?"

His chest tightened, a sickening sensation rising up in his throat as he forced himself to say, "Jun. It must be Jun."

"Jun Chang? Your old nanny?"

"She lived at the house until three years ago. I never understood why my father let her go after she had spent so many years with the family."

"Maybe he caught her stealing information and fired her rather than turning her in."

"I don't know. I wouldn't have thought he would have let her anywhere near the house if that was the case, but she was helping out with dinner when I went home last December."

"How much does your mother know about your father's work?"

"Probably about as much as I did."

"Typically it's the woman who does that kind of hiring."

"True. My dad may have convinced my mom they didn't need Jun full-time, but if he didn't give her another reason for letting her go, my mom wouldn't have thought twice about bringing her in for day jobs."

"It would also explain why your father was so protective of his laptop, even around you."

"I'm still having a hard time wrapping my mind around all this. My dad being involved in intelligence contracts is enough of a stretch, but Jun? I love her like a mother."

"The best spies are the ones you would never suspect. It sounds like she was exceptional to go undetected for so many years," Ghost said. "What are the chances that Jun knows you work for the CIA?"

"I don't know how she would. My job offers and travel information all came to me when I was in school, and she never visited me there." His eyebrows drew together. "Why do you ask?"

"Damage control. We still don't know how Fai found out you're with the agency."

"So if it wasn't Jun who told him . . ."

"Then we have another leak to plug."

"What happens now?"

"The CIA is already working to make changes to the personnel and specifications in the compromised contracts," Ghost said. "I suspect the FBI will arrive in Sedona sometime tomorrow to bring Jun in."

"Please let me know what they find out."

"I will."

* * *

Grace zipped her suitcase and tipped it upright. For such an impromptu trip, it had been more successful than she could have dared imagine. Sean's father seemed pleased with the new stock portfolio she had proposed, and several of the investments were already in place. His expanding business ventures would take more time, but after meeting with him each day, she had a clear understanding of what he wanted and the path they would take to get there.

"Grace?" Clayton called from the hallway. "Can I help you with your bags?"

She stepped out of her room. "That would be great, if you don't mind."

"Not at all." He moved past her to retrieve her suitcase. "I worked you hard enough this week. A woman in your condition shouldn't be carrying anything heavy."

Grace wondered what he would do if he knew she was carrying twins. So far she hadn't been able to share that information with anyone besides her grandfather. The idea of telling someone else before Devin just didn't sit right with her. She focused on Clayton once more and offered a smile. "Did you spoil your wife like this when she was pregnant?"

"Every chance I got." He led the way to the front door. "Are you sure I can't give you a ride to the airport?"

"Thanks, but Jun should be here any minute. She's planning on driving straight from the airport up to the ranch."

"That sure worked out well for everyone. I've only met Jun a few times, but she seems like a hard worker."

"It will be nice to have another familiar face in Colorado," Grace said. A car pulled up outside. "That must be her."

Clayton opened the door for her and carried her bag to the car Jun had parked. The small SUV was the same one Grace remembered Jun driving when Grace had dated Devin in high school, and it hadn't been new then.

"Travel safely," Clayton said. "I'm sure we'll talk soon."

"Thanks for everything," Grace said, climbing into the passenger seat. She shifted her attention to the woman beside her. "Thank you for picking me up."

"It is I who should be thanking you." She put the car in gear and started down the drive. "I look forward to working for you and your grandfather."

Grace forced herself to think positively. "Devin will be so excited when he gets home and finds you there."

"I hope so."

On the drive to the airport, they chatted about the resort and Jun's new responsibilities, then Grace's pregnancy.

"When is your little one expected to arrive?" Jun asked.

"December." Grace mentally added, *I hope*. Every time she thought about the many complications that could come from having twins, she had to fight back the fear and focus on the possibilities. If her babies had problems from coming too early, she would deal with them. Until then, she was determined to expect the best in the hopes that her expectations would be met. At the top of the list was the birth of two healthy babies with Devin standing by her side.

Jun pulled into the airport parking lot, and Grace climbed out of the car, her laptop bag clutched in one hand. The moment she was out of the car, she had the eerie feeling of being watched, but when she looked around, she didn't notice anyone else nearby.

Jun moved to the trunk and retrieved Grace's suitcase for her. "Where are you to meet your friends?"

Grace looked around again, this time at the airfield. She spotted Sean's plane parked a short distance away, but she didn't see anyone near it.

"That's the plane over there."

"Let me carry this for you." Jun led the way to the plane, pulling the suitcase behind her as they crossed the edge of the tarmac. They reached the plane a moment before Sean emerged from the small airport building, a paper in his hand.

"Hey, Grace. Right on time, I see."

Grace motioned to Jun. "Sean, do you know Jun?"

"I've seen her a few times." Sean extended his hand. "It's nice to meet you officially."

"Thank you." Jun bowed her head slightly, then turned to Grace. "If you are okay, I will start my drive."

"Travel safely," Grace said. "I will see you this evening. And call me or my grandfather if you run into any trouble."

Jun lowered her head once more before retreating back to the parking lot.

"Let me get your bag stored, and we'll be good to go." Sean held up the paper in his hand. "Our flight plans are all set."

Grace stood back and waited while Sean stored her suitcase and computer bag. She glanced over at the parking lot and saw Jun standing beside her car, talking to a man and a woman.

It took her a moment to register who they were: Liwei, Devin's family cook, and Maureen, Devin's father's secretary. Grace had seen both of them only briefly when she had been at Devin's house a few months ago, but Liwei had added twenty pounds through his middle since she had first met him while she was in high school, and his hair was nearly all gray. Maureen, on the other hand, hadn't changed much, her blonde hair falling to her shoulders, her sleeveless dress falling several inches short of her knees. Grace hoped she looked as fit as Maureen when she was fifty.

"Here, let me give you a hand," Sean said, breaking into her thoughts.

Grace looked down at her growing baby bump, all too aware of her awkward shape. She accepted Sean's offer, putting her hand in his to steady herself as she climbed into the plane. As soon as they were both strapped into their seats, she sat back and rested her hand on her stomach. The ripple of movement beneath her palm stunned her.

She stared down at her abdomen, reality jolting through her. In four and a half more months, she was going to be a mom.

Chapter 31

FAI FOLLOWED THE HOUSEBOY THROUGH a modest-sized living area and into the home office. The last time Fai had visited here, he had been praised for his work in obtaining the copy of Boyd Shanahan's hard drive. One look at the man sitting at the desk this time indicated praise wasn't going to be the order of business today.

The houseboy announced him and then disappeared the way he had come.

"Close the door," Qing said sternly.

Fai complied and turned to face the older man. Part of him wanted to ask why he had been summoned today, and another part of him hoped he wouldn't find out. He remained silent.

The man across from him put both hands on his desk and stood, then picked up a paper from his desk and waved it.

"Six times." Qing's voice vibrated with barely controlled fury. "Six times we inserted someone into the life of a high-level government contractor only to find out he didn't have access to anything valuable."

Fai fought the urge to squirm. "I don't understand."

"Neither do I." He waved the paper again. "I was told the information copied off Boyd Shanahan's hard drive contained data we had seen before."

"That's correct, sir. Our analysts verified it to be authentic."

"The programs appear to be accurate, but the personnel have been changed in every key area." He dropped the paper onto his desk. "Can you explain how that could happen?"

"You think Devin altered the information."

"That's the most logical possibility." He picked up an envelope. "I received some new information on Mr. Shanahan's wife. I believe it's time he pays us a visit."

"I thought you didn't want to give him access to our operations here in Hong Kong."

"We aren't going to question him here. He is going to take a trip to Shanghai," he said. "Set up a meeting, and keep him under surveillance until then."

"And if he refuses to cooperate?"

"Kill him."

* * *

The weight of Jun's involvement didn't hit Devin fully until he went into work the next day. A plain manila envelope lay in the center of his desk and sent a bevy of nerves rumbling through him. His breath caught when he slid the contents free and stared at the photograph. Grace's face was clearly visible through the window of a small airplane, the red rocks of Sedona creating a familiar backdrop.

Ghost had helped him send the message to Grace in the hopes that she would understand he was all right. What Devin hadn't considered was that she would try to contact his family in search of him.

He thought she would know that contacting her would be more important to him than communicating with his parents. Maybe she hadn't fully understood his message. Or maybe she had gone to Jun because of how much Devin had trusted her throughout his youth. How could he have been so blind? And how could Jun have deceived him so completely?

All his life, she had been the one he had turned to for everything. She had chased away the bad dreams in the middle of the night, patched up his cuts and scrapes, told him stories at bedtime. Many of those stories had been of her childhood in China, but never had he felt like she was trying to undermine his culture. Rather, he had loved seeing the differences through her eyes.

Devin continued to stare at the photo, lowering himself into his seat. Grace's hair looked a bit longer than when he'd seen her last, and her face looked fuller. He wanted to convince himself that this was an old photo, but he had no way of knowing.

He turned it over, hoping to find a date stamp, but the back was blank. It was then he noticed the additional paper in the envelope. The flight plan was dated yesterday and gave much more information than he could have anticipated. Not only did it list the destination as Vail, Colorado, but the pilot's name and address were also listed: Sean Tanner.

Why was Grace flying from Sedona to Colorado with Sean? The two hadn't exactly seemed close when they'd all been in Las Vegas together.

Devin tried to put himself in Grace's shoes. She must have gone to Molly and Caleb in the hopes of finding him. Knowing Caleb, he would have enlisted help from whomever was willing. Devin didn't know how he felt about Sean hanging around his wife.

He looked at a handwritten note at the bottom of the flight plan. The Chinese character for a local restaurant was listed, along with a date and time. *Tonight. 7 pm.*

Devin thought over his schedule. His meetings would go until at least five thirty or six, and the restaurant was halfway across town. He wouldn't have time to meet with Ghost before the scheduled rendezvous, nor would he be able to slip out of the office today in order to send him a text or call without the possibility of Fai or whomever he was working for intercepting it.

Feeling trapped and uncertain, Devin looked down at the photo again. He didn't have a choice. With or without proper backup, he had to go, and he had to make sure Grace remained unharmed.

* * *

Grace gripped the edge of her seat. Sean circled the plane over the Vail airport for the third time, and the turbulence sent her stomach pitching. She swallowed hard.

Sean's normal friendly chatter had ceased thirty minutes before when they'd first encountered the storm front and its accompanying winds. His lack of conversation spoke volumes.

"Let's try this again," Sean said, although Grace wasn't sure if he was talking to her or to himself.

Memories of her parents' crash created another spike in her anxiety. They may have been driving a car, not flying in a plane, but she knew all too well how quickly life could come to an end.

Another jerk to the right caused Grace to close her eyes and send up another round of silent pleadings.

The plane lowered, and she could feel the turbulence lessen. Cautiously she opened one eye enough to see them drop below the cloud cover, and she managed to blink and open both eyes then.

"Check the wing on your side," Sean instructed. "Do you see any ice?"

The idea that there would be ice on the wings in August seemed so foreign, but dutifully, Grace looked out her window. "I don't see any."

Sean kept his hand gripped on the throttle, his tension visibly easing slightly when the airfield came into view below. "Hold on. The landing may be bumpy."

Grace's fingers tightened on her seat. Another crosswind jerked at the plane, but this time Sean was able to recover quickly. A few hundred feet lower and Grace wasn't sure he would have been able to keep them from crashing.

If something happened to her and her babies, would anyone even be able to contact Devin to tell him?

And he didn't even know he was about to be a father.

Her regrets subsided when the plane eased down without further incident and the wheels finally connected with the black tarmac.

Grace let out the breath she hadn't realized she'd been holding. She looked over at Sean, who was looking as relieved to be on the ground as she felt.

Neither of them spoke until Sean pulled into a spot on the side of the airfield and turned off the engine. "Sorry that was so rough. That storm wasn't supposed to move in until late tonight."

"I'm just glad to be back on solid ground."

"That makes two of us."

Chapter 32

DEVIN KNEW IT WAS RISKY, but he didn't have a choice. The moment his four o'clock meeting ended, he headed downstairs under the premise of meeting a client, then hailed a taxi.

He had the foresight to get dropped off at an office building a mile away, walk two blocks, and then take public transit to get the rest of the way to his apartment.

With almost no time to spare, he grabbed the phone he used to communicate with Ghost, sent a quick text message, and secured the phone once more.

Now he was on another bus, this time on the way to the meeting he had been commanded to attend. Standing in the aisle, he wiped one sweaty palm on his slacks. He supposed it didn't bode well for him that his nerves were in overdrive so much that he could hardly maintain his grip on the handle overhead.

The full bus came to a stop, and a dozen passengers fought their way toward the exits. The moment they were clear, several more took their places.

He noticed a man who looked vaguely familiar among the new arrivals, but he couldn't place where he had seen him before.

Two stops later, Devin exited the bus and stepped onto the crowded sidewalk. He started toward the restaurant where he was supposed to meet his contact, assuming Fai would be waiting for him inside. To his surprise, the man he had noticed on the bus stepped beside him.

He felt something poke him in the ribs. "Keep walking."

"Who are you, and what do you want?" Devin managed to ask.

"I'm the person who has some questions for you." He guided him toward the corner of the building.

Devin stopped short of the narrow alleyway, afraid if he moved out of sight of the pedestrian traffic he might not ever be seen again. Another nudge with what felt like a gun barrel convinced him to keep moving forward.

"What do you want?" Devin asked again.

The man didn't answer until they were well into the alley and out of sight of anyone on the street. "Who did you communicate with when you went to your apartment this afternoon?"

"What?"

The slender man pulled his weapon free of his shirt, where it had been concealed, and pointed it at Devin. "Who did you talk to?"

Devin reminded himself to stick as closely to the truth as he could. "I had plans with a friend tonight. When I got the message to meet someone here, I went home so I could get her number and cancel."

A familiar voice sounded from somewhere deep in the alley. "I doubt that." Fai emerged from a hidden niche in the wall. "You don't go out with women. You are too in love with your wife."

Devin turned to face Fai and fought to keep his rising apprehension from sounding in his voice. "Maybe you can tell me what's going on here."

"We have some questions." He continued forward, the look of calm on his face creating the opposite feeling in Devin. "I'm starting to believe you may not have been completely honest with me."

"About what?"

"The information you retrieved from your father has quite a few flaws in it."

"I don't know anything about that," Devin said. "You asked me to copy his hard drive, and I did."

"And you asked for proof that your wife is okay, and I provided it." Fai came to a stop three feet from Devin and held out an envelope. "Now it's up to you to decide if she remains that way."

Reluctantly Devin accepted the offering. He opened it to find an Australian passport with his photo on it, but the name listed was Dustin Sherwood. "I don't understand."

"We're taking a little trip to Shanghai. Consider it an opportunity to prove your allegiance."

"And if I don't go?"

"That would be unwise." Fai motioned deeper into the alley. "Our flight leaves in two hours."

"Hong Kong is a province of China," Devin said. "Why do you need me to go to Shanghai?"

"Because I want to make sure you don't have any friends tagging along while we have our chat."

The man who had forced him into the alley moved forward, his weapon now only inches from Devin's chest. "Let's go."

Fear, adrenaline, and Devin's instinctive sense of survival urged him to react. He let the envelope fall out of his hand. The moment the man's eyes lowered to follow it, Devin grabbed the man's wrist with one hand and the gun with the other and twisted it out of his captor's hand.

Devin barely had time to process that his tactic had worked before Fai's movement drew his attention. Devin tried to step back so he could face both men at the same time, but before he could face Fai completely, Fai's hand connected with Devin's jaw.

Off balance, Devin stumbled back several steps, his grip tightening on the weapon. He swung it toward Fai, a blur of movement causing him to jump back. The kick Fai had aimed at his head missed by inches.

Anticipating another strike, Devin reached out with his free hand, backpedaling away from Fai and shoving the original gunman at the same time. The action caused Fai to strike his ally rather than Devin.

The stunned look on the other man's face as he fell to the ground would have been comical had it not been for the gravity of the situation—Devin was a CIA operative in Hong Kong with two men trying to force him to go to mainland China against his will.

Fai surged forward, mimicking the move Devin had used on his accomplice just moments before. Devin countered by backing up again, only to find himself pinned against the wall.

"It appears my superiors were right," Fai said, his voice still eerily calm. "You can't be trusted."

"It's not me who can't be trusted." Devin lifted the weapon to take aim. He didn't know if he could shoot another human being, but before he could decide, Fai kicked out again, this time managing to connect with Devin's forearm.

The gun fell to the ground as Devin groaned in pain. His arms came up to block the next two blows, a strike from Fai's right hand followed by a left jab. Devin sensed the man's accomplice moving forward as well, undoubtedly intent on regaining his pistol.

Devin tried to lean down to recover it, but the movement left him vulnerable, and Fai kicked once more, this time connecting solidly with Devin's midsection. Another groan escaped him, and he dropped to the ground.

He reached out, his hands grasping for the pistol. His fingers brushed against the rubber grip, a brief moment of hope sparking, but Fai kicked the gun out of reach, and his accomplice rushed forward. Before Devin could fight back, he felt both men grab him. Devin bucked against their grips, but that didn't stop the prick of a needle in his arm.

A gunshot sounded, but Devin couldn't process where the noise had originated from. He tried to focus, but the sights and sounds and even the awful smell of the alley dwindled, and the fading evening light darkened in an instant.

* * *

Grace fought against her exhaustion and struggled to stand when the knock sounded on the door. She had barely moved from the couch since arriving home from the airport three hours earlier.

Her grandfather had taken her suitcase upstairs to her room, but she hadn't been able to find the energy to walk that far. Instead, she had tried to nap downstairs while fighting against the many what-ifs of the morning.

She had spent the past week trying to ignore the truth that she was married to a man who had practically dropped off the face of the earth, a man who had no idea that in a matter of months he would become a father—not once but twice. Now she forced herself to face reality. Sean's father had given her the opportunity to start her new career, but only Devin could give her what mattered most—a future with her husband and children.

Grace went to the door and found Jun standing on the front porch, a suitcase in hand. "You made it." Grace stepped aside and motioned her in.

"Yes." Jun entered and narrowed her eyes. "You look tired."

"A little." Grace motioned to the stairs. "Your room is upstairs. Let me show you."

"I'll find it." Jun pointed to the living room. "You stay and rest."

Before Grace could protest, she heard footsteps behind her.

"You must be Jun," her grandfather said as he entered the room.

Jun bowed her head.

"Jun, this is my grandfather, Quentin Harrington."

"It is good to meet you," Jun said. "I am happy to come to work for you."

"We're happy to have you." Quentin moved forward and picked up her suitcase. "I'll show you your room, and we'll get your car unloaded."

Jun must have known that refusing Quentin's help wouldn't have worked because she obediently followed him up the stairs.

Grace moved back to the couch and lowered herself onto the center cushion.

She looked over at the mantel and the photo that rested there of her with her parents taken the year before they died. When, she wondered, would she have what her parents had? Would she ever have a normal marriage? And would she ever learn why Devin had disappeared from her life?

She heard her grandfather and Jun coming toward her. They were her family now. She prayed that someday Devin would be part of her family again too.

Chapter 33

DEVIN'S HEAD POUNDED. CONFUSION CAME first, followed by memories of the alley brawl. He had been drugged. That was the last thing he could remember. His heartbeat quickened, aggravating his headache as he considered the possibilities. Was he still in Hong Kong? Or had Fai managed to transport him to mainland China?

Though he was afraid of what he would find, he forced himself to open his eyes. Immediately he squinted against the overhead light. Relief flooded through him when he saw Ghost sitting across the room. Devin closed his eyes again, willing his heartbeat to return to normal. He was safe. How he had gotten here, he wasn't sure, but he was alive, and he was still free.

Devin forced himself to wake fully and moaned as he pushed himself up onto his elbow. When Ghost turned to look in his direction, Devin mumbled, "We've got to stop meeting like this."

"I agree." Ghost picked up a glass of water and offered it to him, along with two pills. "Here, take these. It will help with the headache."

Devin popped the two Tylenol into his mouth and washed them down with a swallow of water. He looked around the room, recognizing that he was in the same safe house he'd used with Ghost before. "What happened? How did I get here?"

"I got to the alley right after they drugged you."

"I thought I heard a gunshot . . ." Devin's voice trailed off. "Did you . . . ? Are they . . . ?"

"They're alive. At least they were when I left them," Ghost said dryly. "What in the world were you thinking? You know better than to go to a meeting without backup. Chee didn't even know where you were."

"Someone left a message in my office. They had a photo of Grace and a copy of a flight plan from Sedona, Arizona, to Vail, Colorado."

"You said before that you think she's living in Colorado."

Devin nodded. A jolt of pain accompanied the movement. He pressed his fingers against his temples, the gravity of the situation falling heavily over him once more. "They know where she is, and I have no way of warning her."

"How did she look in the photo? Could you tell where she was? Or if it was even a current photo?"

"She was in a plane at the airport in Sedona. The flight plan listed Sean Tanner as the pilot. He's a guy I know from college."

"Any idea what she was doing with him?"

"My guess is that she went to Sedona looking for me, or at least trying to find out if anyone had heard from me."

"The truth is they may be using Grace as bait to lure you out again."

"And if they're not?"

"Then you're too late."

Ghost's bluntness stunned Devin and sent a stabbing pain into his gut. "You don't think they would . . . ?"

"It's best not to focus on what you can't control. We'll start a search for her again. Assuming she's still okay, our best play is to find the leak. Once we do that, you can safely reunite with your wife."

"What happens now?" Devin asked, a sense of helplessness overwhelming him. "Obviously I can't go back to work now. Fai suspected I double-crossed him even before you shot at him."

"What did they say?"

Devin replayed the conversation and Fai's insistence that Devin go with him to Shanghai. "My guess is the powers that be made so many changes to avoid intelligence leaks that the copy of my father's laptop appeared to have been altered."

"I was worried something like that might happen."

"And you let me go to work every day anyway?" Devin asked.

"Chee was convinced we could use your cover to find the leak. He thought giving you a guardian would be enough to protect you."

"Guardian?"

"Guardian, ghost. It's the same thing."

"Do you work for the CIA?"

"Not exactly."

"Who do you work for, then?" Devin asked.

"All of the guardians at one time or another had some ties with intelligence," Ghost said. "And all of us had someone who wanted us dead."

"Why?"

"Different reasons. Usually we knew too much." Ghost's expression intensified. "I would offer to have you join our ranks, but our way of ensuring no one is following you is to fake your death."

Devin immediately shook his head. "I can't do that. I can't lose Grace."

"I suspected as much," Ghost said. "If you want your life back, we need to find the leak."

"How is it that I was sent over here to uncover leaks for US intelligence, and now I'm a direct victim of what I was trying to prevent? What are the chances?"

"Often these types of situations are related," Ghost said. "Someone set you up here. We need to know who, and we need to know why."

"Where do we start?"

"We start by smuggling you out of the country." Ghost gave him an apologetic look. "I'm afraid your return voyage isn't going to be as comfortable as your trip over here."

"Voyage? As in *sea* voyage?"

"Exactly. I hope you don't get seasick."

"Sounds like I'm about to find out."

* * *

Devin had never been so glad in his life to see land. His stomach pitched with the movement of the waves as a tugboat pulled the freighter into the busy port. The three-day voyage from Hong Kong to Tokyo had taken him through stormy seas, and while the rest of the crew seemed perfectly fine, Devin had spent most of his time on board avoiding food and hoping his stomach would settle.

The clouds overhead blocked out the midmorning sun, but at least the rain had stopped sometime during the night. The twenty-man crew buzzed around the deck behind him, preparing to off-load cargo and bring more on board.

"Happy to see land again?" one of the crewmen asked Devin in Mandarin.

"Very happy to see land again," Devin confirmed.

"A few more days and you'll get used to it."

"Maybe," Devin said noncommittally. Ghost had given him simple instructions when he'd dropped him off at the docks several days after rescuing him from the alleyway. Stay out of trouble on the freighter and go to the meeting place in Tokyo as soon as he put into port.

The meeting place was simply an address Devin had memorized. He doubted it would be anything like the hotel and restaurants he had frequented a few weeks before.

Devin shifted his backpack on his shoulder, not sure what to think about the fact that his belongings could all fit in one bag. As soon as the gangplank was in place, he made his way forward. After a brief conversation with the captain to thank him for his passage, Devin disembarked, stumbling when his feet met solid ground.

He heard the chuckles from the crew. Good-naturedly, he lifted a hand and waved before heading around the huge crane on the dock. Nearly an hour later, he reached the meeting spot, the fish market. He looked around, hoping his stomach wouldn't protest the overwhelming smell.

Huge white signs hung over various booths, black ink creating Japanese characters. Boxes and hand carts impeded the walkways, people bustling all around him. Devin walked the length of the main section and was preparing to turn around when someone jostled him from behind.

"Keep walking."

He recognized Ghost's voice and did as he was instructed.

"Take a left here."

Again Devin complied. He turned a corner and found himself along the back wall of the market. "Please tell me you have a plane ticket for me."

"I'm afraid not." Ghost shifted a duffel bag off his shoulder and held the strap out to Devin. "In here you'll find the essentials, along with a laptop that has everything we know so far on who has had access to your file from the intelligence community."

"Have you found Grace yet?"

"We know she's living near Vail, Colorado. We haven't located her residence yet, but we found a hit on her at a local doctor's office two days ago."

"A doctor's office?"

"That's all I know. The point is she appears to be fine. If Jun or anyone else who is involved wanted to hurt her, they wouldn't have waited five days to do it."

Devin prayed Ghost's assumptions were correct. "What am I supposed to do now?"

"I have you booked as a passenger from here to Singapore on a cruise ship that leaves tonight."

"I can handle a cruise."

"It'll give you some time to research before the next leg of your voyage."

"And what will that entail?"

"You'll spend three weeks in a safe house in Singapore, and then you'll report to your new job working on a freighter."

"Am I ever going to get back to the States?" Devin asked. "It's already been a week."

"It's going to be a lot more weeks," Ghost told him. "The freighter will go from Singapore to Vancouver and finally to Oakland, California. When you reach Oakland, you'll find a car in a hotel parking lot near the docks. The details on the vehicle and its location are in the envelope with the key."

Devin held up the duffel. "In here?"

"That's right," Ghost said. "You'll arrive in Oakland on November 30. Once you get there, you'll find instructions on how to proceed taped under the passenger seat, along with a new cell phone."

Devin's thoughts focused on the date Ghost gave him. "You just said I won't be stateside until November?"

"We need to keep you off the radar while we try to identify who is behind your attempted abduction and hopefully plug the leak that put you in danger in the first place. Like I mentioned before, it's possible it's connected to the one you came here looking for."

"And if you can't plug the leak?"

"We'll get to the bottom of this." Ghost handed him an envelope. "The details for your cruise are in there, and I've left some currency for everywhere you'll be stopping. I suggest you get something to eat while you have the chance."

"Will I see you again?"

"Not if you're lucky." Ghost pointed to the bag. "You have a satellite phone in there. My number is programmed in, and so is Chee's. Call me if you run into any problems or if you make any progress on your research."

Devin extended his hand. "Thanks for all your help."

"Just doing my job." Ghost shook his hand and stepped back. "Stay out of trouble."

"I'll do my best."

Chapter 34

GRACE WATCHED OUT THE WINDOW every day, the leaves turning russet and gold, the pine trees ensuring green remained a permanent part of the landscape. The calendar on her wall marked off the days until Devin would return from Hong Kong. She didn't know the exact date, of course. That would have required some kind of communication between them, and so far he had not made any attempt to contact her beyond the single cryptic e-mail. Based on her estimation, he should finish his job within the next two weeks.

Every day she yearned to call his office again in hopes of talking to him, but the fear that the men in New York wanted to use her to get to him held her back. Why else would they have been at her apartment besides to look for Devin? He had said he was going to be out of town for a few days the last time they'd spoken. Had he planned to surprise her in New York? Or had he truly been trying to break things off with her?

The lives within her were becoming all too real. Dr. Gilmore assured her everything was developing well, and her latest ultrasound confirmed the same thing the last one had: her babies were expected by Christmas.

Though the doctor had offered again to tell her the sex of the babies, Grace had opted to wait. She didn't want to find out without Devin by her side. The fact that they had never truly discussed her pregnancy left her with nearly as many doubts as reasons for why he had stopped communicating with her.

More days ticked by, and the day Devin should have come home passed without any news; her questions and fears intensified. Leaves dropped from the trees as fall gave way to early winter. With the first snowfall, business boomed. Opening day at the local ski resort had brought a constant stream of guests, and the ranch's bookings were already well above what her grandfather and his investors had hoped for during their first season.

Her own business ventures had been limited to managing the investments for Sean's dad thus far, partially because of the demands of the ranch and partially because her nesting instincts had kicked in. The bedroom next to hers now held two cribs; the tall dresser between them was filled with baby blankets and infant-sized clothing. A baby name book rested beside her bed, pages dog-eared with possibilities. Though she had narrowed her list somewhat, the idea of naming her children without Devin's input felt wrong, not to mention she didn't even know if she was having girls, boys, or one of each.

Putting a hand beneath her stomach to support its growing weight, she crossed to the bedroom window and placed her hand against the cold glass. She didn't know what her future held, but no matter what, she was determined to make a home for her and her children.

* * *

"He can't have simply disappeared into thin air." Qing was furious. "You've had five weeks, and still nothing?"

"We traced him as far as Singapore, but he disappeared from there."

"Someone is helping him."

"Our contact in the CIA insists it's not them," Fai said quickly.

"If not the CIA, then who?"

"I don't know."

"Find out."

"We're trying, sir."

Qing paced across the room and looked out the window. "No leads off the girl yet?"

"No, sir. We have her under surveillance, but we haven't seen any sign of Shanahan."

Qing turned to face Fai. "Do whatever it takes to get him to cooperate, or make sure he won't be able to work with anyone ever again."

"Our agent watching the wife said she's pregnant. It appears we will have a new bargaining chip."

"I don't want there to be any doubt as to where his allegiances lie."

"Yes, sir."

* * *

The pain started from somewhere deep inside her, the intensity spreading through her back and abdomen for several seconds before finally subsiding. Grace shifted the pillow beneath her in an effort to get more comfortable. She didn't know what time it was, but she was certain it wasn't time to get up and start the day.

Her body relaxed, and she fell back to sleep. The next pain came on more forcefully, and she struggled to comprehend the cause. Her stomach hardened, and understanding dawned. Labor. Her babies were coming.

"Grandpa? Jun?" she called, then to herself, she mumbled, "It's too soon." The doctor had said he wanted her to make it another three weeks before she delivered.

Jun reached her room first. "Miss Grace, you okay?"

"I need to go to the hospital."

"I will get Mr. Quentin." The words were barely out of her mouth when Grace's grandpa poked his head in her doorway.

"What's wrong?" he asked.

"I think I'm in labor." She felt tears threaten when she added, "Grandpa, it's too soon."

"Everything will be fine," he assured her. "Let's get you out to the car. Do you think you can walk?"

She nodded, relieved when her abdomen relaxed once more.

He turned to Jun. "Jun, can you get her bag?"

"Yes, Mr. Quentin." Jun picked up the backpack Grace had packed over a month before at her doctor's insistence. Dr. Gilmore had stressed the importance of avoiding anything that could bring on early labor, but he had also repeatedly reminded her that she had to be prepared for the possibility.

Every time Grace researched that possibility, fears about her babies' health overwhelmed her. Those fears multiplied when the next contraction started.

Jun and her grandpa helped her out to the car. Thirty minutes and five contractions later, she was at the hospital being examined by her doctor.

Dr. Gilmore spoke to the nurse, giving orders about some medication, then as soon as the nurse left the room, he spoke to Grace. "We're going to give you something to see if we can stop your labor."

"Are my babies still okay?"

"I'm still hearing two strong heartbeats." He wrote something on her chart. "You just try to relax."

Grace nodded despite the tears threatening. She knew her grandfather was still in the waiting room, but right now, all she wanted was her husband and for these contractions to stop.

* * *

Grace struggled to breathe, another pain spreading from her back to her abdomen. Every minute felt like an eternity, and she couldn't tell if she had been in the hospital for ten minutes or two hours. Panic bloomed inside her, the contraction finally easing. "What happens if it won't stop?"

"We'll take care of you and your babies, but right now, I need you to relax and trust me," Dr. Gilmore said.

She managed to nod. The doctor checked the monitor beside her and stepped back to speak quietly to a nurse. Then he turned to Grace once more. "The nurse is going to stay here with you. I'll be back to check on you later."

Grace closed her eyes, a tear escaping as she tried to relax her body. She started at her toes and worked her way up. Another contraction hit, but the pain wasn't as far reaching as the one before it.

Breathe. In, out. She let those words repeat in her mind as she continued to block out the sounds and smells of her room.

Minutes stretched out, the contractions lessening in intensity.

She didn't notice when the last one ended, her exhaustion leaving her drifting in and out of sleep.

Thoughts of Devin crept in, the same old questions whirling. Where was he? Was he really a spy? Was he okay? Would he come back to her? If so, when?

"How's our patient doing?" Dr. Gilmore interrupted her meandering thoughts when he returned to check on her.

"The contractions have stopped," the nurse informed him.

Grace opened her eyes and watched the doctor check the monitor once more. "My labor stopped?"

"Yes, the medicine worked," Dr. Gilmore said.

"Does that mean I can go home now?"

"Not exactly." He stepped closer to her bed. "We were lucky your grandfather was able to get you here tonight, but there's another storm front moving in today. If you go into labor at home, we may not be able to stop it again."

"I have to stay in the hospital?"

"I strongly recommend it." He gave her a sympathetic look before he added, "It's the best thing we can do to make sure your babies arrive healthy."

"For how long?"

"Three weeks. Once we get you to thirty-seven weeks, we'll be able to send you home."

"Do you think I can make it that long?"

"Every day you go is a step closer to healthy babies."

"Thank you, Doctor."

"The nurses will get you settled into your room, and I'll be by to check on you tomorrow."

She watched him go, desperately hoping her babies would wait to come until they could be born healthy. She added her hope that their father would be here before it was time for them to enter the world.

* * *

Devin sat below deck, his laptop open in front of him. After two weeks at sea, he had finally adjusted to the movement of the waves. The motion sickness that had plagued him on his first voyage was now little more than a bad memory.

He worked with the crew for several hours each day, but much of his free time was spent in his quarters searching for answers. This journey would come to an end within days, and time was running out.

His research into the people with access to his identity had been narrowed while he was in Singapore. Ghost had passed him the message that they had reduced their list of possible suspects to three people. As unlikely as it seemed he would be involved, Chee was on the list as well as Jalen and Alison Gerard. He had never met the third person, but apparently she had managed his travel and accommodations.

Devin tried to wrap his mind around the possibilities, but he wasn't any closer now than he had been when he had boarded this freighter two weeks earlier.

Within the hour, they would reach Hawaii, and he would be able to check in with Ghost for an update. Though Devin had a satellite phone, Ghost had instructed him to avoid using it while on board for fear that the crew would overhear him.

Though the laptop Ghost had provided him had been loaded with hundreds of files on the suspects, Devin was beginning to doubt he would find anything useful. He had scoured all but a dozen files already, and so far, nothing appeared to be out of order with any of their suspects.

He rolled his shoulders and shifted his position before opening the next file. The banking records for each of the names on Ghost's list appeared before him, and he scanned through them. He was only on the fourth line when a transaction caught his interest. Not a deposit as he had expected but an expenditure. A single debit card charge for gasoline in Sedona, Arizona, dated almost three months earlier.

Devin pulled up the calendar on his laptop and studied the dates. He counted back to when he had last been in Hong Kong, his eyes narrowing when he made the connection. The charge had been made only a few days before he had received the photo of Grace.

Could this be the person who was working with Jun to recruit him as an asset for the Chinese government?

Assuming Jun really had stolen information off his father's computer for years, someone must have been working as her handler. Apparently Jalen, the personnel officer who had sworn to help protect him, was really the person who was trying to unravel everything important in his life.

"Land ho!" The shout came from the next compartment over, relayed from the lookout above deck.

With his newfound information, Devin secured his laptop and retrieved his satellite phone. It was time to make a call and get some help in proving his suspicions.

Chapter 35

DEVIN STEPPED ONTO THE DOCK in California, relieved to know he would never have to travel by freighter again. When he'd docked in Vancouver, he had called Ghost. Together they had come up with a plan of attack, but first he had to find the hotel where the vehicle had been left for him. He looked out at the vast Oakland port and headed for the area where several taxicabs were parked.

He flagged one down and gave the driver the address of the hotel. The thought that he should take a circuitous route didn't cross his mind until he was only three blocks from his destination.

Too late now, he thought to himself. Surely after all the precautions Ghost had taken, no one would be able to trace him anyway. No one in the agency knew where he was, and Ghost had assured him that the FBI would take care of apprehending Jalen.

He still couldn't believe he had been specifically targeted. The next part of his job was to figure out why, but first he needed to find his wife and make sure she was okay. He hoped she would be able to forgive him for the long silence.

Five months. Those five months had been sheer torture. The long nights of wondering if she was okay. Fai's constant threats against her and their last conversation constantly playing through his mind. She really hadn't sounded like herself that day, and he hated that he had dropped off the radar when she'd been sick.

Morning sickness, she had said. He wasn't sure exactly what morning sickness was, but he was pretty sure he had heard the term before. And Ghost's mention that he had tracked her to Vail through a medical record made Devin wonder if her illness had been more significant than she had let on.

The cab pulled under the overhang in front of the motel, and Devin fished through his wallet to find the correct type of currency. He paid the driver, gathered his backpack and duffel bag, and climbed out of the vehicle. As soon as the cab pulled away, Devin looked around the parking lot and found the blue sedan that had been left for him.

He retrieved the car key from his backpack, relieved when he pressed the unlock button on the fob and the brake lights illuminated. He popped the trunk, loaded his luggage, and climbed into the driver's seat, keeping the backpack containing the laptop with him. He reached down to feel under the passenger's seat and found two envelopes taped there, both containing bulky items.

Inside the first, he discovered a new cell phone. How odd that he had gone through more cell phones in his eight months with the CIA than he had his entire life. He had anticipated the continued use of the satellite phone, but he supposed he would be significantly less conspicuous when using a normal cell phone instead.

He opened the smaller of the two envelopes. This time a hotel key card and a business card for a hotel in Oakland near the Bay Bridge fell out. On the back of the business card was scrawled *Room 416. 3PM.*

Devin glanced at his watch. 11:45 a.m. Though he had hoped to get on the road to Vail, it appeared he had a meeting to attend first, probably a debriefing. If he was lucky, whoever he was meeting with would also be able to provide him with Grace's address and a plane ticket for him to get to Colorado faster than if he had to drive the thousand miles. Eighteen-plus hours in a car didn't sound terribly appealing to him right now, especially after being trapped on a boat for the past month.

Reminding himself to follow protocol, Devin started the car and pulled out of the parking lot. He headed in the opposite direction to where he was going, circling twice before turning toward the airport. He repeated his haphazard turns three additional times, including one detour through a fast-food restaurant's drive-through. Finally, with his lunch on the seat beside him, he reached his destination.

Rather than park at the front of the hotel, Devin chose a spot near a side door. With his backpack over his shoulder, he made his way inside through the closest entrance, using the hotel key card to unlock the exterior door. He climbed the three flights and knocked on the room door when he reached it. When there was no answer, he slid the key into the lock and entered.

The room was simple and appeared undisturbed since the last time the maid service had been there. Cautiously he moved forward, checking the bedroom, bathroom, and closet to make sure he really was alone. Satisfied that that was the case, he picked up the remote control, settled down on the bed with his lunch, and prepared to find out what had been going on in the world since he had last lived in civilized society.

* * *

Devin had expected someone to knock on his door at three o'clock, but instead of a visitor, he received a phone call.

"Ghost. I didn't expect to hear from you again."

"We have a problem."

"What kind of problem?"

"The FBI said we don't have a strong enough case for them to take our suspect into custody. The debit card charge is sufficient to open an investigation but not to arrest him."

"Are you kidding me?"

"I'm afraid not."

"Has the FBI at least questioned him?"

"No. They're planning to put him under surveillance, but that is still in the works."

"What do we do now? After what happened in the alley in Hong Kong, I have to think the people Fai worked for want me dead."

"I hate to say it, but I agree."

It was one thing for Devin to say it, but to have Ghost reaffirm it left him wondering exactly how he was supposed to build a future for himself and his wife. "What do I do now? You don't really think they would try to follow me over here, do you?"

"I don't know, but watch your back. For all we know, they might have it in their minds to make an example out of you."

A healthy dose of fear coursed through him. "Is my family in danger?"

"Since they've threatened Grace in the past, we are concerned that Fai's people could have someone watching her in order to get to you," Ghost said.

"But why? I've never understood what Fai wants from me."

"We believe he was going to push you to go into business with your father so you would have access to everything rather than having to steal it. He would have been the intermediary between you and the Chinese government."

"It surprises me that they thought my father would be open to working with me," Devin said. "Jun had to have told them my father and I aren't exactly close."

"I don't think they care if you're close or not. Your father was proud of your accomplishments at Stanford. They probably assumed he would be willing to use that prestige to expand his business."

"Maybe," Devin conceded. "That's all water under the bridge now. There's no way they'll trust me again."

"Hang in there. It may take some time, but the FBI will get this sorted out sooner rather than later."

Devin closed his eyes. He thought of the months he had spent without Grace as an active part of his life. Frustration overwhelmed him as he considered that he would have to wait even longer to contact her, to see for himself that she was still okay, that she was still his.

"I have to tell Grace what's going on. She needs to know who I work for," Devin insisted.

"The agency approved your request to tell her, but only her."

"Does that mean you have Grace's address?" he asked with new hope.

"Not yet, but the FBI has been working on it. I'll check with them to see if they have her location, but for now, you have a flight to catch."

"To where?"

"Phoenix. You have a rental car reserved under your alias that you can use to drive to Sedona."

Phoenix. The place he and Grace had started to make a home before their lives had turned upside down. He tried to concentrate on the present instead of the past. "Why are you sending me to Sedona?"

"We need to see what your father knows about Jun, and the FBI wants you to help locate her."

"Help locate her? She should be at her apartment in Sedona."

"She wasn't there. The manager said she moved a couple months ago but that he didn't have a forwarding address. We hope you can ask around to find out where she went."

"I'll do what I can. What do you want me to do with the car I have here?"

"You'll park it at the San Francisco airport."

"San Francisco? Wouldn't it be closer for me to fly out of Oakland?"

"It might be a little closer, but the flight times worked better out of San Fran. I'm forwarding the boarding pass to your cell phone."

"Thanks."

"Devin, be careful."

"I have to say I really wish you were here."

"I have someone there watching your back," Ghost said. "Keep your head down."

The line went dead, and Devin looked down at his phone. A moment later, a message popped up with his boarding pass.

He picked up his car key. Finally, it was time for him to move forward in life.

Chapter 36

GRACE READJUSTED HERSELF IN AN effort to get more comfortable. Her stomach contorted as the twins decided to do the same. She put a hand over the movement and was rewarded with a solid kick from one of her babies. Her stomach was stretched beyond what she thought her body was capable of, and she was anxious to have her children arrive—as soon as it was safe, of course.

Only two more days until she would reach the thirty-seven-week mark. That magical day would give her the freedom to go home and make sure everything was as she wanted it to be before the babies arrived. It wouldn't be perfect, though. In a perfect world, she would know where her husband was, or better yet, he would be by her side.

She pushed that thought aside. Worrying about Devin was making her crazy, almost as crazy as being stuck in this bed for the past two weeks and five days.

A knock sounded on her door, and she turned her attention to her doctor.

"How's the patient?" he asked.

"Ready to get out of here."

"I'm afraid we aren't quite ready to let you go." He picked up her chart and studied it silently. "Everything looks good on here."

"When can I go home?"

"Have you been watching the weather forecasts lately?"

"No." She looked at him suspiciously. "Why?"

"We have a snowstorm expected to move in three days from now. I hate to tell you this, but having twins qualifies you as a high-risk pregnancy. As such, I want to keep you here until the storm passes."

"We're in Colorado. Snowstorms are normal here."

"Yes, but you live twenty minutes from the hospital on a good day. I don't want to risk you or your babies by sending you home," he said. "Honestly, I'm surprised you've been able to last this long."

Grace blew out a frustrated breath. What the doctor said made sense, but she didn't have to like it. "Will I at least be able to get up and walk around more? Staying in bed is getting old."

"I'm sure we can ease some of those restrictions. Give it another day and we'll let you take a walk around the floor."

"I'd rather be walking around my own house."

"It won't be much longer," Dr. Gilmore said.

"That's what I keep telling myself."

* * *

Devin navigated the familiar roads in the borrowed car. He supposed he should at least be thankful that after two years of attending Stanford, he was well acquainted with San Francisco and the various routes to the airport. Of course, the last few times he had flown in and out of this airport, he had been shuttling back and forth to see his wife. If only he knew that would be the end result this time.

As he'd been taught, he checked his mirrors to make sure no one was tailing him. Not that he expected anyone would be able to find him here. He took note of the vehicles behind him and turned his attention back to the traffic in front of him. His flight wasn't scheduled to leave until eight, but he knew how bad traffic could be in the city. Besides, he didn't want to take any chances of getting caught in security. The idea of traveling under a fake ID was stressful enough. He certainly didn't want to add to his stress by not having enough time to deal with any unforeseen problems.

He started over the Bay Bridge, the water of the San Francisco Bay mirroring the crisp blue sky. Construction on the bridge had backed up the steady stream of cars to a crawl for the first quarter mile. He checked his mirror again, mentally making a list: green minivan, gold BMW, black Jeep, blue Civic, two silver Camrys that could be twins.

One of the twins shifted lanes and attempted to pass him only to get cut off by the Jeep. The flow of traffic picked up slightly, and he switched lanes to get around a particularly slow Corvette. The red sports car tried to move at the same time, but Devin accelerated and forced his way forward before the driver managed to cut him off.

Why someone would spend ridiculous amounts of money on such a vehicle and then drive like a little old lady was beyond him. He looked to his left to see it was indeed someone on the elderly side driving, but Devin hadn't expected to find himself facing such danger.

The elderly Chinese man turned to look at him, a gun in his hand.

Devin ducked just as a gunshot sounded, the bullet shattering his driver's side window. The whole car shook with the impact, and Devin instinctively pressed on the gas. The brief question of why the man was shooting at him entered his mind, and he quickly dismissed it. He knew who wanted him dead. The real question was how he had been found.

Another shot rang out. Another window shattered.

Desperate for a means of escape, Devin jerked the wheel to the right and ran over two orange cones that cordoned off the closed lane. The tires thudded over the cones, and the front bumper of the car sent a third one flying.

Behind him, tires squealed, and someone honked.

He tried to concentrate on the maze ahead. The actual construction work was more than half a mile away, a dozen men wearing bright orange vests clustered in his lane along with several work vehicles.

Devin glanced behind him at the Corvette trying to follow his path, while the minivan cut the guy off. Devin sped up, bearing down on the construction workers, who were now scrambling to take shelter behind a dump truck.

His breathing coming rapidly, he checked his rearview mirror, no longer able to see his pursuer. With only twenty yards to spare, he slammed on the brakes, cranked the wheel, and cut back into traffic.

Two more cones went flying, and this time the accompanying honks came only an instant before his rear bumper clipped the car he had cut off.

He checked his mirrors again in time to see the driver throw his hands up in anger and the sports car trying to weave its way closer.

Devin was only halfway across the bridge, and the urge to flee overwhelmed him. He crept past the construction workers, ignoring more hand gestures, and analyzed his options once more. The actual roadwork and the work vehicles spanned only a few hundred yards. The moment he was past the last of it, Devin broke back across the barrier and stomped on the gas. He was only a quarter of a mile from the end of the bridge when he saw the sports car follow his path, the distance closing between them.

This time when he broke back into traffic, Devin laid on the horn and even signaled before cutting off a Lexus. Though the driver managed to miss Devin's car by only inches, his reflexes were sufficient to give Devin the wiggle room to enter traffic moments before reaching the end of the bridge.

He managed to move to the left again and tried to hide himself behind a rather large pickup truck. He could no longer see the sports car, but he could hear the revving engine moving at high speeds, followed by screeching wheels and honking horns.

The sounds were too close.

Think! Devin told himself.

He gripped the wheel tighter, his mind going over different routes he could use to evade and escape. He only hoped he could use his familiarity with the city to his advantage.

As soon as he passed the end of the bridge, traffic started flowing once more. He had gone only two blocks before his car shook and the back window shattered.

He ducked, glancing back to see a gun once again pointed in his direction, this time the driver's arm visible as he reached out and aimed.

Devin swerved to his right as the man pulled the trigger again. He jerked the wheel and made a quick turn, slowing enough to keep from letting the hill bottom out the car, and then made the first left.

As he was turning, he saw a glimpse of red. He made several more turns, each time not able to shake the man following him.

With less than a half mile between them, Devin turned onto Filbert Street, the steep hill leveling only at the intersections. As he had done far too often, he accelerated well above the speed limit on the inclines, braking hard right before each intersection. The car bottomed out at the second light, sending sparks flying. Another shot sounded. Devin sped up.

A red light ahead sent a tidal wave of fear through him. He couldn't stop. He couldn't go.

The rev of the Corvette's engine grew closer, and he knew he had little choice. He slammed on the brake, did a quick check of traffic, and cranked the wheel once more. His car skidded into the intersection, drifting as he made the sudden right, two wheels coming off the ground.

He threw his weight toward the passenger side, the car thudding back down with a bang.

Tires squealed behind him, and he looked back to see the sport car not only skid but lose traction through the turn. An oncoming car crashed into it and sent it rolling twice through the intersection before landing hard against the streetlight at the corner.

Devin was still debating whether he should go check the driver's condition when another car weaved past the wreckage and headed straight for him.

His eyes widened. Jalen sat behind the wheel of a gold BMW.

Punching the gas, Devin swerved back into his lane and accelerated. The car behind him already had more speed and quickly pulled up beside him. A man he hadn't seen before sat in the passenger's seat, holding a shotgun.

Out of sheer desperation, Devin slammed on the brakes. His new pursuer blasted past him before braking as well.

Devin did a quick U-turn, this time not pausing to consider the consequences when he blew through the red light. Car horns blared. More people had honked at him in the last ten minutes than over the past ten years.

His car rumbled over the trolley tracks, and his eyes searched for another way out. The simple sedan was designed to blend in, not outrun sport cars.

Three quick turns helped him maintain the slim distance between them, but he knew it wouldn't be much longer before Mr. Shotgun got off a clean round.

A bell rang, and a spurt of hope surfaced. Devin sped up. Anticipating his next move, he reached over and grabbed his backpack, slipping it over his shoulder as he drove. He couldn't let the laptop fall into the wrong hands.

A trolley came into sight, its bell ringing again as it left its stop.

Devin sped up until he was only a few yards from the rear of the trolley, then he screeched to a stop, turning his car so it blocked the entire right side of the road. He shoved open his car door and raced toward the back of the trolley. He hadn't run sprints since high school, but today he had no doubt both his old coach and Grace would be proud.

He didn't look back when he heard the brakes of the oncoming traffic, and he prayed the passengers on the trolley would provide him some protection from the gunman. He leapt onto the back of the trolley, grabbed the pole to keep from tumbling back onto the street, and imme-diately weaved his way through the crowded back section.

Finally, when he was surrounded by a dozen staring faces, he looked back at the havoc he had left behind him.

Chapter 37

DEVIN SHOULD HAVE KNOWN HIS stall tactics wouldn't work. The BMW had taken up position right behind the trolley, and it wasn't going anywhere until these men got what they wanted—him. He forced himself to look away from the men who wanted him dead and focus on where he was in the city and where they were headed.

He was still processing his location when the trolley driver announced, "Next stop: Lombard Street."

The crooked street, he always called it. With its ridiculously steep grade and eight hairpin turns, the one-block stretch of road had a posted speed limit of five miles per hour.

Devin pushed his way to the front of the trolley and exited with a handful of tourists. He managed to shield himself behind a particularly broad-shouldered man for the first few yards. Then the crowd spread out, and he felt his vulnerability.

Though he knew better than to look back, he did anyway. As he'd feared, the men chasing him were right behind the trolley.

The shotgun barrel appeared out the window once more, and Devin sprinted toward the nearest building. He never heard the expected gunshot.

After plastering himself against the brick wall, he leaned out the few inches required for him to view Hyde Street. When he saw the car heading down the brick road, he bolted toward the footpath leading along the side of Lombard Street. It was a more direct route to the bottom of the winding road, but it was also crowded with people.

"Coming through!" he shouted, pressing past a mom and daughter. The thought of these men shooting into the crowd made him add, "Gun! Get down!"

That comment had much more effect. Someone screamed behind him, and the people in front of him ducked behind hedges and scurried into bushes.

With the path now relatively clear, he took the steps two at a time. A horn blared, and Devin glanced over long enough to see the BMW nearly bumper to bumper with the hatchback in front of it.

Hope surged at the sight of the obstacle in its path, and he picked up speed. He made it down the equivalent of four flights of stairs before he had to shout again in an attempt to clear his way. "Coming through!" he yelled, his breathing now labored.

The sound of an engine revving followed by a screech of brakes drew attention once more. The hatchback that had been holding traffic to the snail-paced speed limit had pulled into a parking alcove at one of the bends in the road.

The hand that had previously been holding a shotgun now gripped a pistol.

"Gun! Get down!" Devin repeated with only moderate success. The pedestrians who had ignored his warning all had second thoughts when the gun fired.

Devin ducked at the sound and took a quick look around to see if there had been any casualties. Thankfully, the only people on the ground were those who had taken cover with him behind the low barrier wall that separated the path from the street.

Afraid the next shot would be more accurate, he held his position, searching for an escape.

The brakes squealed again, but this time he heard the crunch of metal against stone, the ground beneath him vibrating with the impact. He looked over the edge and saw that the driver had taken a turn too fast and had hit the wall only a few yards away.

Devin was nearly halfway down the winding path and considered a new option.

As though a starting gun had gone off, Devin sprang up and sprinted once more, only this time, instead of heading toward the bottom, he reversed his course and started back the way he had come.

The grinding of gears and the scrape of metal filled the air as the car started forward again. In the distance, police sirens wailed, and Devin hoped they were heading his way.

On the steep one-way street, his pursuers had to continue forward, and Devin hoped he could disappear before they reached the bottom and circled back to the top.

The muscles in his legs burned, but he forced himself to keep moving. The bell from the trolley rang again, and he was nearly to the top when he saw it pulling to a stop across the street from where he had gotten off a few minutes earlier.

Out of breath, he kept sprinting and jumped onto the running board as the conductor started to pull away. Devin dug in his pocket, paid the fare, and looked back down Lombard Street. The BMW was nowhere in sight.

Keeping his spot on the running board, Devin pulled his cell phone from his pocket and dialed.

"Someone's after me," Devin said the moment he heard Ghost's voice on the line. He noticed some odd glances from his fellow passengers, but at the moment, he didn't care.

"Are you in immediate danger?"

"I lost them, but I don't know for how long. I'm on the trolley, and it isn't exactly the fastest mode of transportation."

"Where are you?"

"San Francisco." Devin looked up at the cross street and relayed his current position.

"There's a market on the edge of Chinatown." Ghost gave Devin the address. "I'll have someone meet you there in fifteen minutes."

"What if they find me again?"

"Keep your head down. We'll get you out of there."

"I'm counting on it."

Devin disconnected the call and willed his heartbeat to slow, but the adrenaline pumping through him kept his body from cooperating. He could feel the energy surging, and he waited anxiously for the trolley to reach his stop.

He hopped onto the street before the trolley reached a complete stop, and he headed for the center of Chinatown. Even though the shop where Devin was supposed to meet his contact was several blocks away, he had enough time to kill that he didn't want to go directly there. Besides, he had been trained better than that.

The smell of Chinese food permeated the air along with an underlying scent of fish and garlic. The signs on the storefronts displayed Chinese characters and only occasionally offered the English translation below them. Round paper lanterns hung on thin wires stretched across the street. He let himself get swallowed up by the foot traffic on the sidewalk, his height betraying him over the locals of Asian descent.

A clothing shop caught his eye, and he walked with purpose toward it. Five other people were inside, a middle-aged Chinese man sitting beside a cash register.

Devin zeroed in on a rack of jackets. He riffled through them, selecting one in black leather. Working his way farther into the store, he found a selection of 49ers apparel. It seemed a bit out of place in Chinatown but fit his needs beautifully.

He took a scarf and a baseball cap from the rack and carried them with the jacket to the cashier.

After exchanging cash for the items, he removed the tags, pulled the jacket over his faded blue sweatshirt, and donned the scarf and ball cap.

Slipping his backpack over his shoulder again, he approached the entrance of the store, looking both ways before stepping onto the sidewalk. He was just turning to his right when he saw a gold BMW turn the corner, a huge dent in the front fender.

Devin mustered every ounce of strength he had to continue onto the sidewalk, his path putting his back to the driver of the vehicle. His breath backed up in his lungs, and he struggled against the urge to flee.

The lessons learned during his summers with the CIA replayed through his mind. *Relax. Move casually with purpose. Don't look back.*

With the changes he'd made in his clothing, he wouldn't be recognizable from the back. He kept reminding himself of that fact as he walked, the sound of each car passing him sending waves of apprehension through him. Less than a minute after he spotted the BMW, it slowly passed by. He tried to keep his gaze lowered enough to avoid recognition, but his effort wasn't rewarded.

The car was only ten yards past him when the driver suddenly slammed on the brakes.

Devin didn't know it was possible for his heart to beat any faster, but he discovered he was wrong when he saw the passenger jump out of the car and start running toward him. Panicked, Devin took off, pushing people away as he wove through the crowd. He was less than a block from the market where help was supposed to meet him, but he'd never make it that far. All it would take was one gunshot into the air for the crowd to scatter and for his pursuer to get a clear shot at him.

Sure enough, a gunshot sounded behind him, accompanied by screams and racing footsteps. Devin reached the corner of a building and ducked into the narrow alleyway between it and the building beside it. In front of him, clotheslines stretched between the two structures, many of them hanging only five feet from the ground.

Devin ducked under the first one, using pants and shirts to create a shield. He zigzagged between articles of clothing, several pulling free and flying through the air.

Footsteps pounded behind him, stutter stepping through the hanging obstacles.

Devin reached the back corner of the building to his left and made a sharp turn behind it the instant a shot fired. The brick inches from his head thudded with the impact, little bits flying into the air.

More low-lying clotheslines hung in his path, and he didn't know whether to bless or curse their presence.

When they were suddenly behind him and he found himself in an open space, he decided he preferred the obstacles to being out in the open.

He saw the cross street two buildings in front of him and increased his speed. The building he was supposed to meet in was right before him if he could only make it.

Had it been fifteen minutes yet since he had talked to Ghost? It felt like an eternity and only an instant at the same time.

He glanced back to see the man behind him fighting his way free of a dangling pair of slacks.

Devin rushed to the back door of the market and barged through it into a storage room. With little time to spare, he continued through the storage area, a meat locker on his right and tanks of live fish on his left.

He noticed a small hallway just beyond the tanks and hoped it would provide him an alternate exit or at least some kind of cover. He was nearly around the corner before he looked up and saw Chee standing in front of him, a pistol in hand.

Devin skidded to a stop, stunned to see his old handler in front of him.

Chee reached out with his free hand and grabbed him by the arm, yanking him into the hallway beside him. "Are you okay?" he asked in Mandarin, his voice low.

"One of them is right behind me," Devin managed to say. "What are you doing here?"

"Ghost sent me to provide support." Chee waved for him to take position behind him. "Stay back."

Devin did as he was told, pressing himself behind Chee just as they heard the back door open again. Chee shifted silently to the edge of the hallway.

Each second seemed an eternity, soft footsteps steadily moving forward, the man clearly searching the locker and tank area before continuing toward their hiding place.

The moment the man came into view, Chee took aim. "Freeze!"

The man didn't freeze. His gun hand lifted, but Chee didn't let him aim. He squeezed the trigger and fired once, which was all it took to drop the man where he stood.

Whatever remorse Chee felt over killing the other man was pushed aside as he immediately turned to Devin. "How many more are there?"

"The only other person I saw was Jalen," Devin responded. "Last time I saw him, he was driving a gold BMW with the front fender smashed in."

"Stay here. I'm going to coordinate with the authorities to make sure we have him in custody before we take you back outside."

Devin nodded his agreement. "Be careful."

"It's not me he's looking for," Chee reminded him. "Don't worry. I'll find him."

Chapter 38

"Good morning, Miss Grace."

Grace looked up to see Jun standing in the doorway. "Jun, come in."

"How are you feeling today?"

"Fat." She put her hand over her stomach. "I think I'm about ready to meet these little ones."

"Did the doctor say how much longer?"

"He thinks sometime this week." Suddenly wistful, she added, "I wish Devin was here."

"I'm sure he'll be here soon."

Though she rarely voiced her fears out loud, she let herself trust the woman who held such a large piece of her husband's heart. "What if he hasn't called me because he can't? For all I know, he could be hurt or even worse."

"Don't think like that. Your husband will do everything he can to make sure you both stay safe."

"In my mind, I want to believe that, but after all these months of not hearing from him, I'm starting to wonder."

"Devin has a good heart. He'll find you. And we'll both be waiting for him when he does."

* * *

Devin watched Chee go, a vulnerable feeling swamping over him the moment his companion left through the front entrance. Unarmed, Devin headed back toward the meat locker to search for anything that would give him a sense of security.

He opened the locker, his only viable option being two huge metal hooks on a shelf near the door. He picked one up, testing its weight. It was heavy and felt unbalanced in his hand.

Deciding it was better than nothing, he exited the freezer and closed the door firmly behind him. When he looked across the wide hallway, he discovered a better weapon. On a worktable near the fish tanks lay a butcher's knife.

He started toward it, but when the rear entrance opened, he lifted the hook and wielded it over his shoulder.

The young woman who entered screamed and scurried back the way she had come.

"Sorry!" Devin called after her, first in English and then in Mandarin. He suspected by the time he'd offered his second apology, she was well out of earshot.

Though he felt guilty for scaring her, he pushed the incident from his mind and crossed the room to retrieve his new weapon.

He turned when he heard the door opening again, expecting that the girl might be returning with the police. Instead he found a nightmare staring back at him.

"You're not an easy man to find," Jalen muttered as he lifted his gun hand. The brief hesitation in his eyes indicated he wasn't the type who was used to doing his own dirty work.

Devin wasn't going to wait to see if the man was capable of pulling the trigger. He lifted his hand and released the knife.

Jalen reacted to Devin's movement and jumped to his right, but he wasn't quick enough to avoid the knife completely.

He cried out in pain when the blade dug into his shoulder, his weapon dropping to the floor. He pulled the knife out of his flesh with another cry of pain and scanned the floor in search of his weapon. Before he managed to locate it, Devin rushed forward and tackled him around the waist, both of them crashing to the ground. Jalen tried to twist away as he continued searching for his gun.

Devin caught a glimpse of it and kicked it hard, sending it skidding across the hall until it thudded against one of the fish tanks.

Once the weapon was out of play, Jalen took a new tactic, his fist shooting out to connect with Devin's jaw.

Devin landed a punch of his own, the two men scuffling on the floor and finally managing to stand. Devin had barely regained his balance when Jalen struck out again and sent Devin back another step. He retreated into the fish room, careful to keep his body between Jalen and where the gun had landed.

"Why me?" Devin asked.

Jalen pressed his hand against his wounded shoulder and glared. "Does it matter?"

"Of course it matters. I don't understand how you could betray our country or why you would want me to do the same."

"You had everything we needed to be the perfect spy. You spoke the language and knew the culture. You had access to your father, something we have lost." He took a step toward the door.

Devin countered his move. "Just because I spoke the language didn't mean I would betray my country."

"You were looking for a sense of family. My employers thought they could give you that."

Devin *had* been searching for something, but he'd found it long before he'd made it to Hong Kong—he'd found it with Grace. "And now you want to kill me because I wasn't interested?"

"It's a matter of pride with the Chinese. You should know that." Whatever hesitation Jalen had experienced when he'd first arrived was gone. Now all Devin could see was his determination. He changed positions again, and again Devin mirrored his movement. "Besides, it was you or me."

"It's not going to be me," Devin stated firmly.

Jalen leaned over, but before Devin recognized his intention, Jalen reached down and retrieved a second gun holstered at his ankle.

Devin stumbled back and dove into the tank room. A bullet whizzed inches from his head, followed by the crack of glass and a flood of water and fish.

Jalen continued into the room, the loss of blood causing his movements to grow sluggish. Devin took another step back, and his foot connected with something solid. He realized what it was and dropped to the ground just as a second shot sounded. Another tank bit the dust, and more fish flooded onto the floor.

Devin reached out and gripped the solid metal hook from the meat locker.

This time when Jalen took aim, Devin swung the hook with all his might. The edge caught Jalen across both arms and sent him stumbling forward. He was still off balance when Devin lifted the hook over his head and brought it down on top of Jalen's back. Though he hit him with the curved back of the hook, the force was enough to send Jalen sprawling.

Devin kicked the second gun away as the back door opened.

Chee walked inside to find Devin breathing heavily, Jalen now lying on the floor.

Not daring to make the same mistake twice, Devin collected the two guns and looked up at Chee. "I found him."

* * *

Devin and Chee stood on the street in Chinatown and watched the police take Jalen away. The officers had taken more than an hour to ask questions and process the scene before finally telling them they were free to go. Devin glanced down at his watch.

"I think I missed my flight."

"I'll get you on the next one," Chee told him. "We need you to see if you can locate Jun."

Devin looked over at him. His hands were still shaking from the adrenaline rush that hadn't yet subsided. He'd nearly been shot a number of times, and now Chee expected him to go right back to work. "You have to be kidding me."

"She's the last link, Devin. We find her and you get your life back."

"I need to find my wife. That's what I need to get my life back."

"We've narrowed the search down to Vail, and we even have her address."

"Then you found her."

"No. We have her post office box."

"Has anyone tried searching for her that way?"

"We tried a couple times, but the FBI's staffing wasn't sufficient to go for more than a couple days at a time. It's possible she only picks up her mail once a week or she has someone else doing it for her."

"What makes you think I'll have any more luck?"

"Vail has less than twenty thousand residents. You'll find her because you won't stop until you do. Besides, when you're in Sedona, you might find someone who knows where she is."

"One of my friends flew her to Vail. He has to know where she lives."

"Then find him," Chee said. "But first, find Jun."

Chapter 39

THE LAST PLACE DEVIN THOUGHT his intelligence career would take him was back to Sedona, and he certainly hadn't expected to come back with a pistol strapped to his ankle and a second holstered in his waistband. Chee had arranged for him to pick up the weapons upon his arrival in Phoenix. A precaution, he had called it. After what happened in San Francisco, he wasn't sure what the agency expected him to find in his hometown.

When Fai had first approached him last July, he had been certain there had been some sort of mistaken identity. How else could Fai think his father could be of use to him? Now he knew better.

Devin followed the familiar route to his childhood home and pulled into the drive beside his father's secretary's car. He drew a deep breath before climbing out and heading for the front door. He rapped a knuckle on the door but didn't wait for an answer before pushing it open.

Instead of finding his parents or Liwei approaching the door, Maureen rounded the corner from her office just beside his father's.

"Devin. I didn't know you were back in the country," she said.

"I just got back yesterday. Is my dad around?"

"No. I'm afraid he is in Zurich this week."

"What about my mom?"

She shook her head. "She and Liwei are in town meeting with a caterer about the New Year's party she's planning. They should be back in a couple hours."

"I don't suppose you know where Jun is these days, do you?" Devin asked, taking advantage of the only source he had available at the moment. "I stopped by her place, but the manager said she moved out a couple months ago."

"She got a job as a nanny out of state. Sorry, but I don't know exactly where."

"That's okay." He took a step toward the door.

"Your mom might have her contact information. Do you want me to have her call you?"

"Yeah. That would be great." Devin started to leave before he remembered he had changed phone numbers three times since he'd spoken to his mother last. "I have a new number. You'll probably want to write it down."

Maureen pulled her own phone out of her jacket pocket and unlocked the screen. "Go ahead."

Devin gave her his number and opened the door. "Tell my mom I'll try to swing back by later."

"I will."

With nothing else he could do at the moment to search for Jun, he headed for Caleb's parents' house. With the loss of his cell phone in Hong Kong, he didn't have any of his contact numbers. Hopefully, he could get Caleb's number from his parents and ultimately track down Sean.

If Devin had to stake out the post office in Vail, he would, but that photo of Grace in Sean's plane made him hopeful that his friend would be able to lead him to her.

* * *

"Caleb!" Devin stood on the doorstep, stunned to see his friend answer the door rather than one of his parents. "I didn't expect you to be here."

"Then why are you knocking on my door?" Caleb asked with a grin.

"Trying to track you down."

"I'm easy to find. You, on the other hand, dropped off the face of the earth." Caleb waved him inside. "Where have you been? I haven't talked to you in months."

"I've been doing a lot of traveling."

"And that means you can't pick up the phone?"

"Actually, I lost my phone and all my contacts with it."

"We might forgive you, then." He headed for the kitchen. "Come say hi to Molly."

Molly's face lit up when they entered the open space, the wide window in the kitchenette displaying the backyard and the Sedona red rocks. "Hello, stranger." She circled the counter so she could give him a hug. "I haven't seen you since our wedding."

"I know. It's been almost a year," Devin said, all too aware that their anniversary was approaching. After all, he and Grace had gotten married the same day. "Any chance either of you have Sean's phone number? I need to ask him something kind of important."

"Actually, he's in the other room talking to my dad," Caleb said. "He's flying us up to Colorado today to go skiing."

"Sean's here?"

"Yeah."

Before Devin could press for more information, Molly said, "Caleb, I'm still not sure about going up with Sean. Flying in a little plane might not be the best idea for me right now."

"Is something wrong?" Devin asked, noting for the first time that she did look a bit pale.

"She's been having a lot of morning sickness the past few weeks," Caleb answered for her.

"Morning sickness? That must be going around. Grace said she had that the last time I talked to her."

Molly grabbed his arm. "Grace is pregnant? No way!"

"Pregnant?" Devin repeated, confused. If Grace was pregnant, she would have told him.

"Yeah." Molly rolled her eyes. "That's why women get morning sickness."

Sean walked into the room while Devin tried to replay his last conversation with Grace in his mind. She had seemed a little put off at his reaction, but he had been so distracted that he thought it had been because he'd said they wouldn't be able to talk for a few days.

"Are you guys talking about Molly or Grace?" Sean asked.

Molly turned to face him, her expression a study in frustration. "You knew Grace was pregnant and didn't tell us?"

"I figured you all knew." Sean looked at Devin, confused. "Wait. How didn't you know? I thought you two were married."

"*What?*" Molly's voice rose to an uncomfortably high octave.

"Back up." Caleb held up a hand. "You and Grace got married? When?"

"The same day you did," Devin said. He turned back to Sean. "You saw her a couple months ago, right?"

"Yeah. I ran into her at her grandfather's in Vail." Sean's eyebrows drew together. "You look like you got hit by a truck. Maybe you should sit down."

"No, I need to see Grace." Devin kept his focus on Sean. "Caleb said you were flying everyone up to Colorado. Were you going to Vail?"

"Yeah. We were going to stay at the resort where Grace lives."

"Can you take me there?"

"No problem," Sean said. "But we need to go within the next couple hours. I don't like to fly into Colorado after dark. Too much chance of ice."

"I'm ready now," Devin said.

Sean turned to Caleb. "How about you guys?"

"Yeah, we're ready," Caleb said.

"Then let's go."

Chapter 40

DEVIN'S THOUGHTS WERE FILLED WITH Grace on the flight to Colorado. How far along was she? Was she feeling okay? When would the baby come? How would he adjust to fatherhood? The questions felt endless, and he couldn't wait to find the answers.

He was beyond grateful that Sean already had a rental car waiting for them when they arrived in Vail. His friends had made a few attempts to clarify why Devin hadn't seen Grace in so long, but other than saying he had been out of the country, he didn't elaborate, and they stopped asking.

The ranch was only twenty minutes from the airport, and Devin was surprised at the size of the house. After seeing the modest-sized ranch house Quentin had lived in last Christmas, Devin had expected this house to be comparable. Instead he found an elegant home probably twice the square footage of Quentin's previous residence.

"Does Grace live in the main house?" Devin asked.

"Yeah." Sean motioned to a nearby bungalow. "That's where we need to check in."

"I think I'll go up to the house with Devin to see Grace," Molly said.

Devin wanted time alone with his wife, especially since his explanation of his disappearance was largely classified, so he was grateful when Caleb put his hand on his wife's arm and said, "Why don't you let Devin and Grace have some time together while we check in? I'm sure we'll have a chance to hang out later."

Before Molly could object, Devin started toward the house and called over his shoulder, "I'll catch you all later." He jogged across the snowy lawn and onto the covered porch, his backpack bouncing against his shoulder. He rapped on the door, waiting for a minute before repeating the action.

When no one answered, he turned back to where his friends had been standing a moment before.

Frustrated, he started toward the welcome bungalow. He was halfway there when a man around twenty rode up on horseback and appeared to be heading to the barn a short distance away.

Devin waved a hand in greeting, and the man guided his horse toward him.

"Can I help you?"

"Yes, I'm looking for Grace Shanahan."

"Sorry, she isn't here right now. Can I get a message to her?"

"Do you know where she is?" The man looked hesitant, so Devin added, "I'm Devin Shanahan, Grace's husband."

Instantly the man's demeanor changed. "I was wondering when you were going to show up. Looks like you're here just in time."

"Just in time?"

"Grace has been in the hospital for the past couple weeks. Quentin is up visiting her right now."

"Is she okay?"

"Seemed to be last time I saw her."

"Can you tell me where the hospital is?"

"Sure." He swung down out of the saddle and gave Devin directions. Digging a set of keys out of his pocket, he unclipped one and handed it to Devin. "Here. You can take one of the ranch vehicles. This key is to the red truck over there."

"Are you sure?"

"Yeah. I'm sure Quentin would offer it if he was here."

"Thanks a lot. I really appreciate it."

"Give Grace my best."

"I didn't catch your name."

"I'm Curt."

Devin shook Curt's hand. "Thanks again for your help, Curt."

With a nod, Curt took his horse's reins and started toward the barn once more.

Devin headed the other direction, his pace quickening as he approached the truck.

He climbed into the work vehicle, adjusted the seat, and headed out. Thirty minutes later, he showed his ID at the visitors' desk and headed toward his wife's room.

He passed a small waiting area and heard someone call his name. He took two more steps, thinking whoever it was was talking to another Devin.

"Devin." A man's voice called out a second time.

He turned as Quentin rose from a chair in the waiting room. The protectiveness Devin had observed at their first meeting was nothing compared to the wave of hostility emanating from the older man now.

Deciding Grace's grandfather deserved whatever explanation he could give, Devin closed the distance between them. "Before you go home and get your shotgun, I promise you, I would have been here months ago if I could have."

"What in the world was important enough to keep you away for so long?" Quentin demanded.

"Grace's safety."

"*Grace's safety?*" The look on Quentin's face made Devin think he should duck to avoid a punch.

"Yes." Devin raked his fingers through his hair. "I can't explain, at least not right now, but I've never stopped loving her, and I've been through a lot to get here."

"*You've* been through a lot?" He folded his arms across his chest. "Grace has been through hell. First those guys break into her apartment, and then she ends up living with me, hoping you would come back but terrified something had happened to you."

"Does she know who broke into her apartment?"

"Some Chinese nationals. The cops picked one of them up, but he had diplomatic immunity so they had to let him go." Quentin lowered his voice. "Grace has a theory as to why she hasn't heard from you. From what I understand, it's not something we would want to discuss in public."

Devin's heart squeezed in his chest. "Please tell me she doesn't hate me."

"Until she ended up here, I'd catch her staring out the window every day. She knew you'd find her eventually," Quentin said. "That's not to say she's going to roll out the red carpet. I imagine you have some groveling to do. Disappearing out of your wife's life for six months isn't exactly something that's going to be forgiven overnight."

Five months, two weeks, and four days, Devin thought to himself.

"Is her room that way?" Devin asked.

"The doctor is with her now."

"Is she okay?"

"She went into labor three weeks ago. The doctors were able to stop it in time, but they kept her here to be safe."

"I need to see her."

"The doctor will come out as soon as he's done."

"But she's okay."

"Yeah, she's okay."

Devin rubbed both hands over his face, his relief over her safety combining with anxiety over how she would react now that he was back. He tried to bank his emotions and looked once more at Quentin. "I promise, I came as soon as I could. I still can't believe I didn't know she was pregnant."

"You didn't know she was pregnant?"

Devin shook his head. "Not until Sean told me today."

A doctor exited a room three doors down and headed toward them.

"Dr. Gilmore, this is Devin Shanahan, Grace's husband."

The doctor extended his hand. "I didn't realize you were in town."

"I just arrived." Devin pointed toward Grace's room. "Is everything okay?"

"Everything is going well. As I told your wife, we expect she will be able to deliver any time now."

Devin didn't want to admit to a stranger that he was unaware of his wife's condition. It had been hard enough to admit his ignorance to her grandfather. Instead, he asked, "May I see her?"

"Go ahead."

"Devin, tell Grace I'll be back to visit her again tomorrow. I think you two need some time alone."

"Thank you." Devin headed for Grace's door and stopped a few feet from the opening. He took a deep breath and prayed that his wife would be happy to see him.

Chapter 41

SHE MUST BE HALLUCINATING. GRACE blinked three times, but instead of the image of her husband disappearing, Devin moved farther into the room and closed the door behind him.

"Devin?" She shifted in her bed, blinking several more times, now to fight against the tears that sprang to her eyes as a result of her conflicting emotions—relief, irritation, love, frustration. First and foremost, she needed to make sure she really wasn't dreaming. "Is that really you?"

"It's me." He crossed to her, and she sensed his hesitation.

"Where have you been? How could you just stop calling me like that for so long?"

"I know you may not believe this, but I was trying to protect you." Devin lowered himself onto the chair beside her bed, and she couldn't help but see the tormented expression on his face. "You must hate me."

"I could never hate you, but I need to understand what happened. Why did you stop calling me?"

"I'm so sorry. I swear if there had been a way to contact you, I would have."

The sharpest edge of the worry and doubts she had suffered over the past months eased when he reached out and took her hand. Not quite ready to forgive him, she kept her hand palm down. "Can you tell me what happened?" Grace asked. "Were you in Hong Kong this whole time?"

Devin looked around the room as though analyzing it, then lowered his voice. "I can't say much here, but there's a lot I haven't told you about who I work for."

Grace drew a deep breath. As much as she wanted to simply accept him back into her life, she needed to know if he was going to stay. "I need to know where you were, Devin. I need to know you aren't going to disappear like this again."

"I'll do whatever I can to make sure this doesn't happen again," Devin said. He pressed his lips together and seemed to muster his courage. "I work for the CIA."

The words felt surreal even after all of her suspicions. "Grandpa thought I was crazy when I said I had married a spy."

"You got my message."

"I didn't understand it, but I knew it was from you." Her eyes met his. "You should have told me who you worked for before we got married."

"I thought I was going to be working in an office somewhere. I never knew I was going to be asked to work in the field until the assignment had already been processed. And I certainly wouldn't have gone overseas had I known it would put you in danger."

"Grandpa told you about the break-in at my apartment in New York, then?"

"He did." Devin looked around the room again. "I wanted to come back so badly, but some of the people there were threatening you. I couldn't risk your safety. You mean everything to me."

The concern in his eyes told her just how serious the threats had been, and a ripple of fear shot through her. "Are we safe now?"

"I think so. I have people making sure we stay that way." He seemed like he was going to say something else, but instead he waved at her enormous abdomen. "I feel like such an idiot. I had no idea you were pregnant."

"I couldn't figure out why you were so casual about it when I said I had morning sickness."

"I didn't realize that meant . . ."

"It's okay." She managed a watery smile. "Although I had a nice little gift I was going to bring to you when we met in London. I was going to tell you then. I hoped you would be excited about the news."

"I never really thought about being a father before, but now I can't think of anything I want more than to start a family with you. I'm sorry I ruined your surprise when I had to cancel our trip." He shook his head. "You must have been ready to shoot me."

"The thought may have crossed my mind," Grace said. "I guess at that point it was a good thing we were living on opposite sides of the world."

"I'm here now," Devin said, stating the obvious. "And I want to stay with you from now on if you'll let me."

Grace blinked, and a tear spilled over. She turned her hand so she could link her fingers with his.

He stood and reached out to wipe away the tear. Then he leaned down, hesitating only briefly before he pressed his lips to hers.

As though the babies knew what was happening, a ripple of movement distorted her stomach further.

When Devin pulled back, she took his hand and pressed it to her stomach. "Here. Feel."

Almost instantly another movement rolled beneath his palm. The wonder in his eyes made her smile. "Pretty amazing, huh?"

"Yeah," he said, though he suddenly looked panicked. "I'm really going to be a father?"

"Any day now." She watched him closely. "Sorry you didn't have more time to get used to the idea, but—"

"You tried to warn me," he finished for her. He hesitated a moment before asking, "Are you okay with all this?"

"I am. How about you?"

He didn't speak for a moment, and a little thread of doubt skittered through her. If he had doubts now, how would he feel when she told him the rest? She opened her mouth, and once again, his words sounded before she could form hers.

"I need you to promise me something," Devin said.

"Okay."

"Promise me we'll be like your family. I want to be like your dad and grandpa. I want to be involved in our kid's life."

"Devin, you'll be a wonderful father."

"I have a pretty big learning curve."

"I don't think it's nearly as big as you think." Grace pushed up in her bed, trying to get comfortable, but the dull ache in her back didn't seem to go away with the change in position. She rested her hand on her stomach and looked down at it. "I never thought it was possible for me to be this big."

He put his hand on hers, his expression serious. "You're beautiful."

Her lips curved. "That was a really good answer."

"I mean it."

"There's something else you need to know."

"What?"

The ache in her back increased, and she shifted again. Within seconds, her breath caught as the pain spread and her heartbeat quickened in anticipation. She recognized the sensation now and gripped Devin's hand as the pain built and her stomach tightened. She closed her eyes, keeping her breathing steady until the worst of it passed. When she opened her eyes once more, concern washed over her husband's face.

"What's wrong? Are you okay?" he asked.

"Devin, call the doctor. I think I'm going into labor."

* * *

Never before had Devin felt so helpless. Nurses arrived within a minute of receiving the call, shuffling around equipment and speaking in terms he didn't understand. The doctor arrived a moment later.

"Let's see how we're doing," Dr. Gilmore said, his eyes lifting to look at a monitor. "Everything is looking good. Can you feel the babies moving?"

Grace opened her eyes, the pain apparently easing for a moment. "I can feel them."

"Them?" Devin's already turbulent emotions turned into a tornado inside him. His eyes darted up to the fetal monitor and back to Grace. "Twins?"

Grace didn't answer. She couldn't. Another surge of pain had rendered her speechless. Her eyes closed again as though that might block any unwanted sensations, and Devin looked over to Dr. Gilmore for confirmation.

"Twins," he stated simply. He examined Grace before speaking once more. "I have a few more patients to check on, but a nurse will stay close by. I imagine it will be a few hours before your little ones will make their appearance."

Stunned, Devin watched the doctor strip off his gloves and leave the room. He couldn't quite wrap his mind around the idea of being a father to one child, much less two. When Grace's pain subsided, he reached out and took her hand. Whether he was ready for fatherhood or not, he was determined to be here for Grace now.

For the next eight hours, he stood by Grace's side and watched her try to shut out the pain. He knew her rhythm now. The moment the contraction began to build, her eyes would close and her breathing pattern would change. At first her breathing slowed as she worked through the contractions, but now her breaths were short and shallow.

Nurses had come in and out to check on them, but now the room was crowded with hospital personnel. Besides Grace's regular doctor, a pediatrician had joined them for the impending delivery as well as two nurses.

"Okay, Grace. Almost there," Dr. Gilmore encouraged her. "One more good push."

Devin watched her body tense, and then it was over, and the baby cried.

Devin looked from Grace to the miracle that had come from her—the miracle that had come from them. The pink little face scrunched in dismay, and their baby let out another wail. The emotions that shot through him were indescribable.

"We've got a girl," Dr. Gilmore announced. He handed the baby to the nurse, who had stepped forward.

"She's beautiful," Devin murmured and reached for Grace's hand. "Just like her mother."

Grace's body relaxed briefly and then, as though her labor had never ceased, her hand gripped his like a vice.

"Okay, Grace. One more time," Dr. Gilmore encouraged.

"I don't think I can do this," Grace said, looking desperate and exhausted.

"You can do it," Dr. Gilmore said. "I see the head."

Two minutes later, Devin watched their second miracle being born.

* * *

Grace opened her eyes, feeling like she was waking up from a nightmare to find the sun finally peeking out over the horizon. The moment she stirred, Devin crossed the room to her.

"How are you feeling?"

"Like I was run over by a truck."

"That's not surprising."

"How are the babies?" Grace asked.

"Beautiful, strong, healthy." Devin beamed down at her. "I can't believe we have two daughters."

"I can't believe you made it back for their birthday."

"I guess it's been a day for miracles." An odd expression crossed his face. "What are we going to name them?"

"I was thinking about Madeline Rose and Lydia Catherine."

"Rose after your mother, and Catherine after mine."

"Is that okay? I know you aren't very close to your parents, but I kind of like the idea of using family names."

"I do too."

Someone knocked on the door, and then two nurses entered, each pushing a bassinet with a baby wrapped in a white, blue, and pink striped blanket.

"The doctor said these little ones did great on their hearing tests."

Grace pushed herself up in her bed and held her arms out when the nurse closest to her settled one of the babies into her arms. The love that flowed through her was instant and overwhelming. The sensation repeated when her second daughter was placed into the crook of Devin's arm.

"We'll give you a few minutes with the babies before you feed them," one nurse said. "I'll come back in a little bit to see if you need any help."

"Thank you."

Grace stared down at the infant in her arms and then studied the baby Devin held. "What do you think?"

"I think I'm holding Madeline."

Her smile was instant. "Then this must be Lydia."

"I hope the nurses can give us some advice on how to tell them apart."

Another knock sounded at the door, and Grace smiled when her grandfather peeked in.

"Come meet your great-granddaughters," Grace said.

"My goodness, are they tiny." He closed the distance between them and reached down to touch Lydia. She wrapped her hand around his finger, and Grace could swear she saw a bond between them developing already.

"Congratulations, Grace. Your mom and dad would be so happy for you."

Tears welled up in her eyes. "I know they would."

Chapter 42

DEVIN HELD LITTLE LYDIA, THEIR oldest, against his shoulder and patted her back. Grace had already fed her, and he had been given the job of burping her.

Quentin's mention of Grace's parents stirred the realization within him that he needed to tell his own of their expanded family.

Lydia burped much louder than seemed possible from such a tiny being, and Devin looked over at Grace to see her amusement.

Awed both by his sudden fatherhood and by his wife's reaction to his return, Devin settled down in the rocking chair beside Grace's bed.

Lydia scrunched her little body, and he kept her firmly against him until she snuggled into him and her breathing grew steady.

"I think you're a natural." Grace moved Madeline to her shoulder to burp her as well.

"Hardly. This is the first time I've ever been around babies."

"You're about to make up for lost time."

His eyes locked on hers. "I'm looking forward to it."

Someone knocked at the room next door, and Lydia tensed. Devin patted her on the back again until she calmed.

"I was just thinking I should probably call my parents and tell them about our daughters."

"Lydia's asleep. Why don't you put her in her bassinet and call now," Grace suggested. "You'll feel better when you get it over with."

"You know me too well."

Devin put his hand against the back of Lydia's head and positioned himself by her bassinet. Gently he lowered her into it, not daring to breathe until he was certain she wasn't going to wake back up.

Not wanting any more secrets between them, he looked down at Grace. "You should know that my parents think we broke up."

"Did you tell them that?"

"No, but I let my dad think it," Devin said. "Our work paths crossed, and I needed to be able to talk to him without our relationship clouding his judgment."

"What are you going to tell them now?"

"The truth." He pulled his cell phone from his pocket to find he hadn't turned it on after his flight from Sedona. He waited for it to power up and tried to rehearse the upcoming conversation in his mind. Realizing that thinking about it would only make it worse, he dialed his father's phone number.

"Hello?" Boyd answered.

"Dad, it's me."

"Devin. We've been worried about you. I haven't heard from you since I saw you in Tokyo."

"I know it's been awhile, but I have some great news to share."

"You already got a promotion?"

"Even better." Devin didn't give him the chance to offer a second guess. "You and Mom are grandparents. Grace delivered twin girls today."

Silence stretched over the line for a moment. "Was child support outlined in your divorce decree?"

"Well, here's the thing, Dad. Grace and I are still married, and we intend to stay that way," Devin said, taking care to be firm without crossing the line into confrontational. "We both hope you and Mom will want to be part of our lives and our children's lives."

"I see," Boyd said tightly. Devin could hear his mother saying something in the background and some whispered response from his father. When his dad came back on the line, he said, "Your mom wants to talk to you."

Devin could hear the phone being handed off.

"Devin, did your father just say Grace had a baby?"

"Actually, she had twins. Madeline Rose and Lydia Catherine," Devin said.

"Lydia Catherine?"

"Yes. We hope you don't mind that we named her after you."

She took a moment to respond, and when she did, Devin could hear the tears in her voice. "Of course I don't mind." She sniffled. "Where are you? When can we see you and the babies?"

A huge weight lifted off his shoulders. "We're staying with Grace's grandfather right now. I got back right before the babies were born, so it will probably be a few weeks before we're up for visitors or trying to travel, but we'll send you pictures."

"Make sure you tell us which baby is which," his mother insisted. "I can't wait to meet them."

"I can't tell you how happy I am to hear you say that."

"Hold on a second," she said, and once again Devin could hear his parents speaking in the background. "Sorry, but I have to go. Your dad has some business he has to take care of."

"Okay. I'll talk to you later."

"Oh, before you go, is this your new phone number?" his mom asked.

"Yes." Devin's eyebrows knit together. "Didn't Maureen give it to you?"

"No. When did you talk to her?"

"I stopped by yesterday morning."

"She didn't mention it, but I don't think I've seen her since then. She probably left a note on your father's desk, and he forgot to tell me."

"You're probably right. I'll talk to you later."

"Okay. I love you."

Surprised by the declaration his mother rarely spoke, he responded automatically, "I love you too."

After Devin hung up, Grace said, "That sounded like it went better than you anticipated."

"Yeah. Who would have known my mother would be excited about becoming a grandma?"

"If you want to invite them up for a visit, I'm sure my grandpa would be okay with it. There's a guest room in the house that isn't being used."

"Thanks, but I don't want to take any chances that someone might follow them up here looking for me."

Devin saw Grace's concern and reached out to put his hand on her shoulder. "Almost all the people who were threatening us are in custody."

"Almost?"

"We believe there's one more." Devin couldn't bring himself to voice the likelihood of Jun's involvement. "We're hoping the man we captured a couple days ago will help us find her."

"What happens then?"

"Then we decide what we want to do with the rest of our lives," Devin said. "I already put my job first once. I'm not going to do that again."

"Are you going to quit?"

He reclaimed his seat beside her and put his hand on hers. "I need to know what you want for your future before I make any decisions about my own."

"Did you like the work you were doing?"

Devin considered the question. "I loved the analysis side of it, but I would never want to go undercover again."

"Are there other options for you there?"

Devin nodded. "A few. I would have the most opportunities to advance if I took a job at headquarters, but I also might be able to convince my employer to lend me out to another agency."

"Why would you do that?"

"If you want to stay here in Colorado, I can see if the Air Force Academy needs any language instructors. Or if we want to try for California, I could try to teach at the Defense Language Institute."

"I would love to stay close to Grandpa."

"I thought you would." Devin looked down at the sleeping infant in Grace's arms. "Here. Let me put her in her bassinet. You should try to get some sleep while you can."

"You're right." Grace handed Madeline over to him and shifted in her bed to get more comfortable. "Maybe you should go to the ranch and try to get some sleep yourself."

"I'll sleep here." Devin pointed at the chair in the corner that converted to a bed before turning his attention back to her. "I wasn't able to help you through your pregnancy. The least I can do is make sure I'm here now."

"I really missed you, you know."

Devin leaned closer and kissed her gently. "I missed you too."

Chapter 43

QING ANSWERED HIS PHONE, IRRITATED at the sound. Every time he had received a phone call over the past two days, the person on the other end had delivered bad news. His superiors would not be pleased.

He checked his caller ID, hope blooming when he saw it was his last remaining operative who could help him out of this corner he had been shoved into.

"Have you found him?" he asked without preamble.

"Your plan worked," she said. "He's in Colorado with his wife."

"Excellent. How soon can you get there?"

"I'm already there," she said. "And so is his father."

"With his laptop?"

"Of course."

"Perhaps we can salvage this operation after all. Tell me everything you know."

"Right now he's at the hospital with his wife. She just had twins."

He pursed his lips in consideration. "Here's what I need you to do."

"Me?" she asked with a hint of panic. "Aren't you going to send someone here to help me?"

"There is no one else. Jalen was apprehended by the authorities, and I can't get another operative to your location in time."

"In time for what?"

"To kill him. I want Devin Shanahan dead. We're not giving him the chance to slip away again."

"Are you sure you don't want to give him one last chance to help us get a real look at his father's computer?"

"He doesn't deserve another chance. He has a laptop with him. I want it."

She gulped before she said, "I'll make sure I get it from him."

"Let me be clear," he said. "Devin Shanahan is going to die before the week is out. It's up to you whether you will share his fate."

Another gulp. "I understand."

* * *

Devin's footsteps broke the 3:00 a.m. silence as he paced back and forth across Grace's room, baby Madeline pressed firmly against his shoulder as he patted her back. Apparently this burping thing was a frequent chore. Unlike her sister, Madeline tended to take her time before exhibiting such unladylike behavior.

The night had been a series of feedings, changings, and burpings, with an occasional hour of sleeping.

Devin hated to think what this whole parenthood thing would have been like for Grace had he not shown up when he did. This was harder work than anything he'd ever done. Except perhaps that chase through San Francisco. Give him a fussy baby over that any day.

Madeline finally burped, and Devin settled her into her bassinet. Immediately, she started to cry. Worried Madeline would wake her sister and Grace, he pushed the bassinet into the hall in the hope that the movement would help her settle. Sure enough, the crying subsided as they made their way past several rooms.

A nurse looked up from where she sat at her station, gave him a look of approval, and then refocused her attention on the computer screen in front of her. A baby cried from behind one of the doors, and Devin stopped long enough to ensure the sound wasn't coming from Grace's room. Once satisfied, he turned and started back the way he had come.

His phone rang, and Madeline let out a cry of her own. Devin quickly leaned down and patted her back. Trying to regain the peaceful silence from a moment before, he pulled the phone free and muted it, surprised to see Ghost's number on the screen.

Devin hit the talk button. "Is everything okay?"

"Where are you?"

"I'm with Grace." Devin used his cheek and shoulder to hold the phone in place so he could use both hands to push the bassinet. "Why?"

"An alert triggered when someone traced the GPS on your cell phone, and intel managed to intercept a call a few hours ago. Qing Lao put an extermination order out on you."

Devin tensed. As though Madeline picked up on his negative emotions, she let out another wail.

"What was that?" Ghost asked.

"That was my daughter. Grace had twins early yesterday morning," Devin explained. "I'm staying in the hospital with them."

"Devin, the Chinese know where you are."

"What?" The baby in the bassinet, Lydia and Grace in the other room— the possibility of them being in danger crashed over him.

"The woman Qing Lao was talking to said something about you being with your wife at the hospital and that she was already in Colorado," Ghost said. "We believe the woman was Jun."

Devin swallowed hard. The idea of Jun being involved still felt like some kind of alternate reality. Now this. Several seconds passed before he managed to voice his disbelief. "You're telling me the woman who practically raised me has been tasked with killing me?"

"That's exactly what I'm telling you."

Memories of San Francisco, of the determination of the men chasing him, surfaced and took on new meaning. All of his efforts to protect Grace, and now not only was she in danger, but so were his precious daughters. "You have to help me protect my family."

"Chee is heading your way, and we put out a BOLO on Jun. She'll turn up, but Chee will stay with you until we're certain she's been apprehended," Ghost said. "Are you armed?"

"Yes. I've kept my weapons with me since I got them in Phoenix," Devin said, now grateful he had followed Chee's instructions so closely. "When will Chee get here?"

"He's already on his way to the airport and should be landing within the next couple hours," Ghost said. "You should also know that Jun has been tasked with recovering your laptop. Apparently they know you've been studying your father's data and our intel on their operations."

"Jalen must have told them what I was working on."

"That's our guess. Unfortunately, he's still not talking."

"What do I do until Chee gets here?" Devin asked.

"I'll put in a fake report about a possible kidnapping at the hospital. That will increase their alert level on your floor without raising any suspicions."

"Then what?"

"When is your wife supposed to be released from the hospital?"

"Today."

"If you had your phone with you at her house, they'll know where that is too."

"It was off when I first went looking for her. It's only been turned on while I've been here."

"In that case, turn it off, and reset the GPS blocker. Do you know how?" Ghost asked.

"Yes. Chee taught me."

"As far as we can tell, that's the only way they've managed to track you."

"I don't understand how they even identified the number," Devin said.

"Maybe they figured out how to track it when you were in San Francisco."

Devin reached the end of the hall and wearily leaned against the wall. "Will this ever end?"

"We'll make sure it does," Ghost said. "Fai Meng is no longer a problem. As soon as Jun is taken into custody, this ends."

"What do you mean Fai isn't a problem anymore?"

"The State Department decided to play hardball with the Chinese. They claim they didn't know anything about his actions. In fact, they claim he isn't even one of theirs."

"He's been disavowed?"

"And wouldn't you know, he just happened to get picked up by the police in Hong Kong twenty minutes ago."

"For what?"

"Remember that little altercation in the alley? The evidence is pointing to him as the gunman."

"Wow. When the Chinese disavow their people, they really make sure they're out of commission."

"Which is great for us."

"What about whoever was over Fai? I got the impression he was working for someone else."

"Fai has been very careful not to leave an electronic trail that will connect him with his superior, but we've narrowed down the possibilities on that too. I should be able to confirm my suspicions shortly."

"What do I do if Grace gets released before Chee gets here?"

"With a heightened alert at the hospital, I can make sure you get out of there without being seen. What's the address to Grace's house? I'll have Chee meet you there."

Devin gave him the name of the ranch.

"Hang in there. Like I said, it's only a matter of time until we find Jun, and we'll make sure your family stays safe until we do."

"Thanks, Ghost. I owe you."

"That's what they all say."

Chapter 44

GRACE AND DEVIN ARRIVED AT the ranch to find a huge banner across the house that read "Welcome home!" Pink balloons were tied to the front porch posts, and several members of the staff had gathered for their arrival, along with Quentin, Caleb, Molly, and Sean.

Snow covered the front lawn, but the driveway and parking area for the guests was clear. Grace turned to look back at the babies, both of whom had fallen asleep within minutes of leaving the hospital. Her decision to feed them right before going home had been a good one.

"Let me get your door," Devin said as soon as he turned off the engine. "Thanks."

Devin climbed out of the vehicle and circled to her side. After helping her out of the car, he opened the back door, draped Lydia's blanket over the top of her car seat, and lifted it.

"Here. Let me help you." Molly hurried toward them and took the baby carrier from Devin.

Grace noticed the way Devin waited until he was sure Molly had a firm grip on the carrier before he released it and turned to get their other daughter out of the car.

Their daughter. She felt an overwhelming wave of love come over her.

"Need a hand?" Quentin asked, walking over.

Grace had to give Devin points for acting like he didn't mind handing their second child over to her grandfather. As he had with Molly, he made sure her grandpa's grip was solid before letting go.

He then took Grace by the arm and helped her to the house. They were walking up the front steps when another vehicle pulled into the parking area.

Grace expected it was one of their guests. Her eyes widened when she saw Devin's parents climb out of the car with Maureen.

Devin had been so adamant about protecting their location from everyone, she was surprised he had shared their address with his parents. "You didn't tell me your parents were coming."

"I didn't know." His eyebrows drew together the way they always did when he was concentrating.

Quentin reached out with his free hand and took Grace by the elbow. "I'll get them inside for you."

"Thanks," Devin said and then jogged back down the steps and approached his parents.

Grace let her grandfather help her inside and wondered if her in-laws' unexpected arrival could threaten their safety.

* * *

"Mom. Dad. What are you doing here?" Devin nodded to Maureen.

"Your mother wanted to come meet her grandchildren," his father said.

"And you?" Devin straightened his shoulders, wanting to hope his father had experienced a change of heart but afraid to let that hope take seed. "Why are you here?"

Boyd shifted his weight slightly before looking Devin in the eye. "I'm still not happy about how this marriage of yours came about, but your mother made a good point."

"What was that?"

"There are children involved now, and it's clear you want to make a life with this woman," he said. "We decided to try to make the best out of the situation."

Though his father's comment was a long way from what he would have liked to hear, Devin forced himself to remain civil. "I think if you give Grace a chance, you'll realize she's the best thing that's ever happened to me."

All of them gasped as a gust of wind bit through their coats.

"Come on. Let's get in out of the cold." Devin motioned them toward the house.

Boyd nodded in agreement and put a gloved hand on Devin's shoulder. "It's good to see you're doing well."

"Thanks, Dad."

"How are the babies?" Catherine asked.

"Adorable." Devin couldn't keep the grin from spreading across his face. He climbed onto the porch. "Come see for yourselves."

* * *

Grace couldn't help but smile when Jun rushed down the stairs expectantly. Grace shifted the babies' blankets so they were no longer over the top of their car seats and tucked them over them as an extra layer of warmth.

"Oh, they are beautiful," Jun said.

Molly, Caleb, and Sean offered similar sentiments before Quentin said, "We should probably let you get these little ones settled."

"Here, let me take her." Jun reached out to relieve Molly of the carrier she held.

"Grace, we'll stop by later. The guys wanted to hit the slopes for a half day," Molly said.

"Go ahead." Grace waved toward the door. "Have fun."

After they left, Jun and Quentin carried the infants upstairs to the nursery.

Her grandpa set Lydia's carrier on the babies' bedroom floor. "I'll go out and get your bag. I don't think Devin brought it in."

"Okay. Thanks."

"Where is Devin?" Jun asked, squatting down on the brightly colored throw rug Grace had chosen for the babies' room.

"He's outside with his parents." Grace wondered how Jun felt about her former employers. Since her arrival, she had rarely spoken of them, and when she had, her comments had been decidedly neutral.

"Mr. and Mrs. Shanahan are here?" Jun asked.

"Yes. I'm not sure what to think about it," Grace admitted. "Devin called from the hospital to tell them about the twins, but the last time I saw them was when they showed up for Devin's graduation. The minute they saw me there, they left."

"Maybe these little ones will help them see what's really important."

"I hope so, although I wonder if they're really here just to visit or if maybe Devin's father had some work in the area. I can't think of any other reason he would bring his secretary with him," Grace said.

"Maureen is here?" Jun asked.

"Yes." They could hear the door opening downstairs, followed by voices. Grace was torn with wanting to stay with her daughters and going downstairs to greet Devin's parents properly. She reminded herself that Jun had raised her husband. "Do you mind staying with the twins for a minute? I want to go say hello." Jun got an odd look on her face, so Grace quickly reassured her. "I'll be right back." Turning, Grace walked out of the babies' room into the hallway and then gingerly started down the stairs.

Devin met her halfway and helped her the last few steps.

"Mr. and Mrs. Shanahan, it's good to see you again," Grace said.

"Congratulations on the babies," Catherine said.

"Thank you." She looked over at Devin's father and his secretary standing right behind him. Boyd stood stiffly, as though he wasn't sure what he was supposed to do now that he was here. "Would you like to see your grandchildren? They're up in their room."

"I would like that very much," Catherine agreed.

"As would I," Boyd said.

Grace motioned in the direction she had come from. "It's this way."

"Grace, those stairs aren't easy on you," Devin said. "Do you want to wait here?"

She looked at the thirteen steps. Reluctantly she nodded. "Maybe I will rest here for a minute."

Devin led his parents upstairs. A moment later, he called down, "Grace, which room is theirs?"

"The one at the end of the hall," she said.

Grace heard footsteps sound upstairs, and in the back of her mind, she didn't understand why they didn't stop when they reached her daughters' room. Then the sound picked up at an almost frantic pace.

Devin rushed back down the stairs, panicked. "Grace, did you leave them upstairs by themselves?"

"No, of course not. Jun is with them."

"Jun?"

"Yes. Devin, what's going on? How could you have been up there and not seen Jun?"

"She wasn't there," Devin said tightly. "And neither were Lydia and Madeline."

Chapter 45

THE FRONT DOOR OPENED, AND Devin whirled to see Quentin walk through the door carrying Grace's overnight bag.

"Did you see Jun outside?"

"No, why?"

"She took the babies."

"What?"

"Devin, I don't understand," Grace said, now heading for the stairs. "Why would Jun take our daughters? She's practically family to you."

"I can't explain right now." Devin turned to Grace's grandfather. "Does Jun have a car here? And how could she have gotten out of the house without us seeing her?"

"There's a secondary staircase that leads from the upstairs bedrooms to the garage."

The words were barely out of his mouth when Devin heard the garage door opening.

"That way!" Grace pointed toward the side hallway that led from the main level to the garage.

Devin sprinted down the short hall and out the door just in time to see Jun behind the driver's seat of her old car, the handles of two car seats visible in the back seat.

"Jun! Stop!" Devin shouted.

Quentin rushed up behind him. "Come on. We'll take my truck."

"No. Stay with Grace. Make sure she stays safe."

"Is she in danger?"

"They all are."

"Here." Quentin tossed the keys to Devin. "I'll call the police."

Devin raced toward the vehicle and quickly started it. He was halfway out of the garage when he saw his parents appear in the doorway. Not able to think of anything but the safety of his family, he shifted from reverse to drive and stepped on the gas.

One way or another, he was going to find his children and bring them home safely.

* * *

This can't be happening, Grace thought over and over again. Five minutes ago, she had been standing in the newly decorated nursery with her two precious daughters and the woman whom she had trusted them with. Now her children and husband were gone. Surely this must be a bad dream.

The doorbell rang, and Grace prayed Devin would be on the other side with Lydia and Madeline.

Her grandfather opened the door, and fear spiraled through her. She had never seen the Chinese man at the door before, but memories of her apartment in New York resurfaced with a vengeance.

Her grandfather must have shared her thoughts because he held his rifle. "I suggest you introduce yourself and state your business here."

The man held his hands out to his side. "Devin. I'm looking for Devin."

"He's not here."

"Where is he?"

"Why should we tell you? For all we know, you're one of the people responsible for this mess."

The newcomer's phone rang. The man's eyes remained on Quentin, and he moved slowly when he reached for his phone.

"Hello?" He paused. "Devin, where are you?"

At the mention of her husband, Grace stood and crossed to stand beside her grandfather. The man continued to listen to the person on the other side of his phone conversation, his gaze shifting to Grace. She saw the moment when the man's concern heightened. "Okay, I'm heading your way."

The man hung up the phone and spoke to Quentin once more. "I'm going to help Devin track down his daughters, but I want you to call the police. Tell them you need a protection detail for the next few hours."

"Who are you?" Grace asked.

"My name doesn't matter. What matters is that I'm on your side." He took a step back and spoke to Quentin once more. "Keep that rifle close by, and call the police."

Grace watched him turn and hurry out to the SUV he had arrived in. For the third time in less than ten minutes, she listened to an engine roar to life and rubber screech on the pavement.

* * *

Devin fought the instinct to pull up beside Jun and force her to the side of the road. The possibility of the newborns being injured in such an endeavor was too real and forced him to bide his time.

He had been following her for the past fifteen minutes, and though he had limited knowledge of the area, he could tell she was heading toward town. But where in town, he had no idea.

Jalen had claimed the Chinese would insist on vengeance. Would Jun really hurt his children to get back at him? Or was she using them as bait to draw him out of hiding?

She took a corner a little too fast, and her car went into a skid.

Devin's heart jumped into his throat.

The car fishtailed to the right and back to the left before Jun managed to control it.

They reached the roundabout leading into the medical center, and Jun looked like she was trying to circle through it, but again, she lost traction with her speed. She had little choice but to continue straight through the roundabout and onto the road leading to the hospital.

He kept a safe distance while still keeping her in sight in case she skidded again. He was almost to the intersection when an ambulance approached from the other direction. One car was already in the roundabout, and it pulled to the side, effectively blocking Devin's forward progress.

Frustrated, he kept his eyes on Jun's car, watching her turn into one of the parking lots near the main entrance. As soon as the path was clear, he revved the engine and blasted through the intersection. He could see Jun in the distance, each arm hooked through the handle of a car seat.

Devin didn't bother with the parking lot. He headed straight for the main entrance, pulling up right in front moments after Jun disappeared inside with his daughters. Jumping out of the car, he raced inside to find the lobby deserted except for an elderly woman sitting at the information desk.

"Did you see a woman come in here holding two babies?"

She reached up and fiddled with her ear. "Sorry. Couldn't hear you. What did you say?"

He noticed the hearing aids now and repeated his question.

"Why, yes. She seemed to be in a bit of a hurry."

"Which way did she go?"

"I believe she went right over that way, by the elevators."

Devin sprinted in the direction she'd indicated. If Jun made it onto the elevators, he didn't know how he would find her. He could have security lock down the facility, but first he would have to find a security guard. The muted cry of a newborn sounded, but he couldn't determine the direction it was coming from. With a sense of determination, he continued in the direction the receptionist had indicated. He heard the elevator door chime and raced around the corner just in time to see Jun stepping toward the doors of the nearest elevator.

"Jun, stop!"

With the burden of the baby carriers, Jun wasn't as fast as Devin. He managed to jump in front of her and block her path.

Jun shifted away from him, shielding the infants behind her, each of them covered by a thin baby blanket.

"Jun, please don't hurt my babies," Devin said, speaking in Mandarin.

"I would never hurt them. And I would never hurt you," Jun said.

"Then why are we here? Why did you take them from us?"

"It was the only way to protect them." The elevator doors slid closed, and Jun hit the up button to call another elevator.

"What?"

"Your father didn't understand either," Jun said.

"Did he know you were stealing secrets from him?" Devin asked. "Is that why he let you go?"

"I never stole anything," she said. "When your father accused me of betraying him, I learned that he worked with government secrets. I didn't share any of them, and I didn't have any way of proving who did."

"Who?" Devin asked. "Who was stealing from my father?"

"Devin!" Jun lunged to grabbed his arm an instant before a shot rang out. She jerked him forward, out of the oncoming bullet's path.

He reached for the gun holstered at his ankle and turned toward the threat. Whoever had shot at him must have recognized his intent because he saw only a blur of movement as the shooter ducked behind the corner.

An elevator door slid open, and Jun quickly lifted the baby carriers. In tandem, she and Devin backed into the elevator, Devin keeping his gun aimed and ready until the doors closed once more.

"Who was that?" Devin asked.

Jun set one of the carriers down and punched the button for the second and third floors. Slowly the elevator car started upward.

"Jun. Who was that?" Devin repeated. "If you weren't the one stealing information for the Chinese, who was?"

"Maureen."

"What?" Devin looked at her in disbelief. As far as he knew, Maureen didn't have ties to anyone in that region of the world. How could she have been involved in espionage? Looking at the woman he considered a second mother, he realized his instincts had been right. Jun could be trusted.

"You have to hide," Jun insisted. "You're the one she's after." As though she wasn't completely sure of her words, she set the baby carrier on the right side of the elevator, shielding it from the door.

Devin picked up the carrier Jun had set down. "The babies . . ."

"Are safe."

Devin didn't have time to process her words or the certainty with which she spoke them. The doors slid open again, barely making it halfway across their tracks before another shot pierced the air, this one impacting the elevator's back wall.

Both Devin and Jun jumped to the side of the elevator, Devin taking a quick glance to make sure his daughters were still okay.

Gun still in hand, Devin sent a warning shot into the ceiling and quickly pressed himself to the side of the elevator car once more. Jun had already hit the close-door button, and the stainless steel once again closed around them and protected them from the woman determined to kill him.

"You need to hide until the police get here," Jun insisted. "Let me take care of the little ones."

Devin shook his head, unwilling to release possession of the daughter he carried. He pulled the blanket aside, his whole world shifting once more when he saw the car seat was empty.

"Where is she?" He pulled off the blanket on the second carrier and discovered the same result. "Where are they?"

"They're safe." Jun took his hand. "Trust me."

She reached out and took the empty carrier from him, tucking it beside the one already on the floor. She then draped the blankets over the top again.

He looked at the bullet hole behind him. "This elevator's too slow. We're going to be pinned down as soon as the doors open again." He looked around, considering the emergency hatch above him. It didn't have internal access, so he opted for the next best thing. He pressed the emergency stop button.

The elevator ground to a stop.

"Now what?" Jun asked.

Devin retrieved his phone and called Chee.

"Where are you?" Chee asked in lieu of a greeting.

"In the hospital. I'm trapped in the elevator."

No response.

"Chee?"

Again nothing.

Devin held out his phone and saw that the call had dropped. He dialed again.

"Dev—" Chee's voice cut out. "Almost—" The call disconnected again. Devin shifted position and hit redial.

"Third floor," Devin said the moment the ringing stopped. "Can you hear me? Check the third floor by the elevators."

"Coming." Chee's voice came through clearly this time. "I'm at the hospital now. Give me three minutes."

"We're in the elevator right now," Devin said. He looked at Jun. "It's not Jun."

"What?"

"It's—" The call cut out again. "Great," he muttered. Rather than try to call him again, he typed a text message. *It's not Jun we're after. It's my dad's secretary, Maureen. She's armed and waiting for me on the third floor.*

"Who was that?" Jun asked.

"A friend who's here to help us." Devin looked at his watch. "We'll give him a few minutes, and then we'll unlock the elevator. He'll make sure the landing is clear."

"Why is Maureen trying to kill you?"

"Because the Chinese wanted me to spy on my dad. I refused," Devin said. He motioned to the baby carriers. "Where are Madeline and Lydia?"

"I promise they're safe."

Chapter 46

GRACE HADN'T THOUGHT ANYTHING COULD be worse than not knowing where her husband was. The constant worry, the never ending questions, the unanswered prayers. Those long months had been nothing compared to this.

How could she have trusted Jun so completely only to be betrayed like this? How had she not seen any sign of a problem? Why had she brought her into their home?

The questions continued through her mind, tears streaming down her face. Her mother-in-law sat on the couch beside her, holding Grace's hand to both gain comfort and receive it.

The house phone rang, and her grandfather rose from the chair across from her to answer it. She could hear his muted voice in the kitchen. A moment later, he returned and held out the receiver.

"Grace, the phone is for you."

Grace shook her head. "I can't talk to anyone right now."

"It's about Lydia and Madeline."

Her hand shot out to take the phone he offered.

"If there's a ransom, I'll pay it," Boyd said quickly. "Anything to get them back."

Grace's eyes met Boyd's, and gratitude filled her before she spoke into the phone. "Hello?"

"Mrs. Shanahan, this is Reuben from Vail Valley Medical Center. I'm calling to tell you your daughters are safe and in our custody here."

Her shoulders instantly relaxed as she let out a sigh of relief. "Thank goodness." She tried to comprehend what had happened in the past hour and asked, "How did they get there?"

"Your nanny brought them in. She said they were in danger and asked me to call you so you wouldn't worry."

"We'll come pick them up right now."

"I'm sorry, ma'am, but we can't let you do that."

"What? Why not?"

"We have a live shooter situation here at the hospital. No one can come in or out."

"What?" Her shoulders tensed again. "My husband? Is my husband there?"

"I'm afraid I don't have that information."

"But my nanny dropped the babies off," Grace said.

"Yes, she did," he confirmed. "I will call you back as soon as the police tell us it is safe for you to come here."

"Thank you." Grace hung up the phone and looked at her grandfather and in-laws. She drew a deep breath. "The babies are okay," she told them, her emotions churning. "But I think Devin is in danger."

"What's going on?" Catherine said.

"Jun dropped the babies off with hospital security, but Devin was chasing Jun," Grace said, trying to put her suspicions into words. "The security guard said there's a live shooter situation. I'm afraid Devin might be right in the middle of it."

Boyd pushed out of his seat and headed for the door. "I'm going over there."

"They said they aren't letting anyone into the hospital right now," Grace called after him.

He didn't slow down until he stepped outside. Then he stopped and turned to look at them, confused. "Where is our car?"

"It should be right outside."

"It's not here." He looked around the room as though seeing it for the first time. "Where is Maureen?"

"I don't know."

* * *

Devin waited an extra two minutes before he pressed the emergency-stop button in the elevator. The moment he did, the car resumed its upward movement. He waved for Jun to take cover in the right front corner of the elevator while he took the spot opposite her.

The doors slid open, and Devin cautiously peeked out, leading with his weapon.

"It's just me," Chee called out to him.

"Where is she?" Devin asked.

Chee's attention immediately shifted to Jun when she edged forward and looked out into the third-floor hallway. "What's going on here?" Chee lifted his gun and took aim. "Hand over the babies."

"It's not what you think," Devin said quickly. "I sent you a text. Jun isn't the one who was stealing secrets. It was—"

A door creaked open behind them, and Devin looked just in time to see Maureen aim her weapon at him. "Look out!" Devin dove to the ground. "Jun, go back down!" Devin rolled to his left, barely escaping a second shot.

"Where's the shooter?" Chee asked from where he had pressed himself against the wall, effectively hiding him from Maureen's line of sight.

"Across the hall, first door on the left," Devin said.

Behind them, the elevator doors closed.

"You said it isn't Jun. Who is it?"

"Maureen. She's my dad's secretary."

A door opened and closed in the direction Devin had indicated. From the corner, Chee leaned out to look, then stopped instantly.

"Drop it." Maureen's voice was like steel.

Devin shifted ever so slightly, now able to see the gun barrel pressed to Chee's temple.

Chee dropped his weapon, but his voice was surprisingly calm when he said, "Stay back, Devin."

Devin lifted his own gun, praying for a clear shot. But it wasn't to be. Maureen remained concealed behind the wall, only the smallest part of her hand visible from where she held it against his coworker's head.

"Come out, Devin. No one else has to get hurt."

"Stay where you are, Devin," Chee said, moving ever so slightly so he would remain between them.

"Do what I say, or he dies," Maureen said.

"Don't do it," Chee demanded. "She'll kill you."

"Devin is going to die regardless," she said. "It's up to him if you go with him."

"Why would you do this?" Devin asked. "You don't have to hurt anyone."

She didn't respond except to shift around the corner enough to take aim.

Chee immediately put himself between them more fully.

"Step aside." She waved her gun at Chee. "You don't have to die."

"I can't just stand by and watch you kill him," Chee said.

"You have a choice. It's either him or all of you."

That was an odd word choice. *All of you.* It was then Devin realized Jun was standing behind him.

He felt her hand on his back, and his shirt shifted, then he felt the pressure of his secondary weapon being pulled free of his waistband holster.

"We can protect you," Chee said. "Tell us what you know about the Chinese, and the government can hide you from them."

"That's not how it works, and we both know it." She spat the words at him. "Now move!"

"How do you expect to get out of here?" Chee continued as though she hadn't spoken. "You won't be able to get through security."

"I have a plan."

"Don't do this here," Devin said, speaking in Mandarin rather than English. "I'll come with you. Just don't hurt them."

"What?" she said.

He repeated the words in English.

"Why should I believe you?" she asked.

"I'll give you my gun."

"Don't do it, Devin," Chee said.

"Take care of my family," Devin said. "And do what she says."

Chee looked over at him and must have sensed that everything wasn't what it seemed. He shifted slightly but not quite enough for Maureen to get a clear shot.

"Drop the gun," she demanded.

Devin engaged the safety and dropped the gun to the floor. He spoke again in Mandarin, his comment directed to Chee. "When I say now, get down."

"Speak in English!" she demanded.

"Now!"

Chee and Devin both dropped to the floor, both reaching for their weapons. Three rapid gunshots sounded.

Devin turned to see Jun beside him, her face pale. It took him a moment to sweep over the rest of the scene to realize the lack of color wasn't from a wound but from what she had done. A short distance away, Maureen lay on the ground, her eyes open and lifeless.

"It's okay," Devin said, gently prying his gun out of Jun's hand. He pulled her into his arms and felt her shudder.

"She was going to kill you," Jun said.

"You didn't let her." Devin pulled back and held both of her arms. "You saved our lives. And you saved my daughters."

Chee collected the weapons off the floor and handed Devin his. "Where are the babies?"

Devin turned to look back at Jun. "I was wondering the same thing."

Chapter 47

WHERE WERE THEY? GRACE SAT by the window, staring out at the drive. The hospital had called to tell them her family was okay and should be heading home anytime. That was thirty minutes ago.

"I wonder what could be taking so long," Catherine said, voicing everyone's thoughts. She stood beside Grace, too restless to sit still.

After the call came, Boyd had occupied himself by standing near the window and staring impatiently.

The rumble of an engine sounded, and everyone strained to see who was coming. A sense of relief flowed through her when she saw her grandfather's truck. What she hadn't expected was to see Jun's car right in front of it. Both vehicles headed for the garage.

"Grace, I'll go help them bring the girls in. Why don't you wait here?"

"I can't wait." Though she was still moving slowly, she stood and made her way to the door leading to the garage. It opened before she reached it, and Devin stepped inside holding one of the baby carriers. Jun followed right behind them carrying the other.

Tears sprang to her eyes, and Devin moved the car seat so he could pull her close.

For a moment, no words were said. They both struggled against their emotions, the unspeakable fear for their children and each other, and the relief that hadn't quite sunk in yet.

One of the babies cried, interrupting the silence.

"I was so worried. Are you okay?" She looked down. "Are they okay?"

As if on cue, the cry grew louder and was joined by another.

"I think they're getting hungry."

"That's not surprising."

Devin ushered her into the living room, where he and Jun set down the baby carriers. Devin lifted Lydia out of her seat, and Jun unbuckled Madeline.

When Jun gently picked her up and handed her to Grace, Grace looked at Jun, confused. "I still don't understand what happened."

Lydia's cry grew more impatient.

"Come on," Devin said. "I'll help you get them upstairs. The police are going to be here in a little bit to question Jun and me."

Reluctantly Grace let him lead her to the nursery. As soon as she was settled in the rocking chair with Lydia, she lowered her voice and said, "Tell me what happened. Why did Jun take the babies? And why is she here now?"

Devin closed the nursery door to ensure some privacy. "Someone has been trying to get me to spy on my father. He works with classified contracts, and some leaks were discovered."

"Seriously?"

Devin nodded.

"What does that have to do with our daughters?"

"The Chinese were threatening you to get me to work with them." Devin paced across the room, trying to pacify Madeline while she waited her turn to eat. "Jun realized who had been sent to find me. She was worried the girls would be used against me, so she took them to keep them safe."

"I get the feeling there's a lot more to this story."

Madeline's impatient cry grew louder. "Let's get these two settled, and then we can talk some more."

"I just need to know one thing."

"What's that?"

"Are they still in danger?"

Devin shook his head. "No. The CIA is making sure of that."

* * *

Devin walked downstairs thirty minutes later holding Lydia. Quentin was trying to entertain his parents. Devin sensed his father's underlying frustration, but he ignored the questions illuminated on his face and crossed to where his mother was sitting on a couch.

"Mom, would you like to hold her?"

"Is this Lydia Catherine?"

"It is. Grace is still feeding Madeline, but she'll be down in a minute." Devin passed the sleepy baby into his mother's arms. "She's already been burped and changed, but you might want this just in case." He set a burp cloth on the arm of the couch.

"She's beautiful," his mom said.

"Just like her grandmother," Boyd said, sitting beside her. He stared down at the infant for a moment before he looked back at Devin. "Can you please tell me what's going on? Why did Jun take the babies, and why is she back here now?"

"She didn't talk to you already?"

"I sent her upstairs to rest for a bit," Quentin said, answering for him.

Devin looked over at Grace coming down the stairs, Jun beside her carrying Madeline.

"Well?" Boyd asked impatiently.

"Maybe everyone should sit down for this," Devin said. As soon as Jun and Grace sat on the couch opposite Devin's parents, Quentin lowered himself into his favorite arm chair.

Devin opted to remain standing and took a moment to gather his thoughts. He chose his words carefully, deliberately not revealing his true employer. "While I was in Hong Kong, a Chinese national tried to recruit me as a spy."

"A spy?" Catherine said in disbelief. "Why would they approach you? You work in finance."

"Let him finish," Boyd said, his own expression unreadable.

"Specifically, they wanted me to spy on Dad."

"That trip to Tokyo wasn't coincidence, was it?" Boyd said.

"No." Devin let out a sigh. "Apparently the Chinese had someone feeding them information on your work. That flow of information stopped around three years ago," Devin said. "Or at least it slowed down."

Boyd's jaw tensed, and he glance at Jun.

"Because Jun moved out of our house around the same time, the government thought Jun was the source," Devin continued.

"If she is sitting here now, I assume you believe it was someone else," Boyd said.

"Yes. It was Maureen."

"What? Are you sure?" Catherine asked. She looked over at her husband. "She's worked with you for over twenty years."

"We're sure. She made her allegiances very clear when she tried to kill me at the hospital today." Several faces in the room paled, and he felt his own face drain of color as he thought of how close he had come to dying today. He motioned to Jun. "Jun realized Maureen was a threat to us. That's why she took the twins."

"I was going to take them to the police station," Jun said. "The car skidded, and I accidentally turned toward the hospital, so I took them there instead."

"I accused you unjustly," Boyd said. "I'm so sorry, Jun."

"It's okay, Mr. Shanahan."

"What I don't understand is why the flow of information slowed after you let Jun go."

"One of the contractors I was working with discovered a breach. I saw Jun coming out of my office a few days later and assumed it must have been her."

"I noticed the door was open and went to see why," Jun said. "That's when you saw me."

"What I didn't realize was that Maureen must have been the person who had unlocked the door. She was probably inside my office when I fired you."

"But Maureen would still have had access after Jun left."

"She would have except that I changed the lock on my office door and started carrying my laptop with me everywhere. I also had a contractor put a lot of security in place in case it was accessed by someone else."

"That makes so much more sense," Devin said. "Maureen would have only had access to what she overheard you talking about or what limited documents she saw."

"Exactly." Boyd looked down at baby Lydia. "What happens now? Will you go back to Hong Kong?"

"No. I'm changing jobs." He motioned to Grace. "We've talked about a few options, but for now, we're planning on staying here in the States."

Catherine shifted Lydia in her arms. "I can't tell you how happy that makes me."

"Me too," Quentin added. He stood. "I'm going to get started on dinner. I thought we could throw some steaks on the grill."

"I'll come help." Jun gave Madeline to Grace and stood.

As soon as they left, Boyd turned to Grace. "If you don't mind, we would like to stay and visit for a few days."

"We don't mind at all," Grace said, and Devin could see his father melting a little when she added, "You're always welcome."

Chapter 48

DEVIN STRETCHED OUT ON THE bed beside Grace, both babies finally asleep and settled in their bassinets. He expected they would sleep for only about two hours. At least he hoped they would last that long.

He pushed up onto his elbow and looked over at his wife, feeling as though he had finally reached the light at the end of a very long, dark tunnel. A wave of love cascaded through him, and he reached out and brushed a lock of her hair off her cheek. "It's hard to believe that three days ago I didn't even know how I was going to find you and now here we are, a family of four."

"I was so scared today." Grace glanced over at the bassinets at the end of their bed. "I never want to go through anything like that again."

"That makes two of us."

"Are you sure we're safe now?" she asked. "What if Maureen told the Chinese where to find you?"

"I'm supposed to hear from my friend at the CIA anytime now to let me know what they've found out."

"I don't suppose you can call him, can you?" she asked. "I don't know that I'll be able to relax until I know this is really over."

"I can try." Devin rolled over and picked up his cell phone from the night table. He dialed Chee's number.

"Devin. I was just thinking about you."

"Do you have any new information?"

"I do," he said. "Ghost called a few minutes ago. Intel managed to identify Fai Meng's superior. He's a man by the name of Qing Yao."

"He worked at Revival Financial too. In fact, I think he was Fai's boss."

"That's right. Unfortunately for Qing, he decided to travel to Taiwan yesterday." He paused for effect. "Evidently someone tipped the Taiwanese government off that Qing is Chinese intelligence. We expect his detainment will last for at least a few years."

"He's in prison?"

"He is, and from what Ghost said, the Chinese government has disavowed him. That means he's lost access to any resources he could have used previously if he was still bent on coming after you."

"So it's over."

"It's over."

"I can't tell you how happy I am to hear that," Devin said. "Thank you so much for everything."

"There is one more thing."

"What's that?"

"I heard from your new personnel officer. Considering your cover was compromised, they approved a temporary assignment to the Air Force Academy if you're interested. You would be teaching Mandarin."

"Seriously? That would be great." Devin looked at Grace, who was obviously confused, and reached out to give her hand a squeeze. "How long would it be for?"

"You'll have some say in the matter. Two to three years is the recommended tour, but it is possible to extend up to five years."

"Thank you so much."

"I'm heading back to Hong Kong tomorrow, but Linda, your new personnel officer, will be calling you on Monday."

"Safe travels."

After Devin hung up the phone, he asked Grace, "How would you feel about moving to Colorado Springs?"

"Are you talking about the Air Force Academy?"

"I am. Chee said I can have a teaching position there if I want it. It could last anywhere from two to five years."

"So we could be kind of close to Grandpa while the girls are little."

"Exactly." Devin nodded. "And I have to imagine I would have school holidays off, so we could come visit pretty often."

"I would love that."

"I can't guarantee I wouldn't get transferred to the DC area afterward, but at least I would fulfill my five-year commitment to the agency."

"After all we've been through, all I really want is for us to be together."

"What about your career?" Devin asked. "We never really talked about what you want to do next."

"I'm doing some financial planning, which I love, but I'd like to keep that part-time." She looked over at the bassinets. "More than anything, I want to stay at home and be a mom."

"You're already doing a great job." He scooted closer and kissed her. "I love you."

"I love you too." She pressed her lips against his and added, "I'm really glad I married you."

"Even after everything I put you through this year?"

"We promised for better or worse."

"We've done the worse," Devin said. "This year let's plan to stay on the better side."

One of the babies let out a little whimper but settled down a moment later. "I think we've already started."

About the Author

Originally from Arizona, Traci Hunter Abramson has spent most of her adult life in Virginia. After graduating from Brigham Young University, she worked for the Central Intelligence Agency for several years, eventually resigning in order to raise her family. And though Traci found her passion in caring for her family, she couldn't manage to forget the action of the CIA, so she turned to writing about it. She has gone on to write a number of best-selling suspense novels that have consistently been nominated as Whitney Award finalists, three of which have won in mystery/suspense. She loves to travel and enjoys reading, writing, sports, and coaching high school swimming.